Viner gets his name from being a water-diviner. The only problem is that the people amongst whom he lives suffer from floods. Viner is blamed and as soon as he's old enough he drifts off to find a place that will welcome his knowledge.

Matters are taken out of his hands soon after he sets out, for he is captured and taken to a settlement where drought problems consume the minds and habits of all the people. Most of all the lack of water worries the rain-king — the scapegoat whose specific task it is to bring water to the dusty land. Within the context of a dishonest social structure, where his working craft is taken for sorcery, Viner soon emerges as a powerful force. But rather than compete with the king, he seeks friendship from this broken man and sets plans afoot to rescue him from what will surely be his fate.

With skill and dexterity Jan Mark shows how the manipulation of a spirit can prove to be so destructive, and in the manner of her highly-acclaimed novels, *The Ennead* and *Divide and Rule*, has created a powerfully compelling read.

Jan Mark grew up in Kent and attended the Canterbury College of Art. She went on to teach art at Gravesend. She started her writing career in 1973, and since then has written a large number of highly successful books, for which she has been awarded the Carnegie Medal and other prestigious prizes. She spent two years as writer-in-residence at Oxford Polytechnic, and now lives in Oxford.

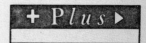

JAN MARK

Aquarius

PENGUIN BOOKS

PENGUIN BOOKS

Published by the Penguin Group
Penguin Books Ltd, 27 Wrights Lane, London W8 5TZ, England
Viking Penguin, a division of Penguin Books USA Inc.
375 Hudson Street, New York, New York 10014, USA
Penguin Books Australia Ltd, Ringwood, Victoria, Australia
Penguin Books Canada Ltd, 2801 John Street, Markham, Ontario, Canada L3R 1B4
Penguin Books (NZ) Ltd, 182–190 Wairau Road, Auckland 10, New Zealand

Penguin Books Ltd, Registered Offices: Harmondsworth, Middlesex, England

First published by Kestrel Books 1982
Published in Penguin Books 1990
1 3 5 7 9 10 8 6 4 2

Printed in England by Clays Ltd, St Ives plc
Set in Baskerville (Linotron 202)

For Freda

Unlike the main character in this book, I am not a water-diviner. I could not find the North Sea with a ten-foot pole, much less an underground stream with a forked twig. I should, therefore, like to thank Arthur and Barbara Cornford, and Bernard Whittleton, for their advice and assistance, and especially Stanley Nicholls, for a practical demonstration.

I

The night the bridge collapsed for the third time in living memory, the population of the village fell by one, drowned, and rose by two, found clinging next morning to the remaining upright of the bridge. As had happened before, the inexplicable occasional force that in spring and autumn sent the river seething back upon itself, coincided with a ferocious rain storm. The bridge was thriftily built at the river's narrowest point within the village boundary, and that circumstance, coupled with the fact that the two piles which supported the centre span forced the water into turbulent rapids, ensured that the bridge was under constant assault from the pressure of the torrent beneath it, the author of its own destruction.

At first light, as the waters subsided, the village elders and the headman made a glumly ritual visit to the river's edge, to see what was left. They waded down another river, which had been the village street, heads bent against the resisting wind and the complaints that rained down on them from upper windows. At the first sign of flooding the inhabitants retired to their lofts, taking with them as many of their chattels and livestock as they had time to shift. A cow looked out of a dormer and lowed dolorously, but the party below had no time to pause and inquire how this feat had been accomplished. A dead sheep floated by, its carcase bobbing jovially on the current.

On the higher ground people were already lighting fires in the forlorn, and totally unwarranted, hope of driving away the rain, but the wood was green and sullen, fuming and sweating, and the sky spat scornfully into the flames until bitter smoke hung in subdued strata above the fires, swelling the clouds.

When they reached the river they saw at once what the night had wrought. The bridge's single surviving upright, all but pounded to kindling, was barely visible above the turbid surface, indicating that in the darkness the water must have reached the very top of the central span and engulfed the lower ones on either side.

'About the highest level I ever saw yet,' said the carpenter among them. He was not encouraged to say more. While no one would have suggested that it was his faulty workmanship that had caused the bridge to fall, it was uppermost in all minds that he had much to gain, since the bridge had to be replaced. Without it they were cut off from all traffic and commerce with the far bank, the hill grazing for the sheep, and they would lose the tolls extracted from traders and mercenaries who needed to pass over, and would otherwise go further downstream where matters were better conducted and there was a ferry. By the time the water level fell in summer the carpenter must have ready, at the village's expense, good timber to erect to build the bridge again. The village annals were punctuated at regular intervals with records of payment to the carpenter for building the bridge, or repairing the bridge; and before that to his father, and to *his* father, before that.

'There's something caught in that pier,' said the carpenter's son, pointing through the vapour of rain and spray. 'Cloth, by the looks of it, a trader's pack, like. Something valuable, maybe.'

'Most probably a corpse, knowing our luck,' said the headman, who had fished out more than one defunct passer-by in his lifetime. In the half light he craned and strained for a better view. 'Washed down from the hills. I don't reckon they *bury* them, Further Up – just pitch 'em in . . . ahoy!' Two or three voices joined his. 'Ahoy! Are you dead, there?'

Out in midstream, from the cradle of shuddering spars, an arm was raised, and a voice.

'No.'

'She says they ain't corpses at any rate,' said the carpenter. 'It's a woman – with a child, I think.'

'How many are you?' the headman called.

'Two. Myself and the boy. Of your mercy masters, save us.'

'Reel them in,' the headman said, resigned to more demands upon his charity, wondering why the stream could not have brought them an able-bodied man in exchange for the one swept away last night, instead of a woman and a useless child.

Further upstream they put out a boat, attached to a line, and with ten strong men on the rope and four more in the boat, recovered the stranded victims from the river. Then the boat was hauled in and the headman himself trod down the treacherous and crumbling bank to help the woman and her child from the bilges. She was incoherent with gratitude and fear, and grovelled in the flood water to thank them, while they tried to raise her to her knees and escort her to shelter. Even when they had coaxed her under cover and stirred up a fire, they could get little sense out of her. When they asked where she came from, and how she came to be marooned in the relics of their bridge, she would only point to the louring sunrise and say, 'From Further Up.' This much was evident. They pressed her for more information in case she proved to be a bad woman, cast off for a good reason.

'They turned us out when my good man died,' she explained, at last, cowering closer to the fire. 'His brother wouldn't keep us, and there was no one to speak for me. I crept out of the house by night and took our boat.' She saw and understood their doubtful looks. 'It was *my* boat, of my dowry, mine by right and I took it; to save our child.'

The child was a sickly-looking creature, male, about ten years old, but they made allowances for his appearance after his night on the water; and in it, and often under it. Moved by compassion alone they would have taken him in, but his fearful mother had claims to press in his favour.

'You'll give us shelter – for his sake? He's nothing much now, but in time he'll repay you a hundredfold. He has the power.'

'Power?' The child seemed to be dissolving before their eyes. What power could he have but over frogs and fish and creeping leeches? Water streamed from his every crevice.

'My husband's brother was jealous of his power. He had the power himself, only not so strong, and he threw us out. He was afraid we'd challenge him, and no one would help us. My son would have been as fine a man as his father was, if they hadn't taken away his birthright, but you good people will know how to use him.'

'Use him?' the headman said, looking at the wretched pair as they crouched by the fire. 'What as, fish bait? What power does he have?'

9

In a voice enriched by motherly pride she cried, 'He's a water-diviner!'

As she had predicted and hoped, the headman was a good man, but she did not know how close he was, at that moment, to seizing the draggled child by the scruff of its neck and hurling it back into the river.

The child found out though, soon enough, and was never allowed to forget it. It was the other children who reminded him, at first when he tried to play with them and later when he avoided them. 'Water-diviner!' they shouted after him, as if it were a term of abuse. 'Water-diviner! Water 'viner! *Viner!*' They forgot his real name, if they had ever known it, and soon everyone came to call him Viner and soon he learned to answer to it. It made no difference to him what he was called. He was called only in order to be insulted, but mostly he was kept at a distance. Following the revelation that he could find water, it was generally assumed that he could summon it, and from that, that he malignly attracted it. Every rain cloud was attributed to his presence. The spring and autumn surges were supposed to be answers to his mere beckoning finger. He could scarcely lift an eyebrow without being vilified, and if he so much as wiped his nose people made the Bad Luck sign. When the river left its course and spread remorselessly over the fields, crushing the green wheat, dredging seed from the ground, fouling the granary, the village knew that the water was seeking its own.

One day, when he thought himself unobserved, he went down to the willows below the village and cut himself a forked twig. His father had trained him to use a hazel, but in that drowned valley willows were the only trees that flourished with any conviction. His intention was to walk round the village, out of sight of the cottages, and see if the rod would work for him. He had more sense than to publish his findings, but he was desperate to know if the power was still in him; however, before he had taken more than a dozen paces a hand grabbed him by the cloth of his shirt, from above and behind, while another snatched the rod from him and set about beating him across the shoulders with it.

'You carny little bastard,' a voice came down to him, shredded by the slashing of the willow. 'Devil's fry! Witch spawn! Vining, were you? I'll vine you till your eyeballs drop out you monster, you soft-shelled slug!' It was the miller who had but lately watched his sacks of flour turn to dough before his eyes. Viner hung limply from his giant fist until the miller, tiring, flung the sinewy whip one way and his victim the other.

'Ever I see you do that again,' said the miller to Viner, lying in the mud, 'I'll tie a stone round your neck and drown you myself – if'n it's possible to drown you which I doubt, you fish-eyed measle, and you may tell your mammy so if she's any complaints. I'll put a gaff through your gills and string you up to dry like a trout. *I'll have them build you into the bridge.*'

That last threat went home for Viner knew it could be done, both secretly and openly all at once. He did not, however, relate the incident to his mammy. He had long ago stopped running to her for comfort. To everyone's surprise she had dried out into a comely young woman and had been snapped up by the recently widowed carpenter, who although a come-down after the reflected glory of her first husband was nonetheless a conscientious provider and would continue to be, as long as bridges toppled. Now Viner had four little half-brothers and -sisters, and one stepbrother, in the person of the carpenter's eldest son, who daily cursed himself for being the sharp-eyed fool who had first noticed his future stepmother and her brat on the bridge. Had he kept his mouth shut they might have been safely swept away. As it was, the carpenter and his family wanted no floods in their cottage and Viner prudently remained outside for as much time as was possible: in the rain.

Even his mother found it politic to revile him, if anyone were listening. She had never again boasted of his power; she had never again mentioned it, and when Viner himself spoke of it, quite piously and in filial remembrance of his father, she walloped him soundly and said that unless he wanted to ruin both their futures he would do well to hold his tongue. Viner had no ideas about his own future, since he had previously been brought up in the belief that he would one day be a dowser as his father had been before him, but he could see well enough where his mother's future lay, and with it his hope of surviving childhood, so he held his tongue, even when clouds obscured the crests of the hills and the children slung stones and clods of earth at him, to save themselves the bother of doing it later, when up to their knees in water.

'The river flooded before we came, didn't it?' Viner protested, just once, when incontinently overcome by the injustice of his position. 'It rained before we came, didn't it? The bridge collapsed, didn't it?'

'All those things happened,' the carpenter agreed. '*But not so often*,' and aimed a leathery clout at his stepson's ear.

Viner left the cottage and went back thereafter only to sleep. He ate what his mother could spare him, after the carpenter's children were fed, and swallowing his memories of that earlier life when he was of consequence and good family, enjoined to take care of his valuable hands, he scratched a living by offering his services to people who wanted sheep herded, chickens plucked, goods hefted. He was never allowed to associate with cattle in case he diluted the milk. Sometimes he earned a penny or two – promptly appropriated by the carpenter – by coming to the assistance of a passing traveller. One such halted by the bridge to rearrange his load before paying the toll and passing over. Viner materialized silently and hovered, hoping to attract attention, ready to run if it were the wrong kind of attention. He rarely spoke if he could avoid it for the villagers, finding his accent outlandish and his vocabulary too extensive, retaliated by treating him as a gibbering idiot, and entertained themselves with crude impersonations.

'Do you want help?' he asked, finally.

'If you want to help,' the traveller replied, equably. Viner saw that he was in the presence of civilization and was about to step forward when the miller's son put his head out of an upper window and yelled, 'You don't want him near you, Master. Yer horse'll rot down to the hooves and you'll find yer pack full of water and yer brains'll trickle out of yer ears. He come out of the river, that one!'

'*Viner!*' Two or three others joined in.

'Sod off!' the traveller replied, not noticeably discouraged, and beckoned Viner towards him. 'Here, catch hold of these straps and don't let go until I tell you.' He set about shifting the packs that loaded his mule. 'You don't seem to be well liked. Been in trouble, son?'

'They say I cause floods,' Viner muttered. He did not explain why. He was growing canny. 'They say I make it rain. Wherever I go water finds me, they say. People throw things.'

'I know of a place where they wouldn't throw things,' the traveller said. 'All right – easy now – bring it round, that's it.'

'What place?' Viner demanded.

'Get your arm round that.'

'*What* place?'

'Place I heard of where it never rains unless they dance for it. They'd like you there, I reckon.'

'Dance?'

'They take a man and make him dance, and when it rains they make him king, and he marries the queen. That's the place for you, don't you think?'

'Where is it? How can I get there?'

The traveller looked at Viner's hungry eyes and regretted his easy words. 'It was only a story, boy. How can you make rain by dancing?'

'How can you make rain by *living*?' Viner said, and wandered disconsolately away, turning his back on the traveller's proffered coin. He had heard too many such stories to be impressed or consoled. Outcasts went into the world to seek their fortunes, married queens and ended with whole kingdoms at their feet. All that lay at his feet was mud, and river slime and more mud, but for several nights after that he dreamed of the fabulous land where it never rained, and a dowser might be king, and woke weeping to another miry dawn.

But he survived. He did survive and he grew, tall enough to make the carpenter think twice about hitting him. He grew hair on his face and began to shave it, when he could lay hands on a razor. He grew broad in spite of his miserable diet. He was sixteen: and then he stopped growing.

He realized that he was now, until old age shrunk him, the size he would be for the rest of his life. There was no longer any hope that he would one day be the tallest man in the village, or the strongest; no chance that he would strike such respect into the hearts of his neighbours that they would refrain from throwing things at him. (He knew that they feared him, but that was not at all the same thing.) His sapling stage was over, and yet no provision had been made for him, as was made for his contemporaries. His stepfather refused to teach him his trade, there was no hope of practising his own, and no one wanted to employ him. He had no prospect of a wife nor of a home, and yet he was seen about the village, day in, day out. What did they expect him to do?

One spring morning, early, he woke as he usually did before the others, and as was his habit took steps to be out of the cottage before they did wake. He backed down the ladder from the loft, took up a crust from the table and slipped out of the low doorway, making no sound. It was this manoeuvre in itself, that made him halt under the eaves. His every action was a deliberate and defensive substitute for his absence. He suddenly knew very well what they expected him to do; they expected him to go away.

Viner, his hand still on the latch, saw the whole of the last six years as a protracted gesture of dismissal. He was not happy to acknowledge it, but he was relieved. As silently as he had lowered it, he raised the latch and went back inside, where he stood looking round the dank cavern of his home in the mildewed twilight. By the hearth, cold and damp as the threshold stone, hung the bait bag in which his stepbrother carried his food to work with him. Viner unhooked it and holding it open before him, prowled round the room. Bacon, onions in strings, dried fish, some kind of sausage – *he* had never been allowed to get his teeth into it – all hung from the beam above the fireplace. From the flitch he clove a chunk of greasy bacon on the bone, bisected the sausage, cut down half a dozen onions and dropped them into the bag; a couple of beets, new bread; all went in after; a pot bottle of beer, too, but no water. No one possessed containers for the uncontainable water and if he should need it, he thought, he knew how to get it. He would have borrowed one of the dried fish, too, but a sound from overhead, in the loft, froze him where he stood, on tiptoe. It was the carpenter, rolling out of bed. Viner heard a long yawn, followed by a cavernous belch in which he thought he detected the vibration of vital organs. Under cover of this he raised the latch again, and went outside, for the last time.

It was, as usual, raining, but not in the torrents that caused filth and curses to be hurled at him. This was a soft spring rain, seasonable, but to his jaundiced eyes it had been going on too long. As he walked along the dismal rill that trickled through the ruts down the middle of the street, the thatch eaves dripped monotonously on either side. Everything was green. Grass grew on the thatch, moss on the windowsills, and a lush, indeterminate silkiness on the walls, under the blebs and running welts of water. Even the sheep, grazing aimlessly by the bridge, had vegetation on their backs, for as it flourished on the roofs so the grass grew abundantly in their waterlogged fleece. They bleated peevishly in the rain, and the shepherd, with his scrip and tarbox, spat and grumbled under the dripping brim of his hat.

Viner, looking over his shoulder to make sure that the shepherd was not watching, turned away from the bridge, into the willows, where he cut himself a forked twig as long as his forearm, springy and green, which he thrust into his belt. Then he went back, past the house of the belligerent miller and without another glance at the village set his foot on the bridge. He could have sworn that his shoe sank a little into the swollen timber, and that moisture bubbled round it. It was too early for the toll-gatherer to be abroad, and Viner walked unhindered over the spongy planks and the ebullient water, to the place where the road diverged on the other side. The right hand fork would have taken him along the river bank, through the marshes, at last to the town. The left fork went uphill among the sheep pastures and into unknown territory, Over the Top. So far as he knew, no one from the village had ever been Over the Top, and to be sure, less than a third of the way up the hillside the road, such as it was, petered out into sheep tracks and then vanished into the grass and the mist.

Whatever people had made the road, long ago, had ceased to need it. In all the time Viner had lived in the village he had never seen anyone come down it or go up it. As he stood at the fork, hesitating between the hill path and the marsh road to town, he knew that the abandoned track was the way for him. He had come, unannounced from Further Up; he would go, unannounced Over the Top, and that, as far as the villagers knew, would be the end of him. He turned left, uphill, over the ochreous slurry that the rain had made of the track, and not until he had left the track and was labouring over the sheer grass path did he turn to look round and down at the village, and when he did, it had vanished, absorbed by the vapour.

'Sunk into the mud. Let it sink, let it lie,' he said, vengefully, and went on.

He was walking blind, inside a cloud, downing lungfuls of unfallen rain. He could judge that he was going in the right direction only by the fact that he was still toiling upwards, skidding on the oozing turf which was already, he noticed, free from sheep droppings. He would have whistled a tune, had he known any, but there was no music in the village, except on rare and solemn occasions, and that not music one would willingly reproduce. Lack of practice had driven from his head the few tunes of childhood that he could swear he remembered his mother singing when they lived Further Up. No one whistled in the village. Whistling called up the wind.

Then he did hear music, a shrill unattached trilling that came down to him through the clouds, and he understood that up here larks rose above the mist and sang in the sunshine. It had never occurred to him before that mist must have an upper limit; he had thought of it as drifting upward for ever, trapping the moon and extinguishing stars, but these larks had found the ceiling, and at that moment he found it too, and looking over his shoulder saw the mist below him at last. He was actually *looking down* on a cloud. There was dew on the grass under his feet, but under the dew the earth was dry. The sun shone all round him upon the hill top, and beyond his hill top upon another, and another after that. He stood in an infinity of hill tops and there was never a cloud in sight, save the mouldering murk below him, at his back. For the first time in his life, or so it seemed to him, he raised his head to stand upright and the rain did not beat in his face.

It would have been sensible to stop there and eat, for he had begun his journey on an empty stomach, but the shallow sweeping expanse of the hillside drew him on, down, into the beautiful bowl and up again. His fatiguing mud-bound shuffle, picked up from the villagers and which had earned for them locally the name of Webfeet, loosened gradually into an easy stride, and as he strode, over the morning turf, he drew from his belt the forked willow wand, and holding it before him he divined his way across the roof of the world.

At first his long shadow loped beside him, but as the morning wore on it seemed to lose impetus and fell a little behind. On the short dry grass he saw that it was a true representation of himself, elongated admittedly, but lean and well proportioned, with buoyant hair, although he could not understand why his feet looked so large, as though they were still shod in clogs. With absent-minded optimism he had left his clogs in the cottage. He had never, till then, been aware of his shadow as an extension of his person, only as one absence of light among many others. All the while the larks rang over his head.

He had expected to be at the foot of the slope within a matter of minutes, but the sheer unfamiliarity of a wide view had deceived him. After walking for over an hour he found that he was still going down, and then something occurred that halted his progress for a long time. As he approached the place where the ground began to level out, the rod moved in his hands. He had almost forgotten that he was holding it and, unprepared, let it spring from his grip and over his shoulder. He stopped then, bending to pick it up, and as he did so memory stirred in him. He recalled the day when his father had placed one of his own rods in his hands, for the first time.

'I shan't be able to hold it,' said the child, fearfully. 'It won't stay in my hands.'

'It will when you've learned to hold it right,' his father said. He was a respected man, dignified by the title of Dowser. Grown-up Viner smiled a little sourly at the thought of a water-diviner being regarded with respect.

'But I haven't the power,' the child protested, looking at his skinned palms.

'Let's have no more talk of power,' the father said. 'I'm *teaching* you. Power is old women's talk.'

'Then – anyone could do it?' said the child, already half jealous.

'Who knows? But it is our mystery. The smith has his mystery, and the parmenter. This is ours. We must all know *how* to do what

17

we do. Any fool could put a boat in the water by our jetty, but how many could take it safely down even as far as the Webfeet's village?'

Mother did, Viner thought. The last thing she did for me – but damn the Webfeet and their bridge. If we hadn't smashed into that we might have gone on to a place where proper men lived; men who needed wells, at any rate, he added.

'Take up the rod again,' said Viner's father, many years ago, and Viner, grown beyond recognition, took up the rod. His father had gone, back into the forgotten past, but he had left his mystery behind him. Viner had at last remembered what to do.

He walked back a few paces and advanced again until the rod twisted upwards in his grip. Then he reached into the bait bag and, bringing out an onion, the first thing that came to hand, placed it on the spot. He moved on, leaving the onion like a sudden mushroom in the grass, until the rod made a second convulsion. He put down another onion, then a third. Pacing back and forth and sideways, with increasing confidence, he deposited all six onions, the bacon, the pot bottle, the beets, the sausage, in slices, and the bread, broken into lumps. By this time his shortening shadow was pointing back the way he had come, uphill, and at his feet lay an enormous edible diagram of five parallel lines stretching in either direction along the valley. He was amazed by what he had done, exhilarated, breathless, and extraordinarily tired, more tired than his unaccustomed walk could have made him. His knees and wrists were trembling and his hands sore, but he hardly noticed that. He looked again and again along the middle line of the five. He had found his stream.

There was nothing he could do about it. At a rough calculation it must be fifteen spits down and deep-running, but he had never intended to dig for it; he had wanted only to prove that he could find water, and he had found it. His shaking legs folded under him and he sat down abruptly by the side of his stream. A grin of pride and guilty pleasure began to stiffen across his features. Spread before him was the evidence of a deed that would have earned for him the thrashing of his life, yesterday, and in another place, yet here he was unscathed, unrebuked, uncursed; free to practise his mystery. He took time off to think for a moment about the other place, far away and below, submerged in mist and doomed to stay so.

One day, he said to himself, one day I'll go back, rich; I'll show them what a dowser can do among people who know how to use him. No I won't; I'll never go back. Let them wonder what became of me for the rest of their lives. He was obliged to admit that far from wondering they had probably forgotten him already, if they weren't actively celebrating his providential disappearance.

By stretching out his hand he could just reach the most appetizing of his markers, the bacon. He ate some, and while wondering if it were worth the effort of crawling across to the far bank to fetch the beer, he propped himself on one elbow, and then lay back on the hot grass and let his eyelids drop. He must have rolled a little way in his sleep for when he woke the largest of the onions lay, white and overwhelming, at the corner of his unfocused eye. For a moment he thought that darkness had come while he slept and the moon had fallen out of the sky.

His shadow had begun to lengthen again when he moved on. It saddened him to erase all traces of his underground stream, but he could not spare so much as a crumb from his rations and after he had rewarded his success with a generous swig from the pot bottle everything went back into the bait bag. He slung it over his shoulder, slid the rod under his belt and started walking; uphill now. There would be no more dowsing for a while; on the other hand, there was no need of it. He had proved to himself beyond all doubt that he still had his power, or at least his mystery. All he needed now was someone who needed him, and he saw that the terrain became drier with every hour that passed. Never a pool or stream or even a spruit did he see. This was a place where men must dig wells, if any men lived here, and he saw no signs of habitation, either. The sun was moving round and down at his right, while his stealthy shadow crept up on him from behind, on his left side.

When he reached the next ridge and looked round he observed that the sun was now reddening and only three fingers, at arm's length, above the horizon. He still had an hour or so of daylight left, but it would take many hours to reach any kind of shelter. On the hill crest ahead of him he could see, glowing in the sun's low light, what looked like the ruins of a stone building. Between that and him there was nothing except the sweeping slope of hill and valley. The ground was smooth, he could surely cross it safely in the dark. There might even be a moon, later, although he had no way of calculating it. It was several weeks since the moon had last shone down upon the Webfeet's valley, and he could not recall whether it had waxed or waned, but he felt certain that in this promised land there would be a moon every night, ever full, round and white as an onion. Encouraged by this fancy he began his second descent of that day, and as he went down, the sun went down, too. He had forgotten what would happen as he left the hill top, not surprisingly, since in the valley the sun, when it shone, had been a dependable lamp that doused itself in the river at evening, or dissolved somewhere above it.

Now it shone still on the stone ruin in front of him, but he found that he was walking downward into deep shadow and, worse, something was coming up to meet him; mist, writhing like a creature over the ground. At one moment he was looking down on it, as he had done that morning, the next he was drowning in it. For a few minutes he blundered on, shivering, and the darkness grew deeper. He could no longer see his own feet, and there were now no larks to cheer him. Instead, a melancholy whooping slewed about his head as a silently flying thing swam through the airborne gruel. His unsuspecting foot was caught in a hollow out of sight, and he fell onto wet grass.

There was no point in trying to go further. He knelt in the thickening darkness and for the first time since he left the village, began to regret what he had done. He was lost in a place that rendered him as cold and wet and miserable as he would have been at home, and it was an alien misery, not the drear monotony of life in the carpenter's cottage, as familiar as mud. He would never be successful, he would never be rich, he had exchanged one bad circumstance for another. From the moment his mother's boat had smashed into the bridge his life had been one long downhill progress towards ignominy, and even if he had set his feet on a different path, he was still going in the same direction. Then he remembered his stream, and his mystery, and trusting that marvellous day would lift the mist for him when the sun rose again, he wrapped himself in the frayed sacking that he wore as a cloak and lay down with his head pillowed on the repellent lumpiness of the bait bag. His unexpected sleep at midday had left him wakeful, he was damp, stiff, the bait bag felt like a cushion full of flints, but he was weary in spite of it and fell asleep at last, dreaming that he strode through the night with his rod, and divined the path of the very sun as it rolled underground between evening and morning.

He got his sunshine next morning, and after a breakfast of beer and beets he moved on toward the ruin on the hill. The ground was hard beneath his shoes; he was unused to walking on a firm surface. His feet hurt and the earth rang like stone under his footfalls. He began to be uneasy. He had left home yesterday in spring, and although he was not fool enough to suppose that he had travelled so far that he had entered another season, it struck him that this place was uncommonly dry for spring, and it was surprisingly warm. Perhaps he had died in the night and come to that Good Place where, the Webfeet had believed, pathetically, they would go one day if they desisted from evil deeds. 'No water there,' they'd said, smugly. '*You'll* never see it.' If this was it, and he was seeing it, they were welcome to it.

As he approached the ruin, about mid-morning, he became reluctant to go any closer. After a low lifetime spent among cottages of clay and plaster, the looming bulk of the stone structure seemed to lean down dangerously toward him, on the verge of toppling. The ascent was very steep here, and he had to tip his head right back in order to see the top of the pile, dark in the blue sky with the sun behind it, and dark birds wheeling overhead. Maybe it was not a ruin after all; might not desperate brigands lodge there, waiting for unwary travellers? Maybe it *was* a ruin, but the abode of ghosts. He was glad that he had not come upon it by night.

In the light of the bright yet unreassuring sun he found himself among the first of the fallen stones that lay about it, bedded deep in the earth and cuffed with the short brown grass that grew on the hillsides. The stones looked as though they had been there for ever, not fallen but emergent. They were grey and freckled with a darker grey, but when he moved his head he saw fiery sparks in the skin of them. When he touched them they were hot under his hands and harder than anything he had ever touched before. He came up and round the side of the ruin, and it was not a ruin; no human hand had ever stacked those stones one upon the other. Either it was the work of giants or else this great building, unbuilt, had shouldered its way out of the very earth, like a stone monster from an egg.

Viner sat down on one of the rocks and looked about him. The world was all in three colours, the blue sky, the brown grass, the grey stone. He thought himself a black unsightly blot upon it. He was still in the land of hill tops, and upon every hill top was a stone castle like the one where he sat, where unseen watchmen guarded an unseen people, and all the world danced in the heat. He reached into the bait bag and took out the pot bottle, but before he had removed the stopper he had thought better of it. This was no place to be wasting drink and no place to be seeking water. The stones sparkled all round him but there was no distant flash of light upon pool or moving stream. The pot bottle was half empty; he did not know how long his journey would be nor where it would take him. He put the bottle back in the bag, stood up and turning his back on the ruin, if ruin it might be, began to walk down again toward the place where the brown grass faded to blue and the blue deepened until it was the sky itself. His truncated shadow stumped beside him, heel to heel and toe to toe; while on his other side fear kept him company, casting no shadow but wheezing dryly through desiccated lungs. It was the only sound in all the silent day.

2

Nightfall found him limping among rubble on a blasted hillside where nothing stood except the dead bracken that crisped and crinkled underfoot. He scraped a pile of it together to make a bed, drank the remainder of the beer and lay down under glaring stars to think of last night's enveloping mist, and beyond it, the village. He heard the roaring of the pent-up river beneath the bridge, the liquid insistence of water talking its way into houses under closed doors, the slapping of wavelets, dripping eaves, the squelch of clogs in sodden grass. His dreams were dank and cold and mouldy, richly satisfying, but he woke in the world's furnace, with cracked lips. He did not know how long a man could survive without water. He still had plenty of food, but he wanted to drink, and after a dry breakfast, masticated, hefted the bait bag and began to walk behind the questing beak of his rod, that seemed to draw him along in its wake, unresisting. So much for power.

He was nearing the end of the fourth day before the willow took pity on him. The stone ruins were left far behind; all was stone now, bleached and barren, with the grass scorched off it. At the head of a little valley, among crookedly stretching shadows, the rod started expectantly, and when the spasms became too strong for his enfeebled grip he went down on his knees and tore at the scree with his hands until he uncovered a little stream that broke out of the hillside, where rocks had rolled down and buried it. He lay on his face and sucked in the water; then he filled the pot bottle; then he crouched among the stones and, scooping up water in his cupped hands, sluiced his dry skin and prickling hair. He spent that night by the stream and sent his nostalgic thoughts of the Webfeet packing, back to their valley where they belonged, like the watery wraiths they were. In the morning he drank again, and moved on.

He managed to make the water last two days, but even after the pot bottle, upended, refused to yield another drop, he continued to walk, and all that kept him moving was the pride, still flickering in him, that after his years of grovelling, all his years of contriving to avoid trouble, he had had the courage to walk into the unknown instead of turning back to face safety and defeat. He imagined that he would die soon.

What a waste, he thought, vaguely, biting his tongue to make the spittle come. Over before I've begun. He was so dazed by now that he continued to walk, on his flayed and tortured feet, before he realized that the rod was on the move again. He went back, then, to a little muddy hollow through which he had staggered, unnoticing. He dredged a cavity in the mud and after a long while it filled with soupy water that tasted of iron and brimstone, but nevertheless slaked his felted tongue and filled the pot bottle; and so he lived another night.

The rod ignored him for a time, after that, but he continued to follow it because it had saved him twice and he hoped, since there was nothing he could do but hope, for a third deliverance; but the third time it deceived him. He had come to an open space ringed by standing stones of great height which made him think of dragons' teeth, so that he almost expected a huge reciprocal jaw to swing down from the sky and consume him in everlasting darkness. The rod had drawn him across the circle to the far side before it leaped in his hands, but when he dug, with his shaking fingers, he found no water. He found a cracked urn that cut his hand, and ashes, and among the ashes a gold ring with a red stone in it. He sat for longer than he knew by the dry hole, licking the blood from his hand while it was still wet, and sucking at the wound for more, before creeping to his feet again and following the rod where it beckoned him on toward a brooding hunchbacked hill, with three summits, that floated above the horizon, beyond the stones.

When he saw the trees on the hillside he thought at first that they must be witched, so featly did they dance on their stunted trunks, but when he drew near he found that they were rooted in the earth and that between them ran a track; that on the track were the prints of hooves, wheels, human feet; and that from somewhere people were approaching. The dry fog behind his eyes lifted

24

like a morning haze. He was a stranger, alone in a strange land, bearing valuable trove and an instrument that might yet lead him to his death. What was power to his mother, a mystery to his father, a curse to the Webfeet, might be taken for sorcery here, and who could tell what a strange land thought of sorcerers? He drew back among the trees and stooped to hide himself, for although he recognized them as oaks from the time when he lived Further Up, they were so dwarfish that his eyes were on a level with the topmost branches. He would have thought them standing corpses had he not seen spring buds blistering the twigs. He slithered downward until he was safely concealed behind a stout trunk, and peered out towards the track he had just left. From one direction came an elderly peasant with a herd of refractory pigs; from the other, four young men on horseback, leading a pack-ass and moving slowly, wary eyes cast in all directions. They were armed. When peasant and horsemen were within talking distance of each other they all halted, and after a brief conference two of them dismounted and advanced toward the swineherd on foot. The taller of the two was dressed in an extraordinary jerkin made of red and tabby cat-skins which gave him what Viner guessed to be a misleadingly soft appearance. He raised his hand. 'Is it peace, friend?' he said. His accent was broad and glottal but Viner, accustomed to foreign tongues, understood him well enough.

'Are you free men?' the swineherd asked, at once.

'Harmless travellers, as you can see,' Catskin said. Suddenly his hands were empty and innocent, while the two young men behind him raised their arms to show their swords safely sheathed at their sides. Only the prognathous youth beside Catskin made no move to show that he was unarmed, and his elbows were oddly akimbo beneath his cloak. Viner imagined that he was already drawing a bead on one of the pigs, for there was now no sign of the short bow that had hung at his back. 'What is the name of this place?'

'We call it the Low Forest, sirs,' the swineherd said.

'We?' The bowman's arm twitched beneath his cloak.

'Easy, Hern,' said Catskin. Hern subsided, but his right arm flexed.

'We in the village down there, sirs,' the swineherd said. 'It's half a day's journey, sirs, on foot. No one comes up here except I myself,' he added, unwisely, at which news Hern raised his bow and spitted the nearest pig. The drover, seeing no future in conversation, fled downhill among the trees, with the rest of his beasts. The two riders who had waited behind rode forward. The one who led the pack-ass said nothing, he had the look of a servant, but the other, who wore his hair so long that it was plaited into a queue between his shoulders, slid from his horse and went with Hern to inspect the pig.

'Was that an honest man?' he asked.

'More honest than we were,' Hern said, matter-of-factly, as he tugged his bolt from the body of the pig. 'Let's find a good camp site and start a fire. We'll be left in peace tonight if that fellow goes telling tales that we are free men, and there are no true ones about.'

Viner, holding his breath and trembling like the dry twigs all about him, pressed his body nearer to the tree trunk where he leaned, and prayed that his dark head would not show conspicuous among the bony branches. He gathered that free men were men who felt free to do as they pleased, and if the marauding quartet on the road were not free men then they gave a convincing imitation. Moreover there might, as they seemed to think, be true free men about. What did free men do, to demonstrate their freedom? Compressing his dry lips until they split, and the blood trickled, he held himself silent and still while Hern, Catskin and the other remounted and rode away. It did not escape him that the pack-ass, plodding in the rear, was laden not only with bedding and utensils, but with two great skins of water. He knew already what he was going to do. Armed or not, they must be persuaded to part with some of that water, and if they were looking for a camp site he would follow them until they found it, and wait until dark, and then creep out, and if he did die with Hern's bolt through his heart he would die with a drink inside him.

He would have preferred to approach the drover, but there was no trace of him or his pigs, and in any case, he had carried nothing about him save a gnarled staff; no bait bag, no bottle. Viner moved upright and eased himself stiffly between the trunks until he stood among the trees that fringed the track. In the distance the four riders could easily be seen, head and shoulders above the tops of the gibbous oaks. He stooped his own shoulders lest one of them, glancing back, should mark his head as a likely target, and started in pursuit of the ambling horses, himself as bent and painful as the trees on either side.

They did not travel far. When he caught up with them again they had ridden round to the far side of the forest, uphill of the place where he had first seen them, and halted in a hollow where boulders formed a natural windbreak and a flat stone lay in the grass, offering itself as a hearth. Viner left the track and crouched down among the trees again to watch them. The sun was setting and he was now only one shadow among many others. The party prepared to settle for the night. The servant, addressed as Anvil, hobbled the beasts and turned them loose to graze on the uninviting turf. Catskin went into the wood to gather kindling while Hern settled by the hearthstone to skin and joint the pig which he had carried behind him, pillion. The fourth man sat himself down on a boulder and drew dour silence round him like a blanket. A gold ring glittered in his earlobe. He looked unsafe. He seemed to be the leader, since he did no work and was asked to do none; also he was the guardian of the treasure, for at his feet were the water skins. Viner lay in the soft rot of leaves and bracken, sucking a pebble, staring with lascivious eyes through the failing light at the water skins, and wondering if his thirst would overcome his fear.

Hern looked up from his grisly work and said quietly, 'Cleaver?'

Viner thought he was asking for one, to pursue his business with the carcase, but he was addressing the fourth man who looked round, perceived that the other two were occupied and distant, and answered, 'Yes?'

Cleaver? *Cleaver?* What kind of a name was that? What were these people?

'Where do we go tomorrow?' Hern said, his knife shining with blood and sunset.

'We go back,' said Cleaver, looking away from him. 'Back home. We can't stay here for ever. People are going to start wondering where we've got to.'

'I thought we were supposed to be on a hunting trip.'

'Supposed?' Cleaver gestured towards the meat. 'No hunting

trip ever lasted nine weeks, not even one of ours. Questions'll be asked.'

'They'll be asked anyway – especially if we go back with nothing.'

Cleaver sighed moodily. 'We *shall* go back with nothing. Even if we found anything this far out it would be no use. We could hardly take it back with us.'

Hunters? Mercenaries? What were they looking for?

'Can't we just disappear?' Hern's guttural voice turned wistful.

'Don't I wish we could? But what about the King?'

King's men. Which king?

'What about him?' Hern said. 'We go back and the King dances. The King dances and nothing happens. Nothing happens and –'

'Something may have happened since we've been gone,' Cleaver said, uneasily. He seemed reluctant to continue the conversation and when Catskin returned with an armful of branches, tossed it down and turned away to fetch more, Cleaver stood up quickly.

'I'll go. You see to the fire.'

'Anvil's collecting too.'

'We'll need as much as we can get. I don't fancy scratching around in the dark when we run out.' He moved hurriedly between the trees and Viner pressed himself into the humus as he passed, not a dozen paces away.

A *dancing* king?

Catskin knelt to erect a little cone of bark and twigs, and produced flints from his wallet. 'What was all that about?'

'The King.' Hern laid a finger to the side of his nose.

'No wonder he cleared off,' Catskin said. 'He doesn't care for that kind of talk.'

'He says we're to go back tomorrow.'

'It's his choice. It was his idea to come in the first place.'

'I said it was a pity. I said it was a pity we couldn't just disappear.'

'It's a pity the King can't just disappear,' Catskin said. A flame sprang up between his hands and he gave Hern a sinister look across it.

28

'He certainly doesn't care for *that* kind of talk,' Hern said.

'He should worry. When we have a princess will be time to think of a new king. No point in fretting ourselves beforehand.'

'And if it isn't a princess?'

'We'll worry about that when it happens ... another two months, yet ... he's coming back,' said Catskin, between conservative breaths into the cradle of his fire.

Cleaver reappeared bearing a single log as thick as his own waist, which he dropped alongside Catskin. Catskin sighed into the flames. Hern leaned forward to cast small sticks onto the burning touchwood. Viner, dry as tinder, scorched, mouthed, Go away, all of you. Go. *Go*. After a moment, Catskin rose and left them.

'What will you worry about when it happens?' Cleaver asked, suspiciously. He tweaked his plait forward and dusted his fingers with it, absent-mindedly.

'Oh, ways and means. I say we should sacrifice.' Hern's knife gleamed in the infant firelight.

'Sacrifice?' said Cleaver. 'It's not the custom.' In the deepening dusk he clasped his hands about his shoulders and pulled the cowl of his cloak higher round his neck. 'Where did you learn of sacrifices?'

Hern said, 'There's nothing to stop us making a sacrifice, is there? No one would know.'

'Will it work if no one knows?' Cleaver asked. 'Will it work if we sacrifice here? Shouldn't we do it at home?'

'It must be a black sacrifice. A goat or a cock: or ... a man. They're more dark-featured round these parts than we are at home. What say we took someone back with us?'

'You can't mean that?' Cleaver sounded more hopeful than certain, and his voice struck a falsely optimistic note above Hern's urgent whisper. 'The King would never allow it.'

'The King will never know. Let him dance. That's about all he's good for, and he's no good for that, either. Or the other thing.' He sniggered, and this sound of good cheer struck more fear into Viner than anything that had been said before. He fixed his eyes on the water skins, to screw his courage to the sticking place. 'A black sacrifice,' Hern was saying. 'The blacker the better.' He stooped and plunged his knife into the earth to cleanse it. Viner thought he looked as if he were cutting the world's throat. His mind was made up. He would not stay another minute in the vicinity of these plotters and murderers who belittled their king, planned sacrifices and did not trust even one another. He would slide silently away in the darkness, and if he lived till morning he would go down, across the track, and if he lived one half day longer he would find the swineherd's village, or the rod would find him a stream, or he would die. He started to rise and was instantly knocked flat again by the impact of something enormously heavy that struck him down from behind. As he tried to roll over to free his face from the stifling humus, to breathe, to *see*, he felt the pressure of fur against his skin and thought that a wild beast had attacked him, until a human hand gripped his arm and dragged him to his feet and a human foot kicked him toward the fire that now blazed beyond the trees while a human voice shouted, 'What have we here, then?'

He had been caught by Catskin. It was Catskin who man-handled him to the fireside, threw him down in the ashes and made him sit with his hands clasped behind his head and Hern's knife before his eyes. In the confusion Anvil wandered up with his load of firewood. Hern pointed toward the pack-ass, silhouetted against the last redness of the sky.

'Fetch a rope.'

They were going to hang him. He wondered how they would hang him when the nearest available trees were so much shorter than he was.

'Oh, look at that,' Hern said, with horrid, breathy pleasure. 'Look at that. Black hair, black beard, black clothes. Look at his eyes: like damsons.' The blade in his hand quivered with anticipation. In spite of his extremity Viner was flattered to hear the sparse fluff on his face described as a beard.

Cleaver regarded him from a little way off. 'Who are you?' he said. 'Why were you watching us?'

'Where are the rest of you?' Catskin said.

Viner's raw lips opened a little and closed several times before he was able to speak. 'I meant you no harm,' he said, but his voice came out in a hiss and they all leaned frighteningly close to hear

30

what he said. 'There's no one else. I was looking for water.'

'Water!' Hern snapped, and the knife jerked, dangerously near his neck.

'No!' he cried. 'No, no. Not water; no. I never wanted water. I wasn't looking for water.' He knew what happened to people who went looking for water.

'Looking for water on a hill? In a wood?' Catskin jeered. 'Water flows upwards for you, does it?'

'No. *No*. A mistake . . . not water . . . not . . .'

'He's raving,' Cleaver said. 'Of course he wants water, look at his mouth. Give him some, Catskin. We might get some sense out of him, afterwards.'

Catskin shook his head at this prodigal suggestion but he did as he was told. Viner heard the water, and smelled it, and felt it poured down his throat until he choked on it, but he would not admit that it was that for which he had been searching. Then he guessed that they would probably search *him*, and the first thing they would find was the rod. Would they know what it was for?

'I hid in the wood when I saw you were armed,' he said. 'I was afraid. I didn't want your water.'

'Didn't you?' Cleaver looked sadly at him. Anvil came softly out of the dusk and stood at Cleaver's side with a rope in his hands, twisted into a skein and about to be untwisted; untwisting now.

'I wasn't *looking* for it. I don't know how . . .' If this gang disapproved of dowsing, they wouldn't stop at throwing things.

Hern pulled the bait bag from his shoulder and opened it. He drew out the empty pot bottle, the blunted knife, and the bacon bone.

'How long have you been travelling?'

'I don't know. A week, maybe.'

'Are you a free man?'

'Free to come and go,' Viner said. 'I went.'

Cleaver hit him across the face more, he thought, from nervousness than from a desire to punish.

'No jokes here,' Cleaver said. 'Where were you going?'

'To find work – a place to live,' Viner said.

'Work? Who are you, what do you do? What's your name?' Catskin shook him. Viner remained mute.

'Who cares what his name is?' Hern said. 'He won't be needing it much longer.'

'Viner,' said Viner, with an unexpected flare of contrariness.

'Is that what you are, or what you do?'

'It's my name.'

'You grow vines?' Cleaver looked bewildered.

'It's my name,' Viner said. 'Not what I do.'

'What do you do?'

'Nothing!' He almost screamed it. 'I don't do anything.'

'Perhaps he carries the tools of his trade on him,' Catskin said. He took the rope from Anvil and swung it, idly. 'Have a look.'

Hern, without lowering the knife, ran an expert hand over his body. 'All bone and gristle,' he said. 'Hello, here's a spare bone.' From inside Viner's shirt he drew out the forked twig. 'Your weapon?' he said, derisively, tossing it to one side. It fell across the hearthstone and Viner, disregarding the knife, forgetting the danger he was in and that the world is full of twigs, remembering only that the rod was his mystery that had saved his life, flung himself after it. He had it in his roasting fingers before he realized that he had probably given himself away, and by then they had hauled him out of the ashes, singed and fatuously clutching a willow twig that was beginning to char at the ends. He had not given himself away.

'It's his charm, maybe,' Cleaver said. 'Let him keep it.'

'I never meant to burn it,' Hern growled. Viner had accidentally kicked him in the stomach in passing. 'He's a madman, that's all. Worships a stick. I've heard of people like that. Tie him up, Cat, before he kills one of us.'

Catskin wound the rope several times round his waist and his elbows, knotted it, cut off the remainder and tied his ankles with it. Viner, now on his back and helpless, did not fail to notice that there was now no rope left, and still they had not hanged him. Then he remembered the knife, the swords, the bow; who needed rope? Hern went to work again, searching in places where Viner would never have expected to hide anything, before turning his attention once more to the bait bag, upending it and shaking it. This time he had more success. In the firelight they all saw what fell from it, into the grass. It was the gold ring with the red stone that Viner had found in the urn with the ashes, earlier that day, or yesterday, or once upon a time.

Catskin retrieved it and passed it to Cleaver.

'Is this yours?' Cleaver said, holding it up close to his prisoner's face.

'No, that is –'

'You stole it?'

'I found it.'

'He stole it,' Catskin said, flatly.

'I found it.'

'Where did you find it?'

'In the ground.' Involuntarily his eyes swivelled to where the rod lay beside the hearth. He struggled to his knees, off balance with his arms pinioned. 'Perhaps I could find more.' He could not disguise the hope in his voice.

'Your god finds it for you, perhaps,' Catskin said, nudging the rod with his foot.

'It's no god,' Viner said.

'Wishbone,' Hern said. 'Great big wooden wishbone.' He sounded drunken; drunk on the prospect of killing?

'But it found gold for me,' Viner said, certain, now, that he was pleading for his life. 'If we went back to the same place, there might be something more.' Only, not water, not water, not this time. This lot had plenty of water. Better nothing at all . . .

'Nothing to lose by it,' Cleaver said. 'We might as well have something to take back. The Queen would like that ring, and if there's anything else we can sell it. That would lay any questions,' he said to Hern. 'Where did you find this?' He held up the ring.

'In the ground.'

'*What* ground?'

'The other side of the wood. Half a day's walk, on foot. You have horses.' He was not at all sure about the distance. He had not been aware of it at the time, but he was unwilling to admit that it might be several day's walk away. He thought it was this morning, but –

'You'll be on foot,' Hern said. 'You and your magic wand.' His look said, Don't think for a moment that you're going to escape

33

me; gold or no gold, I'll have you. He glanced at the others. 'What say we move off at first light?'

'First light,' Cleaver agreed, 'and then home.'

They seemed to forget him after that, and busied themselves with cooking the pig, but Viner soon found that his slightest movement was rewarded with a visit from Hern or Catskin, and when they finally sat down to eat he was seated carefully between them, and the knife was still unsheathed. They gave him more water, bread and some of the meat. It was not easy to eat with his arms so constricted, but by curling himself head almost on knees he contrived to get something down. They were taciturn over their meal, cagey, each looking round at the others before venturing on a single word, and he discovered nothing new, listen as he might, before they banked the fire and settled to sleep. He knew it might be his last night, ever, as he lay looking into the embers, but recently he had passed so many nights that had promised to be his last that the prospect did not depress him as much as it might have done. At all events, it did not prevent him from sleeping. At all events, he wasn't dead yet.

He heard their voices in his sleep, woke, saw that it was morning and closed them again, knowing that he would learn more if they thought he could not overhear them. They squatted in a huddle on the far side of the hearthstone, feeding the fire while they talked, and he strained to catch their words above the clack and snap of the flames as they bit into the wood.

'I know you suggested it,' Hern said, 'but is it worth a detour?'

'It won't be a detour. If we're turning back we'll be going more or less in that direction anyway.' That was Catskin. It seemed that he really was called Catskin, but why was Cleaver called Cleaver? He seemed the most pacific of them all. And why Anvil, why Hern? Hern, *Heron?* If Hern resembled anything it was a toad. He had no forehead and no chin.

'How do we know he's telling the truth?' Hern again.

'We don't, so let's find out.' Cleaver, this time.

'Kill him now.' Hern. 'We don't need the gold.'

'We may be glad of it.'

'I want to see how that thing works, that he carries,' Catskin said. 'How can he find gold with a forked stick? How can he find anything?'

Viner broke out in a sweat of terror. He did not expect to find gold. Gold did not run in molten streams through the earth. What would they do to him if he found water instead? It was possible that, charred as it was, the rod would not find anything. Today he would die.

'He'll die anyway,' Hern said.

'Not if he finds gold.' Cleaver again, and quickly. Viner knew then that Cleaver had suggested the treasure hunt to save his life, or at least to prolong it. Cleaver knew that Hern wanted the prisoner dead; Hern had wanted the prisoner dead from the moment he first saw him with his black hair, black eyes, black clothes. Cleaver might be the leader, but Hern would have his way. Viner was to be the black sacrifice, today he would die. Before he died he would ask them what he was dying for, but until then he would keep his mouth shut. It was not something he wished to discuss.

Anvil trod heavily toward him and shook him awake.

'Time to be moving,' Anvil said. He bent over Viner to free his ankles but left his arms fastened. 'You'll be walking. Get up.'

He moaned and swore as the blood returned to his cramped limbs, but they took no notice of him. They were too much occupied in breaking camp, packing up the remainder of the meat, stamping out the fire. Anvil brought down the horses and the pack-ass and they loaded up. Hern attached Viner to his saddle bow with a short length of rope and kneed him into action.

'Show us the way,' he said.

Viner began to walk, and they followed. If he knew the way at all it was as a series of landmarks, hazily noted, without sequence or significance, and if he could not recognize any of them he might as well confess as much to Hern and die on the spot. It would at least save him many hours of fear and pain. He looked round and up at their implacable faces. Catskin carried the divining-rod.

'If you lead us into a trap,' Hern said, evenly, 'you'll fall before any of us. We're all armed and I ride with my bow strung, if there's any chance of danger. Lead on.'

They came out of the Low Forest, along the track, and he looked

35

up at what might be his last view of the world, but the first thing he saw was a cleft in the hillside, through which he remembered passing, yesterday.

'That way,' he said, inclining his head. 'Follow me.' They proceeded in silence across the hillside, past a dead goat. 'Follow me.' Past a ruined hut. 'This way. Follow me.'

'How can you tell we're on the right road?' Catskin asked.

'We're passing all the places I passed yesterday,' Viner said.

'We're on no road. It's a trap,' Hern said.

'Why should I lead you into a trap?'

'Why not?' Hern evidently tended to judge people by his own motives. 'How do we know you weren't sent to decoy us?' The still hot air was heavy with suspicion and mistrust. Cleaver slumped over his horse's neck and said nothing. 'You said half a day's journey, on foot. We've been travelling half a day already. What say we kill him now, Cleaver, and take his rod? It may work for us.'

'It won't work for you,' Viner cried. 'It will only work for me.'

'He could teach us to use it,' Hern said, 'before we killed him.'

The sheer cheek of this suggestion stung him to retort. 'If you think I'm going to teach you my mystery so you can murder me sooner, think again,' he said. Hern leaned down from his mount and struck him between the shoulders.

While they paused to argue Anvil had gone on ahead a little way, and stood up in his stirrups to see what lay in front of them. He called back, 'We're coming to a ring of big stones. I can see their tops from here.'

'That is the place,' Viner said, and he shivered as he had never shivered while they doubted him. Delaying time was over. It was divining time.

'It seems that his god guides him after all,' Catskin said, and switched the air with the confiscated rod.

'It still took longer than it should have done,' Hern said. 'From now on I ride with my weapons showing.' He threw back his cloak so that any hidden watcher could see his bow, his knife, his sword, his quiver full of arrows. The others, though less defensively dressed, did likewise, and the party advanced in a single file, very slowly, with Viner in the van, on his leash and leading.

'Where do you think the attack will come from?' Cleaver asked, with some irony in his tone that made Viner glance back at him, sharply. They were proceeding across a dusty plain where nothing raised itself above ground level except for the big stones, growing bigger by the minute, as they approached. The same thought had occurred to Viner, who could see no hiding place in any direction, but he had expected no kind of humour from this crew.

'This is a trap,' Hern reiterated. 'He has brought us here to die in the dust.'

All the while, before them, Viner walked on, and did not look back again.

The sun was at their backs when they finally reached the stones. They halted in the shade of the nearest that towered fifteen arm-spans above them. On either side the next stone, seemingly identical, was all of two hundred paces away.

'Now,' said Hern, his face lit with sunshine and cold malice, 'where did you find that ring?'

'At the foot of a stone.'

Hern smiled his lipless smile. 'Which?'

Viner looked all round him and saw only himself as he had appeared there yesterday, desperate and near delirious, on his knees and scraping like a dog in the dirt. He had been close to a stone, but which indeed? There must be a hundred of them and in the bright light the ground where they stood ruptured and rippled like water. They lurched, shuffled, continually changing places like lumbering children engaged in a sly game.

'Which stone?' Hern said again.

Viner was staring at the ground. Out of the corner of his eye he could see, among some pebbles, the urn that he had thrown away the day before, discomforted rather than disappointed by its contents. He knew bone-ash when he saw it. He pointed as well as he could with half an arm. 'That one.'

'How do you know?'

'I know. If you'd let me loose,' he said, 'I could find the exact place where I was digging yesterday.' Hern unhooked his end of the rope and Viner, trailing it behind him, began to prowl across the withered grass, with bent head and close attention.

'What if he runs?' Catskin said.

'Ride him down,' said Hern. The bolt was in his bow.

Viner, walking carefully to save his chafed arms further distress, found what he was looking for. He was vaguely surprised to see how far down he had dug. Among scattered rocks his excavation was elbow-deep; no wonder his nails had gone.

'This is where I found the ring,' he said. 'Will you dig in the same place or shall I dowse again?'

'Dowse?'

'With the rod.'

'Give him the rod,' Cleaver commanded, and Catskin handed it down.

'Will you loosen the rope?' Hern was ready to argue, but Cleaver dismounted and slackened the knot. As soon as the rod was in his hands again he was filled with confidence and with as much despair. Whatever he found would not save him. If he found water or nothing, Hern would strike at once. If he found gold he would live a little longer, but not much; he was the black sacrifice. Nonetheless, hampered as he was by the rope round his elbows, he caught hold of the forked ends and, taking no more notice of his captors, began a steady pacing that took him away from them. He sensed, rather than saw, Hern raise his bow in readiness, and with all his will tried to fill his mind with thoughts of gold, but the dust clogged his nostrils and furred his throat, and all he could think of was water.

After a dozen paces he stepped aside and continued at a different angle.

'How does it work?' Cleaver was saying. 'Does it lead him?'

'Perhaps it speaks, only, naturally, we don't hear it,' said Hern, sarcastic, but in a cautious undertone. '*Ayyyy*,' he cried out, caution abandoned, as in Viner's hands the rod was convulsed, and swung upright.

'It *has* spoken,' Catskin muttered, nervously twirling the striated tails that hung from his jerkin.

'Mark that place,' Viner said, unable to keep the arrogance from his voice. 'Use my bacon bone.'

'Is this, too, magic?' Cleaver asked. He took the bone almost reverently from Viner's bag, and placed it in his hand. Viner stopped and put the bone on the ground, at his feet.

'No, but I use it as a marker. It's all the marker I have left, except the pot bottle. I ate the rest. You'll have to find something else to mark the other places.'

'Ate them?'

'What other places?' Hern cut in, as Viner began to move again, remembering too late that gold did not flow. 'Stop that!' He stamped on the end of the rope and Viner was brought up short. 'He's playing for time,' Hern said. 'There is no gold. If we dug all day there would be no gold.'

'There *is* gold,' Viner said, shivering again. 'That is, there was yesterday.'

'Then we'll dig for it now,' said Hern. 'We'll dig just where you put that bone, and there'll be no more what-d'you-call-it, dows-ing. If we find no gold then you die.' He walked to the waiting ass, dragging Viner with him, backwards, and tugged a shovel from under the pack strap. 'Anvil, dig there, where the bone is. See how the shadow of the stone is moving? When it reaches you, stop, and if you've found nothing this Viner dies in the grave you've dug for him.'

Viner looked away from him, to where Cleaver stood, morosely declining to intervene, and he knew what he was thinking. Hern might dress like a warrior but he did not want to fight, he wanted to kill. He did not demand honourable combat with a worthy adversary; he would be equally satisfied by the death of a bound and helpless prisoner. Any sacrifice he made would be to himself, and all Cleaver would do, was doing, was to hope that Anvil's spade would strike gold before the stone's advancing shadow struck Anvil. Viner, now fully admitted to Hern's own mystery, stood back from the deepening pit and stared into it with sick eyes. He was closer than Anvil to the shadow, and when he felt it growing on him his eyes quivered shut, and stayed shut, so that he would not see when it reached the edge of the pit.

'Now,' said Hern, striding forward. 'Where's the gold?'

'There is no gold,' Anvil said.

He heard Cleaver and Catskin approach and stand close by him. Neither spoke. He opened his eyes a fraction and looked down into the hole; there was nothing in it but gravel and loose earth. Hern laid down his bow and unsheathed the knife at his belt, moving slowly round the side of the pit to where Viner stood alone, wide-eyed now.

'No gold, Viner,' Hern said. 'There is no gold. There never was any gold, was there? It was a good try, but it's over. As a matter of interest, before you go, tell us where you really did get that ring. If we can go there ourselves and find more at least you'll go knowing that you paid for your extra time. Did you think to cheat it from us?'

'I found gold here,' Viner said, not looking up. His voice had turned very thin and dry. 'I didn't *promise* more, but you would have me look.' Rare and distant, in his mind's eye, he saw the valley, the rain, the river, the Webfeet in their mud-caked clogs; heard the water slurping vulgarly in their footprints.

'You lied to us,' Hern said. 'Or did the rod lie to you? It's a poor god, your rod. Put not your trust in forked sticks, Viner.'

'If you're going to kill him, kill him; don't read him a lecture first,' Catskin snapped. Hern stepped round behind Viner and flung an arm across his throat, jolting back his head and raising the knife at the same time, and at the same time Anvil shouted, 'Look! Look in the hole!'

They followed the line of his pointing finger, Hern too, although he neither relaxed his hold nor lowered his knife. Viner saw what they were looking at and felt the last dregs of hope drain out of him, like a haemorrhage, leaving him bloodless. The bottom of the hole was full of water.

Cleaver leaped across the pit and struck the descending knife from Hern's grip in the same movement. With his other hand he gave Hern a great shove that sent him reeling back. Viner staggered under the impact and, unsupported by Hern, sat down backwards. Cleaver seized him by the shoulders, shaking him and shouting in his face, 'I knew damn well you were looking for water. Is that what you found? Did your rod find that?'

Viner gaped at him, realizing, only very slowly, that the face above him was twisted not with fury but with *relief*.

'Yes,' he said, blankly. 'The rod found it. It works with water, too.'

'This is the truth? You can find water under the ground – and bring it out?'

'And gold.'

'Bugger the gold. You can find water.'

'If it's there, yes. I can find it, with the rod.'

Cleaver looked over his shoulder at Hern, spread-eagled in the dust. 'You stupid bastard!' He went over to Hern and kicked him, soundly. 'You and your sodding sacrifices! He's just what we need and you wanted to kill him, you damned brainless stupid son of a *whore* . . .' His powers of invective were, it seemed, endless. While he stamped and shouted Catskin and Anvil joined in, delivering a few kicks of their own before hoisting Hern to his feet, whereupon they flung their arms around each other's shoulders and performed a manic caper in the dust that rose in clouds around them.

Viner, dimly aware that he was the cause of the celebration but past caring about anything aside from the fact that he was going to live after all, stared down into the dingy pool that had, against all odds, saved his life. Behind him, Cleaver and his boys were whooping and cheering and hurling stones into the air. One aimless rock missed him by a hand's breadth and crashed into the water.

'How could I know what they wanted?' he said, plaintively. Another rock sailed over his head to strike sparks from the standing stone beyond the pit. He thought it would be a pity if they killed him now, by accident.

3

'How could I know?' he said later, when they had all calmed down. 'How could I know you wanted water? You never mentioned it, even when I was in the wood, listening to you.'

Cleaver shook his head, still bemused. 'When you said you were looking for it, I didn't know you meant that you could find it.'

'I didn't want you to know,' Viner said. 'Where I come from, no one wants water. They've got too much water. They drove me out because they thought I could call it up.'

'Can't you?' Hern said.

Viner hesitated. He could not call it up, but did they want to know that? He compromised. 'If it's there.'

'But didn't they want gold, those people where you lived?' Catskin said, seeking some evidence of rational behaviour in that incredible place.

'I don't think they ever saw gold in their lives,' Viner said. 'They wouldn't have known what it was.' He did not care to reveal that neither he nor the Webfeet had had any suspicion that the rod would answer to gold.

'You knew what it was,' Hern said, swiftly.

'I wasn't one of them. I came from Further Up.'

'Were you looking for it, by the big stones?'

'No.' He was able to laugh, now. 'I was looking for water, and when I found the ring, I was afraid. I wanted to get away from that place.' They might as well go on thinking that he had known about his power over gold. The less they knew about his mystery, the stronger the power.

'So was I afraid in that place,' Cleaver admitted.

'Old woman,' Hern murmured.

'The ring was among ashes and bits of bones. I was afraid I would become bones too, if I stayed there.'

'So you would have done – if the pit hadn't flooded,' said Hern.

Viner, looking at him, knew that Hern was still unsatisfied, and would remain unsatisfied. The sacrificial victim had become a valued comrade, more valuable than the gold ring; no less valuable than the treasure at the bottom of the pit, that he had revealed to them; water. He knew now why they were on the road.

As soon as they had rested and recovered from their excitement, they put as great a distance as they could between themselves and the stones, lingering only long enough to redistribute the ass's load amongst their horses so that Viner might have a mount of his own. He was pleasantly startled to find them grateful enough to offer him the ass, but relieved that they were not so grateful as to offer him a horse, for he was distinctly uncomfortable in the saddle, although he was so close to the ground. He had never ridden on anything before, except his father's shoulders, and he would have been quite happy to travel on foot, once he was free of the rope – and he had been freed at once, but their ill-natured lethargy had given place to a tangible sense of urgency. They wanted to get home; they wanted to get him home. Only later did it cross his mind that they had not *asked* him to go with them. He gathered that they were not used to begging for favours.

At first they retraced their path from the stones until the ground rose toward the edge of the plain, and among foothills they altered course, to rejoin the route they had been following when they first came to the Low Forest.

'Not that it was a route, precisely,' Cleaver explained, as they prepared to camp for the night. 'We were wandering rather than travelling. As soon as the stars come out tonight, I'll plot our course for home.'

Anvil was sent off to find firewood. Catskin and Hern melted into the soft twilight and returned after a couple of hours with an indefinable animal, ready skinned. Viner wondered where they had obtained it, but observed that no one else asked questions. When the fire was well alight and the carcase roasting over it, they settled in a circle beneath the darkening sky. Viner, marking where Hern sat, chose a place on the opposite side and found himself where he wanted to be, next to Cleaver. Although Cleaver had done nothing, had not even protested, to save him when the knife was at his throat, he inferred that Cleaver had not wanted to see him killed. In spite of the fact that Cleaver had hit him in the face only this time yesterday, he felt that he liked him already; better than he liked the others, at any rate; and that Cleaver knew it. It seemed a good opportunity to supplement his power with a little information.

'Why were you wandering?' he remarked, casually, picking up Cleaver's earlier comment. 'When I first saw you I thought you must be mercenaries, but you spoke of a king. Are you king's men?'

'After a fashion,' Catskin interrupted, from the other side of the fire. 'Our king is a Rain King, only latterly,' he said, looking sideways, down his nose, 'there's been no rain.'

'Are the wells failing?' Viner asked, eagerly.

'Not yet, not at home; that is, not when we left. But we've seen villages out here where they say the wells have been dry two summers running.'

'No; we haven't lost our wells yet,' Cleaver said. 'It's a mere detail, really; our river dried up. Nothing to worry about.'

'Talk straight for once, why don't you?' Catskin said. 'We've lost our river. Is that something to laugh at?'

'Who's laughing?' Cleaver said, grimly. 'The King sent us out to look for the source, but we soon saw that it wasn't only our river. The world's drying up all round us. The grass dies and the cattle die and the seed stays in the ground all summer.'

'But you have plenty of water.' He pointed to the skins.

'Who'd refuse us?' Cleaver looked at Hern. 'But soon there'll be none to beg or demand.'

'And the King dances,' said Hern, bitterly. 'He may dance till his feet wear out and he stands on the bare bones of his ankles. It won't rain for him.'

'Why should it?' Viner asked.

'Because that's what he's for; to make rain and to get children. He's done the first thing once and the second thing once, as far as we know,' said Catskin, 'and once is not enough.'

'It wouldn't matter about the rain,' Cleaver said, 'if there were some other way of getting water –'

'Is that why you were going to sacrifice me?'

'Of course,' said Hern, with no false protestations of remorse.

'A black sacrifice brings rain – don't you know? But it doesn't matter now. You'll get our water for us, one way if not the other.' There was the slightest tremor of regret in his voice.

'For the King,' Cleaver said, and stared moodily into the fire. Viner watched him covertly and felt a warmth for him that might have been the first stirring of affection. It was a long time since he had liked anyone, and he was out of practice.

'Here are your stars,' he said, as the sky thickened above. Cleaver leaned back on his elbows and counted the constellations that blinked over his head.

'There's the Dial . . . the Torque . . . the Bow . . .'

Viner looked in the other direction. 'And here are ours; the Frog, the Louse, the Three-Legged Sow . . .'

Hern looked blankly where he pointed. 'Never heard of them.'

'That's what the Webfeet called them.'

'Webfeet?'

'The people from my village; always ankle-deep in water,' Viner explained.

'Did they really have webbed feet?' Anvil asked, hopefully.

'No, that's what people called them. They were human beings – just.' He permitted himself a sarcastic smile in the darkness and again, looking sideways, saw the same smile on Cleaver's face. In spite of Hern's menacing presence on the far side of the fire Viner felt himself among friends, and forgot his brush with murder, his terrible journey, in the relief of having escaped one to achieve the object of the other; people who needed him; in a country where it never rained. It was only later, when he woke briefly during the night, that he recalled his long forgotten encounter with the traveller who had told him, jokingly, of the land where a man danced to make rain, and was called king for it.

This memory accompanied him through the next day. There was little opportunity for questions as they were now moving with all possible speed toward the place where they had seen the stars of the Dial rise last night. It took Viner's entire concentration to keep his ass in step with the horses, and frequently the others had to slacken speed while he caught up with them. He sensed their impatience, but no one complained. They did not care to offend him. He was still necessary and he was still free; they expected him to stay with them of his own will. He wondered what would happen if he indicated that he did not will it; glad that he did.

From time to time he caught fragments of conversation, mainly concerning the King and the Queen, but he had no chance to join in and had an idea, moreover, that his queries would not be welcomed. The remarks were uttered sporadically, almost unwillingly, as though the subject were a nagging pain that insisted upon attention even while one longed to forget it. All he could deduce was that the King and Queen were in the place where he was going, so knowing that his curiosity must be satisfied eventually, he was content to wait.

Toward nightfall, on the third day, the spirits of the party rose noticeably. Anvil and Catskin even sang a snatch or two of genial tunes. Cleaver whistled now and again. Hern was silent. *Why* was he called Hern? What was there of the smithy about Anvil? What had Cleaver cloven? Perhaps as with the Webfeet and the stars, in other places men's names had other meanings.

As darkness fell he saw lights sprinkled on the hillsides. Cleaver, dropping back to keep him company, explained that these were from the villages of his own country. 'We know where we are, now. These are our people.'

'Is that why you're so cheerful?'

'Does it show?' Cleaver sounded surprised. Perhaps he had never noticed how grim they all were in company. 'Everyone feels happy when he knows home is near.' By his tone Viner judged him ill at ease.

'I wouldn't be,' he said lightly.

'There's a cave on this hill, just above a stream – and that's the last stream in our land, assuming that it still runs,' Cleaver went on, less cheerfully. 'We'll camp there tonight. After that we should be home in three days. You'll see, in the morning.'

Viner did see, in the morning, although it was the last thing he saw for some time. While Catskin and Anvil packed up the gear and loaded it, he stood in the mouth of the cave and surveyed the view. At the foot of the hill ran a stream, clear brown and clean, although he could tell that the bed it ran in must normally accommodate a much broader river; drooping willows, alder and hazel grew along the banks (he must cut himself a new rod before they moved on) and smoke rose straight from the settlements. He heard the sound of fowls and goats; a cow lowing. It almost reminded him of home, except that the sky was brilliantly empty, the sun shone, and the river bubbled over its stony bed without threat. No mist obscured the horizon and he could see clearly the way they had come the day before, over heath and hill, back and back to the edge of the sky that hid the last hill of all; the triple-peaked giant that overhung the plain of the big stones. Should he ever need it, there lay his road home.

'This is our land,' Cleaver said, behind him. 'Welcome to it.'

'I'm happy to be here,' Viner said, and turned his back on the way home, swearing that he would never go home again, and came face to face with Hern, standing behind him with a long thick scarf in his hands.

'It's all right,' said Hern, as Viner fell back a step. 'Come back.' He might have been calling ducks to the slaughter. 'I'm not going to strangle you.'

'It's not all right. What are you going to do?' Viner said, backing off as Hern advanced. Hern would hang him yet. Hern did not trust the rod; he wanted his sacrifice.

'Only blindfold you,' Hern said. 'Hold still, you fool. It won't hurt. You can still ride the ass and we'll lead it.'

'What a sense of occasion you do have,' Cleaver was mumbling, irritably. 'I've just been making him welcome. Can't it wait?'

'No.' Hern took the last few paces at a trot and had the scarf wound tight round Viner's eyes before he could dodge it, tying it in a very tight knot at the back of his head. 'We don't want to lose you,' said Hern.

'Lose me?' He was lost already. Hern was an evil voice in his ear. The night was in his eyes. 'You don't want me to find my way back again.'

'Something like that.'

'It's not necessary,' he protested. 'I *want* to come with you.'

'We want you to *stay* with us,' Hern said, cosily.

'Time to be moving,' Catskin said, in the sudden darkness by daylight. A hand took Viner by the upper arm and led him firmly across the grass to where the ass stood waiting. Viner's groping

47

fingers touched its rough coat a moment before Hern said, 'Here you are. I'll help you get on – all right? And I'll ride behind to make sure that your blindfold doesn't slip off.'

'Slip?' Viner said, worrying at the bandage.

'And to make sure that you don't slip off. Anvil will lead you – hold tight.'

'Why don't you tie my hands again?' Viner said, bitterly.

'You're not a *prisoner*.' Viner could tell that he was already walking away. He could tell also, by the sound of Hern's voice, exactly how he looked as he said it, and as the day wore on all his hatred and fear returned to plague him in the night at noon.

Did not any of them trust anyone?

They let him remove the blindfold in the evenings, slipping it over his head and each time taking some of his hair with it, in the knot, but before he could open his eyes in the morning, it was replaced. He had to take their word for it that beyond the scarf the sun was shining, although the heat would have told him as much had he not been so thoroughly chilled by fright and suspicion. As far as he was concerned they were moving through perpetual night. The knowledge that Anvil's unimpeded vision guided his ass did nothing to combat his certainty that they were all as blind as he was. Convinced that at any moment they might plunge into an unseen chasm, or a swollen river; that they might be attacked by hidden enemies that advanced with silent stealth; that they were irredeemably lost, he clung to the animal's back with hands and knees, his head tucked into his shoulders and his whole body aching with the tension of being ready for the catastrophe, should it happen. At night, when they sat convivially round the fire and in response to their questions he inflated his few successful divinations to a dozen wells and springs, he forgot his day-time miseries, so anxious were they all to make him forget. By day he cursed and wondered why he had not taken advantage of the dark to be quit of them once and for all. The only thing that stayed him was the knowledge that they must want him and his mystery very badly indeed. He would surely be requited.

By the third afternoon he was in such panic that when he heard Cleaver calling upon them to halt he was ready to fling himself from the ass's back and crawl on all fours at their feet, begging them, without any remnant of pride, to let him see; but before he could put this thought into practice – and behind the scarf he could picture himself doing it and blushed – Cleaver's voice came again, this time at his side.

'This is the end of the journey. Viner, forgive us, but you know why we did it. This is the palace of the Rain King. Now you can look.'

The scarf was pulled suddenly from his face as blinding night exploded into blinding day. His eyes were so filled with tears of shock that all he could comprehend was brightness, red, white and green by turns as he blinked and blinked and shook his head to escape from it. Cleaver, unthinking, had left him facing the sun, and it was low in the sky, but at last he could look up, and he saw where they had brought him.

They were halted upon an open plain, in three directions tree-less as far as the eye could see, and barren; but when he turned away from the sun, to the east, he thought for a moment that he stood at the foot of a mountain, for the building before him was so immense that he did not know where to begin looking at it. Taller than the tallest of the big stones, longer than the Webfeet's entire village, it filled both eyes from the left of the left to the right of the right, from lower lid to upper. Stunned, he calculated that it might take as much as five minutes to walk from one end to the other, but he did not sense that there were rooms behind the windows, that the great doorway would admit him to an interior; it was all flatness, a tapestry of pillars and pinnacles, turrets and many windows, without depth; a picture of a palace worked upon un-bleached cloth, and the cloth was fraying at the edges. The pillars were cracked, the pinnacles crumbling, the battlements gap-toothed; there was not a whole feature upon it, but before he had time to take in the ruin that gnawed at the splendour he became conscious of sounds that drew his eye from the dizzy parapets, over the windows, down the columns, to the terraced forecourt from where the sounds issued. The land all around and in front of the building was level, but Cleaver had dismounted his party on a small hillock, at some little distance, so that Viner could see down onto the terrace to observe what was happening inside the walls.

49

From either end of the building, like encircling arms from shoulders, a balustrade curved out and round to enclose the terrace, and where the fingertips did not quite meet, a flight of shallow steps ran down to the open plain without.

On the half-moon of the terrace was a circle of people, four or five deep; more people than Viner had ever seen assembled in all his life; more people than there were in the Webfeet's village. He had never imagined that people could gather together in such large numbers, like rooks or starlings. There must be all of three hundred of them, down in that courtyard, and they were not moving. They crouched low, knees level with their shoulders and palms flat on the ground. Behind them, against the wall of the palace and placed two on either side of the wide dark doorway, stood four brazen gongs, hanging from wooden frames, and in the doorway, side by side, two life-sized silver statues. He forgot the broken stones and stared at the silver. Here was richness.

'Well, well, well,' Hern said, with a look of sour amusement, 'we're just in time to see the King dance.'

Viner felt a spasm of unprecedented excitement; he was going to see a king. The king of his own country lived far away from the village, and ranged further, waging war. He was so remote from life in that drowned valley that Viner had heard him mentioned only two or three times in the six years that he had lived there, aside from the annual ceremony, grudgingly performed, when Majesty's envoys came from the city to gather the wool tax and went away again on the same day, bearing the best of the fleeces with them. Viner had imagined him ever in the saddle, mailed head to toe like a mercenary and smiting his enemies all day long. Even in the tales of his earliest childhood the king had been a fabulous figure, associated with might and mayhem, faceless behind his visored helm, and yet now, here, was a king who was going to come out among his people and dance.

Viner said, 'Why is he going to dance if it won't rain for him?'

'He has to keep trying. That's the only reason he's here,' Catskin said. 'To dance and to get us a princess.'

'But he doesn't do *that* in public,' Hern murmured, through an immodest leer.

'If he does it at all,' Catskin said.

'He did it once,' said Cleaver. 'He must have done it once.'

'Once,' said Catskin. 'He made it rain, *once*.'

Viner stared at them, discomfited by their tone. He was accustomed to hearing a king cursed, especially after the yearly taxing, but he had never heard him mocked; and never spoken of so lewdly. What kind of a king was this? He turned away and looked toward the courtyard, where in the reddening light an utter stillness had fallen over the waiting people. Their silence was almost visible, manifest in the quivering air above the sun-burned stones where they knelt.

Then he saw a flame leap up in the shadows of the doorway, and immediately after, a man sprang out between the two silver statues, holding above his head a blazing torch. Without pausing he began to run round the circle, swinging the torch at arm's length so that it dipped and looped, scoring fiery lines across the eyes. He flung it up, caught it as it fell, bounded to the centre of the ring and stood there, drawing bright streaks of fire, and as he stood, a solemn booming rose from behind him, and fell, and rose again. Viner looked for the source, and saw that the gongs were being struck with muffled sticks.

'First the lightning,' said Cleaver, as the booming died to a rumble, and faded; 'then the thunder.'

'And then the rain?' Viner asked.

The others looked at him.

'That's a good question,' Hern said.

At first Viner thought that it *was* raining, in spite of the cloudless sky. His ears were filled with a soft pattering that swelled as the thunder had done until it became itself thunderous. In the courtyard the people were drumming with their flattened palms upon the stone pavement.

'Rain?' Viner said.

'Rain,' Cleaver said.

'But where is the King?'

Cleaver pointed to the doorway. Viner looked and saw no one. Then the taller of the two silver statues stepped down from the doorway and advanced to the centre of the throbbing circle. It raised its arms beneath its cloak, spread the cloak like wings and shrugged it back so that it fell from the shoulders to the ground

51

behind, and lay there like a sloughed-off skin. It was all done very slowly and it took Viner as long to understand that the statue was a man; that he was looking at the Rain King.

His first impression was that the King was a very aged king, for his hair, held close by a band round his forehead, was as silver as his cloak; but his body, dressed only in a kilt, also of silver, looked even from a distance firm and hard; not an old man's. He began to move, turning slowly upon the spot, scarcely lifting his feet from the ground, and there came from him a faint ringing sound. Viner realized that the hair was not hair, but a wig of silver filaments, and that the kilt itself was of leather or cloth, hung with fine chains, from the waist. As the dancer picked up speed the chains began to move until at last, as he spun and stamped, arms out-stretched, they swung away from him, flailing the air. Now he leaped, now he crouched, now he ran, stooping, and leaped again, and all the while the drumming rose around him. If the Webfeet danced, as they occasionally did, at funerals, they stumbled to and fro, earth-bound in their clogs. This dancing king seemed to spring fully to his own height as he went, faster and faster, round the circle, and as he went the people rose from their haunches and stood, clapping their hands together first at knee level, at shoulder height and finally above their heads. Then, at the moment when it seemed that if the spinning figure rose again it would continue to rise and never come down any more, the second statue left the shadow of the doorway.

'Here she comes,' Hern said, 'with her faggots.' The silver woman was loaded with more silver, long javelins, held across her forearms. She offered them to the King.

'The Queen?' Viner said.

'Herself,' said Hern. He turned to Cleaver. 'What do you think? One of his better days, isn't it?'

Viner wished they would be quiet. He could not take his eyes from the King and the Queen, one whirling, the other motionless, and to hear them discussed critically, as one might discuss one's neighbours, tarnished the silver. The King was holding the jav-elins now. He broke out of the circle and down the steps, from the terrace to the open land beyond it, and there he threw his javelins; not levelly, as a hunter would, but straight up, into the sky, where they gleamed one after the other at the climax of their flight, stalled, and fell back to earth, as straight as they had risen.

'Remember when he first did it?' Catskin said, 'how they all came down flat?'

'It rained, though,' Cleaver retorted.

Hern said, 'It's not raining now.'

Viner looked up. The air was as dry and clear as it had been when the dance began. He looked down. Below them the King knelt among his fallen javelins where they stood, arms outspread, palms up; head tilted back and eyes fixed on the uncooperative sky.

'Now,' Cleaver said, touching Viner upon the arm, 'do you see why we need you?'

Viner nodded, unhappily. Until he had turned his eyes to the sky, and seen it blue from one side to the other, he had been determined that the dance would end in a deluge. Hern's carping comments had made no impression on him. When he saw the javelins go up he had waited to see rain come down from the charmed sky. He was relieved, therefore, when the party descended from the hillock to approach the palace. He did not want to stay and see the defeated King stoop to pick up his weapons in the ruthless light of the setting sun.

'The Queen looks well, don't you think?' Hern's tone of playful evil was back again.

'Well enough,' Catskin said.

'Shall we see a healthy child, this summer?'

'Here's hoping.'

'One of his javelins found its target,' Hern remarked carelessly, to Viner. Catskin spat, over his shoulder, and Viner, shamed, stared at the ground. He had seen for himself that beneath her robe the Queen carried a seven-month child, but it startled him to think that the King had sired it. He had always visualized kings safely sealed inside their armour – but this king wore no armour. For all that he dressed in silver and stood like a statue, he was a living man. He danced.

They turned aside from the terrace and did not enter by the gaping doorway where the little silver Queen stood waiting for her husband. Cleaver led off to the right, following a track that ran below the sheer side of the palace. Viner saw at once why his first sight of the building had made him think of a picture, without depth. It had no depth. The great façade concealed a ruinous pile of masonry that fell away, like a collapsing staircase, from the pinnacles at the front to a warren of low-roofed outbuildings at the back. Once, he supposed, straining to imagine the enormity of the original structure, it must have been a three-sided shell, enclosing a spacious courtyard, but as the building disintegrated the stone had been cannibalized and resurrected in the form of annexes built against the walls and encroaching upon the courtyard until they engulfed it. He saw the carpenter's cottage, multiplied a thousand times, stacked upon itself, and still it would not equal the tottering mass above him; and he had thought the outcrop on the hill top a giants' dwelling. This was a giants' dwelling, and yet in it lived people no bigger than himself, like mites in a cheese.

Stone and tile gave place to mud and thatch, sheds and hovels. A kind of stable yard had been levelled among these, and Cleaver led the way in. Viner's sense of exaltation, already ebbing rapidly, left him entirely among the familiar proportions of barns and stables, the domestic smells of midden and kitchen, the chime and clatter of stithy and hearth. Anvil, as was ever his fate, disappeared with the beasts; Catskin with a glad yell of recognition threw himself upon a passing girl, barely giving her time to utter an answering squawk before bearing her off to some long-awaited tryst behind the stables.

'Who takes him in?' Hern said, jerking his thumb toward Viner.

'I do,' Cleaver said. 'You'd do better to wash off all your bloodstains before Madam Mere sees you.'

'Any excuse will do, to delay seeing Madam Mere,' Hern answered sharply. 'You take him along, then, and lay it on thick. Let Himself know we've done him a favour. He should be about ready for a favour after that performance just now.'

'He'll know we've done him a favour soon enough. As for Madam, where's the ring?'

'The ring?'

'The gold ring.'

'What gold ring?'

'If you remember,' Cleaver said, heavily, 'Viner here had a gold ring with a red stone in his bag, when we found him, and you had it last. We were going to give it to Herself. Where is it?'

Hern had the grace to look away. 'I don't remember.'

'You're not going to give it to that trull you keep in the kitchen?' Cleaver said, sounding deeply disgusted. It had been in Viner's mind to request the return of the ring, at a propitious moment, but he could see that he was not going to get it.

'You're thinking of Catskin. My trull's in the dairy.'

'Give.'

'I haven't *got* it,' Hern said.

'Very likely, very likely. Give.'

'If you must know . . .' Hern turned his back and looked across the yard, '. . . I threw it into the hole.'

'What hole? Not the one where we found water?'

'No; the other. It went back where it came from. I was afraid of that place.'

'So were we all afraid of that place,' Cleaver said. He watched thoughtfully as Hern, ashamed even from behind, made his way round the side of the building. 'But I didn't think he was afraid of anything.'

When Hern was out of sight he turned in at a low doorway, Viner following. 'Listen,' he said, 'now that you're here, forget Hern; forget how we found you; forget how we brought you here –'

'Why should I?' Viner said, emboldened by finding himself alone for once with Cleaver, and a match for him. 'Why should I forget that you knocked me about and tied me up and kept me blindfold? Why should I forget that Hern tried to cut my throat – he wanted to sacrifice me!' He felt a startlingly knowing grin on his face. 'Will it go badly with you if the King finds out?'

They were in a dark passage now and although Cleaver laughed Viner could not see how he took this. He answered amiably enough, however; 'No, nothing like that. I was being friendly. All I meant was, you'll be honoured here, if you really can do what you say you can do.'

'You saw me do it.'

'Once. I saw the King make rain, once. Anyway, that's as it

may be, but you won't be threatened. If you come across Hern he may scowl at you but he certainly won't cut your throat. He might even greet you. Just forget that we ever took you prisoner, you're no prisoner now.'

'So if I don't like it here I can just walk away?'

'Not quite that . . . but why should you want to go? When the King knows what you are, you'll want for nothing. Don't make yourself a prisoner –'

'By trying to leave.' Viner finished the warning for him, and surprised himself by his quickness on the uptake. He was becoming wise in the ways of the world. If he ever went back to the Webfeet's village, how they would grovel! He would not go back. 'I don't want to leave,' he said.

And he would not forget.

The passage opened into a high-ceilinged room, well lit, with benches round the walls. Cleaver threw himself down on a bench and motioned to Viner to do the same. Viner perched more formally and looked round the room with cautious eyes. It was still habitable, and clean overall, but grimy cracks flawed the faded paintings on the walls, a film of pale dust powdered the floor, and the echoes of their voices were impure, shingly, as if something, somewhere, were coming loose. Immediately in front of him an impressive flight of stone steps, with a broken banister, led up to a curtained entry at the far end of the room.

'What do we do now?'

'We wait. They'll be here presently – once they've allowed a decent interval for the clouds to arrive; which they won't. It would be bad luck to turn away too suddenly, just in case.'

'In case the clouds were offended?'

'That's it.'

These people are mad, Viner decided, recalling the fate of the gold ring, and Hern's insistence on a black sacrifice. What will they make of my rod?

'Who are we waiting for?' he said.

'The King and the Queen, of course. Himself and Herself.'

'Madam Mere?'

'Forget about the Madam. That's just a – a –' Cleaver's mouth became wry, 'a pet name. We don't worry about titles in private.'

56

'I can't just call her Mere, not the *Queen*,' Viner objected.

'Few of us do, but if she should speak to you, remember it's her name.'

'And the King? Surely –'

From behind the curtain came the sound of footsteps and voices, raised and lowered in some hurriedly suppressed dispute. Cleaver pulled Viner to his feet, but instead of approaching the stairs he turned sharply and led Viner out, the way they had come in.

'What's wrong? What are you doing? What . . .?'

'You can see him,' Cleaver said, 'but you're not going to meet him; this isn't the time to introduce you. You can meet him later.'

'Because they're quarrelling?'

'It wouldn't do any good. Wait till you've got something to show him.'

'You mean water?' Viner struggled with furious disappointment. 'You're afraid I won't be able to do it, aren't you? It's a pity you didn't think of that sooner – at the big stones.'

'If I'd thought of it sooner you'd be dead by now. It doesn't matter what I think,' Cleaver said, 'it's what he thinks that matters, and he won't be in the thinking vein right now, I can tell. Stay here, if you want to see him. Look round the curtain.'

Viner found a convenient rent in the fabric, at eye level, and squinted through it, just as the curtain at the far end of the room, at the head of the steps, was swept aside. In the archway, thus revealed, stood the silver figures of the King and Queen, she still shrouded, he with his cloak thrown back, naked to the waist but glistening all the same.

'How he sweats!' Viner said, involuntarily.

'We need more than sweat,' Cleaver replied, and left his side to advance into the room. He strolled to the foot of the stairs with his arms held wide in greeting.

'I've come back,' he said cheerfully, and in a voice so devoid of reverence that Viner was shocked all over again. 'Aren't you pleased to see me?'

'What did you find?' the King asked. His voice was raw with exhaustion. Viner could hardly hear what he said. 'What news have you brought?'

'Oh, all kinds,' Cleaver said, adopting an easy stance, with his

57

thumbs tucked through his belt and all his weight on one leg. 'Some good, some bad and some atrocious, enough to make you weep –'

'We need more than tears,' the Queen said, and *her* voice was incisive in the grainy air.

Cleaver ignored her. 'And some to make you smile again, maybe. What'll you have first?'

'What'll you tell me first?' the King said, as though he dare not commit himself even to choosing.

'Oh, stop playing at statues!' Cleaver bawled, losing patience. 'D'you want me to shout it out loud so that every fool in the building can listen? Come down and hear it, Morning Light.'

4

Finding the curtain crumbling to sand beneath his fingers, Viner enlarged his spy-hole until he could see through it without squinting. The fibres parted soundlessly to frame the group as it re-assembled at the foot of the steps. The Queen remained standing, leaning back a little to balance her burden and gazing light-eyed at a point somewhere above Viner's head. He would have thought her pretty but for the empty eyes and her small mouth, crimped into a quirk of chilly resignation. He could not tell whether the cause were Cleaver, now lounging again on the bench, long hands dangling between his thighs, or the King who sat beside him with knuckles clenched like whitened bones, the man with the extravagant name, whose head drooped with fatigue so that the silver wig fell forward and screened his profile; Morning Light. Viner, breathing shallowly, stood behind the curtain and watched them: Cleaver, Mere and Morning Light. Cleaver, Hern, Anvil, Mere, even; strange names but meaningful, practical even. *Morning Light?*

'If I'd come home only one day sooner,' Cleaver was saying, 'I'd have brought you nothing but bad news.'

'I thought you were never coming back,' the King said. 'Is the source of the river so very far away?'

'We found the source after fifteen days,' Cleaver said, soberly. 'That is, we found the place where the source once was. We found the place where the marsh once was, where the source once was.'

'Is this becoming a ballad?' the Queen cut in, tongue like flint. Cleaver flicked a look of pure dislike in her direction, before continuing.

'We couldn't come back and tell you there was nothing left, not after fifteen days –'

'It would have been thirty days, by the time you got back –'

'Lady, it would have been thirty-one. We lay down and wept for

59

one whole day out of clean disappointment,' Cleaver said. Viner, unable to picture the grotesque image of Cleaver and his cut-throats prostrate with grief, angled and craned his neck for a better view of the King's face, but it remained shadowed under his wig; while his wife and his friend sniped at each other over his head.

'We thought it best to see how the rest of the world fares, before we came back.'

'And how does the world fare?' the Queen asked. 'How did it fare after you and your gang had ridden through it?'

'We travelled far beyond this land,' Cleaver said, 'and it was the same wherever we went. The rivers run dry, the wells fail, ponds sink into the ground. All the world wants rain, and none falls.' The angry formality of his voice softened and he laid his hand on the arm of the man at his side. 'Morning Light, it isn't your failure only. The whole earth is drying up.'

'Is that the good news?' the Queen said, 'that it's not his fault?'

The King withdrew his arm, not haughtily, but as if kindness could only cut him deeper. 'You said you had good news,' he said.

'Why, yes.' Cleaver paused, until the King raised his head. Viner saw cheek-bone and chin and a sector of eye, before the wig swung forward. 'All the world wants rain, and none falls, except in one valley we heard of, where it never stops, and the people have webbed feet.'

'You cannot bring that valley here,' said the Queen.

'No,' Cleaver said, with threadbare tolerance, 'but we heard tell of another thing. One of these Webfeet is a sorcerer who wanders over the world to bring water where it's needed; by his art he can call it up out of the dry earth. When he holds out his wand rivers spring from the ground, wells are filled; lakes appear at his bidding.'

Viner, appalled, listened to this catalogue of wonders conjured from a muddy puddle in a ring of stones by no greater art than his own boasting and Cleaver's vaulting imagination.

'Can he make rain?' the King asked, jealously.

'He doesn't need to,' said Cleaver.

'Can you find this sorcerer?'

'I don't know,' Cleaver said, 'but if I can, I will.'

'Do that,' said the Queen. 'I should like to see a man who can summon water without dancing – that is, I should be happy to see no more dancing.'

The King, without looking at her or at Cleaver, rose from the bench and passed out of sight, head bowed beneath the silver tresses, his cloak unfurling like a moonglade behind him.

'But why did you tell him I was a sorcerer?' Viner demanded, plaintively. 'He believed you. Now he'll expect miracles.'

'Anything wet will look like a miracle to him,' Cleaver replied. 'Of course he believes me. He dare not disbelieve.'

Viner looked at the doorway through which the King, followed by his cross-grained Queen, had passed a minute before. 'But I'm not a sorcerer.'

'Are you not?' Cleaver plucked at the rod beneath Viner's shirt. 'Isn't this your wand?'

'I'm a dowser, not a magician.'

'And this is your mystery?'

'Knowing how to use it is the mystery.'

'That's sorcery enough for us.'

'But I can only find water if it's there to be found. I can't *make* it come,' Viner protested. While he was perfectly prepared to assert his power, and with it acquire power, he had somehow to establish his limitations, and leave himself a means of escape if he failed, but if he failed, Hern would be at his throat again, greedy for sacrifice. From what he had heard of Cleaver's remarks to the King, he was being advertised once more as a man who could infallibly summon water to him. From what he had seen of the voiceless desperate King, nothing less than infallibility would do. He held the rod close, under his shirt. If willow or hazel grew in this desert he must cut another, and it must not fail him.

Cleaver was watching him, cleverly.

'Are you afraid?'

'*No.*'

'And you wondered why I wouldn't let you meet him,' Cleaver sighed. 'You needn't be afraid of me – I understand. Sorcery's a chancy thing. Wait till you've found water and then we'll tell him.'

'Yes,' said Viner, knowing only too well that Cleaver did not understand. Cleaver believed in sentient clouds and obedient streams, and in this mighty ruinous maze were hundreds of others who thought as he did. Still, in the country of the credulous, a liar might be king. In a desert, a dowser might be king. He did not want to be king, but one could have power without kingship just as one could, it seemed, have kingship without power.

'Meanwhile,' Cleaver said, breaking in on his thoughts, 'we'll have to lodge you somewhere, and I need food; don't you? Come with me.'

Viner could not help noticing, as they walked through rooms and anterooms and passages, that although many of the ceilings were exquisitely decorated and moulded, others had vanished entirely. Whole tracts of the palace had no roof at all; a corridor might suddenly become an alley; the second of two rooms a sty, open to the evening sky. At one point there were no walls either, and they found the way blocked by a pile of masonry. Cleaver attempted to climb over it, but after ascending a little way he found it subsiding under him, and slithered down again.

'This is new, since I was here last. We'll have to go back the other way.'

'I don't mind where I sleep,' Viner said. He amended hastily, 'So long as I've a roof over my head.'

'I'd as soon sleep under the stars. I may have to,' Cleaver remarked, as a lump of plaster, dislodged by their footfalls, crashed to the ground behind them. 'I can only suppose my room's still standing.'

Viner, disturbed by Cleaver's placid acceptance of the fact that his home was disintegrating over his head, said indignantly, 'Why *is* this place falling down?'

'It's drying out,' Cleaver said, briefly. 'Just as well, in a way, it doesn't rain.' The moon shone suddenly down upon them. 'There's no one to build it back again.'

'But all those people . . .?'

'They don't all live here. Half of them will have come in from the villages to see the rain dance.'

'Aren't any of the other half builders?' Viner asked, waspishly. 'Even the Webfeet could build.' He refrained from enlarging upon the quality of their building.

'Not a one,' said Cleaver. 'Most of them couldn't build a mud pie. If it did rain I guess someone might get round to putting the roof back, but it'd only fall again. The foundations are shrinking.'

'But it's water that shrinks things.'

'Drought shrinks things too.' He nodded at a stately door, massively carved. Thick lamplight poured through the cracks between the planks like honey through diaphanous lace.

'Then why stay here? Why not go somewhere else and start again?'

'Why don't the Webfeet go somewhere else if they don't like water? Let them come here, huh?'

Viner pondered. 'It's their home.'

'This is a home, too. Not everyone wants to go off cantering over the countryside,' Cleaver said, pointedly.

'*You* do.'

'Yes, but I like to come back here. Perhaps it's the thrill of not knowing if there'll be anything to come back to.' They were passing an apartment gorgeous with murals and carved furniture, where the window frame had fallen out, taking a major part of the wall with it. 'Why should you care? There's still plenty of room.'

'All I thought, was, so *many* empty rooms, does it matter which one I sleep in?'

'There's an order of precedence here, same as anywhere else,' Cleaver said. 'Suppose I gave you a room that was better than Catskin's; I doubt if Cat would mind, but the fellow up the scale from him would mind very much.'

'Does Catskin live here?'

'We all do, somewhere about. Hern, Catskin, me – Anvil out at the back. We don't meet very often. In this place we don't have to meet very often.'

'But –' Viner halted in a doorway, 'what are you?'

'We wait on the King and Queen. They may not be royalty, but they need a retinue.'

'What do you mean, not royalty?'

'They don't rule over us,' Cleaver said, 'they are here to make rain.'

'Is that why you call them just Mere and – and – Morning Light?'

'Yes; no – not that way. The floor's gone,' Cleaver said. 'I broke

63

my ankle there once. What's the matter? Why shouldn't I call him Morning Light?'

'I was just thinking, it's a strange name.'

'I suppose it is, for a birth name.' Cleaver did not seem particularly intrigued, however. Viner thought that his own name was odd enough.

He said, 'I can see why Catskin's called Catskin, because he wears cat-skins, but –'

'He wasn't born wearing them,' Cleaver said. 'That's the prerogative of kittens. His name's Lintel. He was born before his time; in a doorway, he says.' He saw that Viner was no more enlightened. 'Catskin's his given name. Our birth names are the first things our mothers see after childbirth. My mother saw a meat axe. Cat's mother saw the lintel of the door. She didn't get as far as the bed.'

'Suppose they see something nasty?' He hesitated. Was a meat axe a desirable thing to see?

'Oh, well . . .' Cleaver smiled. Viner was not sure whether he took the point or not. 'Mistakes can happen, but a canny family takes care to surround the childbed with appropriate things; that's why we paint our walls. We can control the naming up to a point. It's the improvident ones who end up with babies called Broken Plate, Slop-Bucket, Fluff-Under-the-Bed. I knew a man once called Dead Brother. He was a twin,' Cleaver said.

'And Mere?'

'It was a little lake, in the gardens – a lovely place; all reeds and willows. I used to fish there. It's dried up, now,' he added, shortly.

Viner began to understand. Presumably Anvil was the son of a blacksmith, Hern had been born near marshes. Given all this, Morning Light was not such an unusual name; but it was still a very odd name. 'Then the King was birthed at dawn?' he suggested.

'Or in a very empty room,' Cleaver said. 'I don't know where he was born. I don't know anything about him before he came here. He's the Rain Dancer and that's all I need to know. That's all my care. Perhaps he fell out of the sky,' he said suddenly. 'On his head.'

'But aren't you his friend?'

'I'm a better friend to him than most. I don't like his wife, for one thing. Here, this should do for you, for the time being.' He halted before a cranny at the very end of a decrepit corridor. 'You'll be given something better – much better – as you rise in favour.'

The room was frugally furnished with a pallet and a chest.

'Shall I rise in favour?'

'Oh yes,' Cleaver said, tonelessly. 'You'll rise. Like water you'll rise. Nothing will keep you down. Now, I should sleep, if I were you. Later on I'll bring you some food, and clothes. Something of mine should fit you. We're about the same size.'

'You're very kind,' Viner muttered, not insensible to the change in Cleaver's demeanour since they parted from Hern. He was condescending, but he was easy with it. Could he be contemplating a transfer of allegiance; paving the way for a more profitable friendship elsewhere?

'I called you a sorcerer,' said Cleaver. 'Better you don't go round dressed like a night-soil man longer than necessary.'

He went away, and Viner spread himself gingerly on the bed, with due regard for his painful bones. He intended to lie there and take stock of his marvellous change of fortune, gloating over the bygone miseries of life among the Webfeet, scarcely two weeks behind him, but as soon as his head was down and his feet were up he was conscious only that aching could be an actual voluptuous pleasure, a grateful surrender to overpowering exhaustion. As sleep numbed him he thought he began to understand the nature of this amazing sensation: he was enjoying himself. He was not happy, but he was enjoying himself.

He had not noticed the slit window the previous evening, having found his dark room in darkness, but he woke to see morning light filtered through an aperture, high up in the wall, and heard, somewhere outside, a voice raised in cheerless melody. He remembered where he was. Morning light had now a different meaning.

On the chest at the foot of his bed was a pile of clothes, evidently left by Cleaver, as promised. He shifted them and found that by standing on the chest he was able to see out of the window, one eye at a time. His confused sense of direction, fuddled by fatigue and

65

last night's complex journeys, had led him to believe that he would look out over the stable yard where they had entered yesterday. Instead, he discovered that his room must be in another part of the building altogether, for beyond the window his view of the plain stretched uninterrupted for a great distance before he could find anything to look at, a village in a grove of trees, whose outlines broke the very horizon, already restless in the brilliant sunshine. The remains of a road, overgrown with grass that had withered in its turn, ran from the village and passed from his sight, somewhere to his right hand. Not until a black bird crossed his line of vision, cruising on warm air, did he notice that the landscape was utterly empty. There was no thing and no one moving in it.

There seemed to be no one moving indoors, either. Viner stood down from the chest and pushed open the raft of planks and battens that served as a door and separated his room from the end of the corridor. It was not a room at all; it *was* the end of the corridor. He acknowledged that Cleaver had been supremely tactful in his choice of a place that would offend nobody's sense of superiority. The corridor itself was deeply shadowed, lined with doorways and recesses and occasional piles of rubble, and only in the far distance could he see a transverse beam of sunlight that indicated the presence of an intersection. It lay thick, like a strip of matting across the floor. As Viner approached a man entered the corridor ahead of him, along the line of light, and halted where the two ways crossed. With a choice of three directions it could have been simple indecision that made him pause, but to Viner he appeared to have arrived at the place where he wanted to be, and there stood, absorbing the yellow light. He shone. With his feet astride he raised his arms and stretched as though he stood in a cascade of warm water, shook his head to clear his hair of droplets, or to wake himself – for it was still very early. The tousled hair sprang away from his face and the sun burned so redly and brightly through it that his head gleamed wholly, without features, and unidentified he disappeared, as suddenly as he had come, into the shadows of the corridor. In his place came Cleaver, from the same direction. Cleaver waited at the corner for Viner to approach.

'Sleep well?' Cleaver said. 'I looked in on you last night, but kicking wouldn't wake you so I left you to it. You didn't seem very hungry.'

'Did you see that?' Viner asked him: and blinked. The outline of the golden man was still under his eyelids.

'See what?'

'That man – him – in the sunshine. He was . . . shining.'

'He was wet. He's just come from bathing. *He* can have as much water as he likes, of course, but to give him his due he doesn't use more than the rest of us. Unlike Herself.'

'Then who was it?' He did not want it to be anyone, holding fast to the intangible bright image; but he could not ignore the damp footprints on the floor.

'It was the King, you fool. Didn't you recognize him?'

'But yesterday, he was all silver.'

'And today he's flesh and blood? Disappointing, isn't it? Did you think he was silver through to the spine?'

Viner was thinking something quite different. If these people were truly named for the first thing their mothers saw, then Morning Light had surely entered the world several hours too early. He should have been named for noon, strong sun and short shadows, high and mighty heat. Viner thought of the shining man at the crossways, drowning in sunshine, the golden skin, the rufous halo of hair. He had never in his life seen anyone less suggestive of wet weather. No wonder they dressed him in silver when he danced, to hide the truth from the undeceived clouds. No wonder he could not make it rain. (No man can make rain, he said. He did not believe that a man could make rain, any more than he himself could summon water.)

'I was coming to find you,' Cleaver said. 'I thought you might want something to eat and no one would bring you anything; no one knows you're here. Eat with me, until you can make yourself known.'

Two women carrying a basket between them glanced incuriously at Viner as he stood aside to let them pass. He watched their receding backs. 'I should have stayed in my room. Supposing someone asks who I am?'

'Nobody will do that. This place is full of strangers, coming and going. You could stay a year and never know everyone who lived here. Still, if you are asked, just say that you've come to serve the King. It's true. No one will question it. If they do, tell them you're here to help me. That's true, too, but who cares? Tell them what you like.'

Viner detected considerably too many ifs and buts.

'But what do *you* do?' He foresaw a period of subterfuge in which he, an unaccomplished liar, unused even to telling the truth, out of practice in the habit of speech, would be forced to lie continually.

'I wait on the King, I told you.'

'That's all anyone seems to do here – wait.'

'What else? We, me and Hern, are his companions.'

'What about the Queen?'

'She has her own companions. Catskin, for one.'

'That's not what I meant,' Viner said. 'Doesn't she keep him company?'

'Not if she can avoid it.' Cleaver lifted a curtain that hung in a doorway at the foot of a staircase, and beckoned Viner to follow him. They entered a room that faced the sunrise, as Viner's did, but here the sun poured through a wide window, with casements of horn, thrown open to the morning. The room was large, as it needed to be to accommodate the most impressive item of furniture in it; an enormous bed awash with quilts and cushions.

'Is this your room?'

'You can come here when you like, don't wait to be asked. But never go up those stairs. The King's apartments are up there, and the Queen's. Sit down, won't you? The maid should have brought food . . . yes.'

'Is this your bed?'

'Who else's?'

'*All* yours?'

'I share it sometimes.' Cleaver smiled, slyly. 'I'm not greedy.'

Viner thought of the communal couch at home, in the loft, with eight of them wedged together in unsociable proximity. 'But isn't it too big?' It was bigger than the whole slip of corridor allotted to him. 'There's no room for anything else – hardly room to walk.'

Cleaver sidled round the bed, carrying a tray with a plate and a jug on it.

'I don't come here to walk, I come here to sleep. I know I don't need so much bed, but I'm entitled to it; so I have it.'

Viner rode side-saddle on the extreme edge. 'What do you mean, entitled to it? Did you earn it?'

Cleaver poured milk into two mugs and handed him one, with a haunch of bread. 'Listen,' he said, between mouthfuls, 'it's my right. I have certain rights and I don't turn any of them down. They're little enough but you'd be a fool to turn anything down in this place. We all have *something*, according to our station. The King and Herself are entitled to all the water they need – or all they can get. I'm entitled to this bed. Hern's entitled to hunt where he pleases. Catskin's entitled to drink what he pleases, and he does. Even the girls in the kitchen can take away bread and bacon grease. We're all entitled to something. For the rain's sake, Viner, why else do you think we'd stay? For the roof over our heads?'

'Don't you live here?' The milk was not quite fresh and the bread was not quite stale. Cleaver's rights did not, apparently, extend to good food.

'I live here while I work here, but it's not my home. The Queen lives here because she is Queen and she was born here – I wasn't. The King lives here because he's married to the Queen. We are here because we serve the King, or because we are his friends. He's here to make rain and we're here to help him make it. It's my job to help him. I don't do it because I like him.'

'I thought you said you were his friend.'

'I did. It's as good a job as any other.'

'Being his friend is a *job*?'

'It's not an entertainment; but it's not as bad as it sounds; I *do* like him,' Cleaver said, thoughtfully.

Like the man who shone? *Like* him? Worship him sooner, surely?

'And not Herself,' Viner said.

'Did I say that? True: she's a captious little lady. Catskin's her friend. She has her own following.'

'I thought you and Catskin were friends.'

'No, just in the same line of work. Do you know what a friend is, Viner?'

'I never had one.'

69

'Good. It will save you having to learn all over again. You'll be sounded out sooner or later. Questions will be asked. Nothing outright, you understand.'

'You said no questions.'

'No questions yet. But once you start to be useful, there'll be questions asked. People will want to know where you stand.'

'I'll stand where you stand,' Viner said.

'Wisely spoken, very. Because of me, or because of him? Not that it matters in the long run.' Cleaver lay back on his monstrous bed and addressed the ceiling, grinning. 'What a clever dowser it's turning out to be. Haven't I done well?'

I'll stand where the King stands, Viner thought. And I'll choose my own friends.

'I'll show you where the well is,' Cleaver said, at last rousing himself to get up and leave the room. Viner followed him, looking curiously up the proscribed staircase; no one stood on it. 'The important thing,' Cleaver was saying, 'is to find out how much water you're entitled to. I may have two bucketfuls brought to me, and two more if I fetch them myself. You may have one – nobody's denied at least one, if you go to the well, but don't presume to take any more until you're told you may. A thief of water is a thief of life.' He must have seen by Viner's look that Viner found the observation out of character. 'I'm quoting. It's written over the well head; can you read?'

'And write. *And* tally.'

'Hoity-toity,' Cleaver said. 'Not that it matters, there's nothing else to read. I'm losing the skill myself.'

'It's a long time since I learned,' Viner said, apologetically. Cleaver spread his hands.

'Most people here can't read. Why should they? Herself can only just write.'

'And Morning Light?'

'Oh, *he* can. One of these days,' said Cleaver, 'I should like to find out why.'

'Why shouldn't he be able to write?'

'For most of us there's no need. My father's a scribe, so of course I learned young. But who knows what Morning Light's father was, if he had one. I told you, for all I know he fell from the clouds.'

'Talking of things falling from clouds,' Viner interrupted with new firmness, 'such as rain, such as water, when do I go out dowsing?'

'Tomorrow, after noon,' Cleaver said, 'because tomorrow, after noon, the King dances again, so there's no chance of his sending for me. He probably wouldn't, but I shouldn't like to be away if he did, not after having been gone so long and only just returned.'

Viner perceived that Cleaver considered himself needed, by the King, and pleased to be. Viner hoped for that pleasure.

'Don't you want to watch him?'

'No,' Cleaver said. 'You saw him yourself, yesterday. Would you want to?'

'I thought it was wonderful,' Viner said, defiantly.

'I suppose it is, the first time, but after two years . . . it would be a sight more wonderful if something came of it. You do realize that it's meant to rain afterwards, don't you? Rain, think of it; the crops would grow, the pigs would fatten, we could all have a bath, Morning Light would smile again and Herself might for an hour or two look less like a vinegar mother than usual. Here's the well. Draw yourself a bucketful, do.'

'What's a vinegar mother?' He sent the bucket jumping down on its rope, down, down, very far down.

'Why,' said Cleaver, 'it's that grey cloudy thing that sits on top of wine and turns all sour beneath it. She should take care, should Madam, while she's carrying, or she'll give birth to a pickled walnut.'

'Will that child be the next king?' Viner said, as he began to wind up the bucket.

'Oh no, that's not how things are done. If it's a boy it will be nothing, just another child; if it's a girl she will be the next queen, and her husband will be the next king.'

'But a baby can't wed.'

'A baby princess can wed,' said Cleaver, 'and her husband can wait. Madam's mother was married and her husband waited. What else could he do? Madam's mother was married at three months. Meanwhile, we're all waiting.'

Viner, in some disgust, said, 'Is that how Morning Light became king?'

Cleaver laughed. 'No, no. It was only two years ago, and Herself was already a grown woman, but she didn't need a husband until her mother died, the old queen that was. I served her once. The queen marries the first man who can make rain.'

'And Morning Light did it?'

'After six weeks' drought, and six-and-twenty dancers, along comes Morning Light from no one knows where, and dances for an hour. By the time he'd finished the courtyard was under water and she wed him before the week was out.'

A forgotten remark, somewhere overheard, pricked at Viner like a splinter under a fingernail but, splinter-like, it would not come to the surface; only he was certain that the birth of a princess would not be an unqualified blessing.

'This babe won't be a queen yet, then?'

'Not unless Herself dies in childbirth.'

'And Morning Light will still be King.'

'Unless the Queen dies.'

'What will happen to him if she does?'

'I don't know,' Cleaver said. 'I don't know what happens to a failed king.'

And what happens to a failed dowser? Viner wondered. If the King should dance and rain should fall, he would no longer be needed. Would they then throw him out again? He reminded himself that the King could not make rain, that no man could make rain. His time would come. Cleaver had said he would rise, but how far would he rise, and who would he displace as he rose?

Cleaver went about his bitter business and Viner, with his entitlement, returned to his room where he set up house by stowing Cleaver's loaned garments in the chest, with the rod wrapped among them, and transferring some of the water to the pot bottle. He looked doubtfully at what remained in the bucket and then, casting caution aside, washed and changed his clothes. The Webfeet had rarely washed except in spring, when they broke out of the clouts wherein they had been sewn all winter, reckoning that they got wet enough by accident, without making any effort; but he seemed to remember that it had been quite unexceptionable behaviour Further Up, and it did feel pleasant to scrub and shave, slay fleas, sluice away the grey bracelets round his wrists. He rinsed out his shirt and hung it across the chest to dry. He was at home.

Having established his tenancy, cat-like, he spent the next few hours wandering about the palace and getting his bearings. Rather than explore the whole building which seemed from the inside to be boundless and organic, thrusting out corridors like tentacles and rooms like tumours, he confined himself to making mental maps of certain journeys; from his room to the well; from the well to the kitchen; from the kitchen to his room; from his room to Cleaver's, half hoping to see again the gold in the gloom, the Rain King washed in sunlight, but the only person he met, whom he knew, was Hern. When he saw Hern, lounging in an alcove and whetting his knife upon a broken stone, he doubled back to take a different turning and found himself unexpectedly in the yawning doorway that led to the terrace, where yesterday had stood the silver statues of the King and the Queen. There were no statues now, although the great gongs blared silently in the sunlight, and sooty fibres lay on the hot stones where the lightning-maker had flourished his torch. Afraid that he was in a place where he should not be, Viner advanced hesitantly toward the balustrade, where the steps dropped away to ground level. The earth was fissured like the skin of an enormous basking reptile, the fabled corkendril, but he could see by the skeleton shrubs and clemmed hedges and shallow, brick-lined graves that had once been ornamental ponds, that all round the palace had lain gardens; once. Nothing remained now but an arid paddock, stark as winter, where a score or more of youths and young men were scuffling over the fired clay in pursuit of a ball that they kicked to one another when they could find it.

Viner recalled similar games, involving an inflated bladder, from his days in the valley, although he had never been invited or permitted to join in, and he paused to watch, faintly surprised to see grown men so ferociously occupied with a children's game, especially when he recognized among them Cleaver and Catskin. When they could not kick the ball they hacked at the nearest player instead, and when the ball vanished, as it often did under cover of the churned up dust, they chased each other, their feet thudding on the hardened ground, and their shouts rebounding from the wall of the palace where Viner saw, on looking up, and away from the game for a moment, a woman watching from an upper window, her head propped on her fist in an attitude which even from that distance he could interpret as weary distaste. There must be many women in the place who might pause at a window to watch the young men running, but surely only one who could watch with such displeasure, although he wondered if the Queen did not perhaps derive a certain perverse satisfaction from watching something she despised; superior in the knowledge that it did not please her, and that anyone who was pleased was also a fool. Did her anger need regular meals?

Had she wanted to marry the man she'd had to marry? At least she had not been wed, like her mother, at three months old; she had not grown up to find the deed already done. How did it feel to grow up with your spouse as firmly and unalterably designated as were your parents? And how did Morning Light feel? He looked for him, in the game.

The players were now so far and so fleet that he could not tell one from another, and if the King were among them, all were equals in the mêlée. When he glanced back at the window, the Queen had gone. Perhaps it had not been the Queen.

He sat on the low wall and looked out over the plain to where the King was surrounded and hidden by his friends, or lost among them. Friendship here was a trade, like carpentry, or water-divining. No; dowsing was his mystery. Maybe he could make friendship also his mystery. He would not practise it as a trade.

The game grew wilder. Those who were not in possession of the ball at any one moment laid hands on each other to prevent anyone else from gaining possession. By sound and appearance it was still all very good-humoured, but he could imagine very well what might happen should it get out of hand; if, for instance, just one of the players laid on too roughly, or let slip a remark that was not entirely amiable. Presently, when several made a concerted dive for the ball, they ended up on the ground in a heap. No one, it seemed, was damaged, but how easy it would be, he thought, to do damage; to end a man's life as he lay helpless at the bottom of the heap. How easy to do it even by accident. Such things had never occurred in the presence of the bladder.

What happened to a failed king?

As it had reached its climax so the game subsided, gradually, until the players were seen to be making their way back towards the terrace, loafing rather than running, chucking the ball aimlessly to one another, and as they mounted the steps a woman came out to meet them. This time Viner had no doubt that it was the Queen, and was as certain that she was the same woman who had watched from the window. As she paced across the terrace a figure detached itself from the jostling group, hurrying to greet her, and Viner turned expectantly to see the King, ready to kneel before the silver statue or the golden colossus with the flaming aureole. But there on the terrace stood a young man, only middling tall, whose hair, not red but brown like a marten, clung in little points to his damp forehead and framed a face that was at once friendly, eager, and utterly undistinguished by any flaw or feature. His nose was straight, his brows level, his teeth regular in his hopeful smile. Viner did not kneel, could not kneel, but nevertheless, it was the King.

'It was a good game?' he said, with almost childish anxiety for her approval.

'It was better done than the dancing,' she said, and stepped aside before he could touch her. Viner saw Morning Light wince away, crushed. How much better his friends must have seen it as they clustered at his heels. There was no further exchange and they all went inside, Cleaver with them, although he gestured to Viner as he passed, and grimaced suggestively at the Queen's back. The Queen walked, with careful pregnant gait, toward the place where Viner was sitting, where the low stone coping made a convenient seat. When she was close enough to speak without raising her voice, she said, 'I should like to be alone out here.'

Viner leapt from the wall at once, and then wondered what to do. Did she expect him to bow to her? She made no sign that she expected anything except, like the Webfeet before her, that he should go away, but as he started to leave she said, 'Who are you?'

'I am Viner, Madam,' he said. He thought he said it well, and stored it up as an occasion to be reviewed and enjoyed later. *Today*

I spoke with a queen. Then he recalled that Madam was not her name or her title, and that it might be a term that she was not supposed to hear.

'What are you?'

'I do many things,' he said, lying through his teeth. Mindful of Cleaver's caution, he could not reveal his mystery.

'And why are you here?'

'I came to serve the King, lady.'

She looked him up and down.

'Serve him right,' she said, and moved away, leaving Viner to interpret that remark as he liked.

5

His pallet was no narrower that evening, and no harder, than it had been the night before, and he went to it as gratefully as he had done then, but as he lay in the darkness he saw Cleaver, lounging on his own great raft of a bed and smiling obliquely. *I share it sometimes; I'm not greedy.* Viner turned restlessly from side to side between the confining wall and the bed's edge, knowing the impossibility of sharing this strait crib with anyone wider than a willow wand. He was not homesick for the suffocating company in the carpenter's loft, but he wished he could feel something at his flank other than the wall, and gradually, not thinking, half sleeping, he gathered the blankets together into a bundle in his arms, which he gentled against his shoulder as he lay, pressing it to him. Resting at last he saw the day unravel before him, from evening back to morning, from supper to the game of ball, to the well head, to Cleaver and his bed, the golden man, shining in the dark corridor, the plain man humiliated in the sunlight. All the while he drew the body of the bed linen closer, and fell asleep with his face pillowed in it.

Cleaver came to wake him at a very early hour. Viner peered at him unintelligently from under the ploughed-up bedding, dredged from a dream in which he was entertaining Cleaver in the carpenter's cottage, surrounded by his family which had swelled to tribal proportions. They were sitting on shelves, all the way up the wall.

'It's a lie about the feet,' he said, when Cleaver shook him. 'Look at them. It's not their feet that are webbed, it's their ears.'

Cleaver took no notice and continued to shake him until the family, with their flapping leathery ears, had faded into the dawn. 'Get up. I want to leave before anyone else is about.'

Viner pushed the blankets aside and sat up. 'What hour is it?'

'The sun's not risen. Let's get away before it shows.'

Infected by his urgency, Viner scrambled into his clothes. 'Will someone stop us?'

'No – but I don't want any questions asked until you've found something.'

'Won't questions be asked when we get back?'

'You'll have found something by then.' Viner hoped very much that he was right. 'I've packed food. We'll eat on the road.'

Viner hurried at his heels to the stable block, and was not pleased to see that Cleaver had saddled an ass for him. He was uncertain, but he thought that it was the same animal that he had ridden on the journey from the big stones, and they eyed each other with mutual distrust. He wondered if Cleaver would believe him if he were to claim that his powers of divination were weakened if he lost contact with the earth, but Cleaver was mounted already, and leading the way out of the yard past the byres where beasts stamped and snorted in their straw, to the road that led to the village on the horizon. They skirted a shallow depression ringed by the bleached stumps of dead trees.

Cleaver said, 'Remember the mere Herself was named for?'

'Yes?'

'That's it.'

He was still unable to judge distances accurately. The sun rose as they left the environs of the palace, and the village was hidden from them by a slight swell in the ground. By the time it came into view again, the sun was well up in the sky and the red haze in which they had begun the journey had lifted into the dry air, disclosing that what he had taken for buildings and tall trees were in reality a grove of bushes, overhanging ruined walls.

'Where are we going to try first?' he asked.

'I thought the village. There was water enough there once, and might be again, if you can call it,' Cleaver said.

'Wouldn't it be better to try somewhere closer to the palace?' He was growing tired of Cleaver's hole-and-corner caution.

'We will later, but you mustn't be *seen* failing. If you fail out here, today, no one will know.'

Viner could not argue. He did not want to be seen failing. He did not want Cleaver to see him failing, but most of all he feared to fail the King. One instant of success there would wipe out for ever the six years of contempt and disdain among the Webfeet. When he looked over his shoulder he saw the palace reduced to a quivering pile in the distance, a cairn of hot stones.

He was feeling stiff again by the time they reached the village and halted in the shade of the bushes by what had been a pond. Nothing remained but the basin, littered with flat stones and bones and the other domestic refuse with which the villagers had fouled their lifeline before it was taken from them. He thought that he saw the dome of a human skull among the perforated cauldrons and potsherds; that must have caused a stir when the truant waters exposed it. Cleaver dismounted, suggesting that they tether their horses to one of the trees, sit down and eat. Viner was looking at the trees.

'This one's a hazel.'

'So?'

'Hazel makes fine rods,' Viner said.

'But you've got a rod.'

'It's too dry. The wood must be green.' He took out his knife, ready sharpened, and cut a fork. Cleaver watched him as he trimmed it.

'Is that part of the mystery, green wood?'

'Yes, it must be cut at sunrise.' As far as he knew it made no difference to a rod whether it was cut at noon or evening. 'Or at midnight, in the full of the moon.'

'I don't understand your mystery,' Cleaver replied, sulkily. 'Rain can come down at any time, so we call it at any time, night or day, it makes no difference.'

'No, it doesn't, does it?' Viner said, spitefully. They ate their unappetizing breakfast in offended silence. Viner would happily have poured his sour milk into the ground, only he perceived that to be caught wasting liquid of any kind would be the ultimate offence. He swallowed, his face writhing in protest, and recalled Cleaver's comment about the vinegar mother. Could Herself turn the milk?

When the last of the curds was lurching in his stomach he thought of suggesting that it might be time to start. He inferred that Cleaver was thinking the same thing, but unwilling to suggest it. Cleaver, in spite of the big stones and Viner's own boast about his prowess, was still afraid that the whole thing might turn out to be a terrible mistake.

'Where will you begin?' Cleaver asked, reading his thought. 'Here where the pond was?'

'No, over on the other side, beyond the ruins.'

He was not prepared to admit that he had no idea where to start looking. His memory of his father's instructions did not stretch to include the lore of likelihood. He must rely now on his own good sense, and the breakfast interval had given him time to observe that the trees on the far side of the ruins, for all they were scrubby and little more than bolted bushes, were greener and more plentiful than those which stood round the crazed cup of the pond. If they had found some means of survival, he too might find it. As Cleaver packed up the remains of their meal he went down into the dry pond and, deliberately avoiding the thing he thought was a skull, began to pick up stones and put them into his bait bag.

'Is that part of the mystery?' Cleaver asked, when he came out again, the bait bag hanging heavy at his side.

'I need them for markers.'

'How many times do you expect to find water, then?' Cleaver said, with no optimism in his voice.

'You don't think I'll find it even once, do you?' Viner said. 'Now it's time to put me to the test, you're afraid I won't be able to do it.'

'How can I help it?' Cleaver had the grace to look ashamed; 'living with Morning Light day in day out; we were sure of him, once.'

'If there's water here, I'll find it,' Viner said. 'But look, it's not just a puddle down there. It'll be a stream, and I'll have to chart the course of it. I have to know how wide it is – how far down.'

'You can tell all that – from up here?'

'Yes.' And you're not going to learn how it's done, Viner added, under his breath. 'Every time the rod moves, I have to mark the place. Pegs or sticks would be best, but we'd never get them into the ground without a hammer, it's that dry.'

Cleaver looked very dubious, as if he suspected that Viner intended to make a fool of him and was playing for time. 'When you found water at the big stones,' he said, 'you only put down one marker, that old bone, and we dug where you put it.'

'Only because Hern wouldn't let me go on. It was sheer luck that I chanced on the best place, first time.' Viner knew that it would be hard not to make a fool of a man who was so anxious to be fooled. 'If you remember, we weren't looking for water, we were looking for gold. Once is enough, for gold, it doesn't flow.' He still refrained from telling Cleaver that the discovery of the ring had surprised him as much as the water had surprised them.

'Do you mind if I watch?' Cleaver asked.

'No, but don't talk to me. I have to concentrate.'

Cleaver was silent immediately, and in silence they left the animals and walked through the ruins of the village. What had happened here was now happening at the palace. Not a wall was left standing above shoulder height, and the houses had become lidless boxes, filled with the rubble of tumbled roofs. They had been built of unfired clay brick, and in falling into disuse they had fallen indeed. They were turning back to the earth from which they had been made.

'What became of the people?'

Maintaining his imposed silence, Cleaver shrugged.

'When did they go?'

Cleaver shook his head. Viner thought of the people who had lost hope and fled, unnoticed and unmourned by their nearest neighbours. Beyond the most distant of the outlying buildings they passed a deep pit, filled with more refuse.

'What's that?' Cleaver shrugged again. Viner lost patience.

'I didn't mean you couldn't say anything at all. Only while I'm dowsing.'

'It's the clay pit,' Cleaver said. 'Where they dug out the mud for their building.' It did not escape Viner that he had, however unintentionally, given an order and that Cleaver, however misguidedly, had obeyed it. Cleaver was coming to heel. Viner looked into the pit.

The rubbish was all piled on the side nearest the village. Not only unthrifty but bone idle, he said to himself. The bottom of the pit, where it was exposed, was quite flat and quite dry. He held out the rod, over the edge. It did not move. Cleaver, breathless, watched him. Dismissively, Viner turned his back on the pit and walked away, among the dead and dying trees, towards the few that retained green leaves. Once he was past these he halted and taking the rod in both hands held it out at arm's length, as if dedicating it, before tucking his elbows into his sides and assuming the dowser's grip. Had he felt only slightly more sure of himself he would have muttered obscure imprecations over it, but even the true simple ritual, unadorned, had the desired effect. Cleaver halted respectfully, and at a distance.

Viner began to walk. He remembered his father telling him that children could dowse because their heads were empty, and he knew it was essential to clear his mind of all thoughts except those of water, but while water remained strongest, he was still aware of all its tributaries: Cleaver watching with hot intensity from beneath his tree, out of sight but oppressively present; Morning Light, dancing his maniac dance to no purpose; the people of the deserted village trekking forlornly away from their crumbling homes; the skeleton in the pond; the big stones and the urn of ashes; Hern, Catskin, the man called Dead Brother . . . the rod leaped in his hands.

By noon he had mapped out his stream, a hundred paces each way, the banks and the parallels that flanked it and from which he would calculate the depth and width. His wrists ached abominably, but he dared not stop walking until he had measured his distances. He had no intention of letting Cleaver find out how he did it, and while Cleaver remained awestricken under his tree he could not see clearly what Viner was doing. He must not come any closer until Viner had all the information that he needed; then he could walk where he liked and marvel at the sight. For once Viner was glad of his shaking arms; Cleaver would be impressed by his physical exertions as he had once, presumably, been impressed by the King's torrential sweat. He no longer needed the rod, but he kept it held out before him, to impersonate the charm that Cleaver thought it was. He mouthed soundless chough-talk with his lips, and made his calculations in his head, and Cleaver never moved. Viner did not look at Cleaver and imagined that it was the King who stood there, pinned to the trunk by fear and admiration. He put the rod under his belt and walked toward the trees.

Cleaver never took his eyes from him as he approached, but he said nothing. Viner had earned his right to silence.

'How soon do you want it out?' Viner said.

'Out?'

'The water. You'll have to dig, remember. If you and I start now, and go on till sunset, and come back tomorrow, and the next day, and maybe the next, you'll keep your secret. If we go back and bring out four or five with us, tomorrow, you'll have it by nightfall the same day.' He was amazed by the authority in his voice, he who had spent his life cringing under the impact of others' authority. Just a little over a week ago Cleaver, who now hung on his every word, had struck him across the face for answering out of turn, Hern had threatened his life; they had bound him and dragged him across country on an ass, blindfold. If they thought he would forget that, they were mistaken. One day, sooner or later, he could wait, he would have his revenge, when they were least expecting it. For now, he stood face to face with Cleaver, and gave orders, and Cleaver heard him. That was balm enough, to be going on with.

'Let me see it,' Cleaver said, hoarsely.

'I can show you where it is.' Viner sat down and waved Cleaver away in the direction of his rows of stones. He was half asleep when Cleaver returned, and he had no idea how long he had been gone, prowling up and down the stream that he could not see and scarcely dared believe in. Cleaver came and sat on his heels, at Viner's side.

'Are you sure?'

Viner could not blame him for his doubts, after so many disappointments at the dancing place, but he concealed this and answered with hauteur, 'I'm sure. It's a long way down, and it's shallow, but it's there.'

Cleaver looked through the branches to the broken walls of the houses. In the midday sunshine there was no sound but the high drone of passing insects on the wing. 'They went away because they had no water; now it's come back. They won't.'

'You brought picks. Do you want to start now, or will you come back tomorrow?' Viner could see that Cleaver was torn between his desire to reach the stream as soon as possible, and the drama of keeping it a secret and presenting the water as an accomplished fact. He also knew, at that moment, that unless he were careful it would become Cleaver's miracle, and not his own: the King would be as far out of reach as ever, distantly shining but unattainable, as was the sun, and Viner would never come close even to the brown-haired man with the small, anxious smile. 'Which is the more important, secrecy or water?'

'Can't we begin now?'

'Alone? We shouldn't get far, with the ground so hard, but we could make a start and come back tomorrow at first light. Who would you bring with us, Hern and the others?'

Cleaver nodded, but he was already on his feet. Viner watched him run through the trees and into the ruined village in his haste to fetch the pickaxes. That is, he amended, *you* can make a start. I'm fit for nothing. All the same, while Cleaver was out of sight, he rose and cut himself some more likely twigs from the hazel branches over his head, and stowed them in his shirt.

It was dark when they returned to the palace, and Viner could hardly summon the strength to stagger to his room. Cleaver was not in much better shape, being no more accustomed to manual labour than was Viner, but in spite of their blistered hands and aching shoulders a certain exhilaration had kept them digging until the sun set. Viner had dreamed of food all the way home, but when he reached his room he had no thought of eating. He was asleep almost before he found his way to the pallet, and he moaned and buried his face in the blanket next morning when, still in darkness, Cleaver came to rouse him.

In the courtyard by the kitchen he found a company assembled, all armed with shovels and picks; Catskin, Hern, Anvil and a reassuringly hefty youth with shoulders like the quarters of a war-horse. They all nodded to him without speaking, and Viner thought there was respect, rather than condescension, in their reticence. He looked round for his ass, but Anvil led up a horse. Viner did not know whether this was in acknowledgement of his power, or because it could move faster than an ass. Whichever the reason, he would have preferred the ass, and he did not enjoy his precarious journey to the ruined village.

They dismounted, tethered the horses and sat down to eat. The meal was hurried, and although all eyes were turned to the hazel trees beyond the ruins, no one spoke. When it was over, he and Cleaver led the way between the walls and through the scrub to the site of the stream, where the lines of cold stones gleamed whitely in the dawn light, and the hole that they had dug yesterday gaped at them. Everyone looked at Viner, but still no one spoke until Hern said, almost casually, 'How far down must we dig?'

'To twenty spits,' Viner said.

'If there is no water after that,' Hern said, 'then this time I will certainly cut your throat,' but the others looked at him with such scandalized faces that he said no more. Viner had thought that Hern had been joking, in his homicidal way, but he could see that the rest thought it was no moment for jokes. Viner, with his charmed rod, now had also a charmed life. There were no further exchanges. As one, they threw off their jerkins, bent over their shovels and began to dig. They did not stop all day. Viner would have said that it was not possible for men to work so hard, for so long, but by his magic he had made it happen. From time to time, unable to maintain the furious pace, he straightened up to rest, and although no one joined him, no one rebuked him: he was one apart. As darkness gathered their efforts intensified; apart from the occasional cry of a night animal in the ruins of the village there was no sound save the grating of spade blades in gravel, the thud and mutter of falling stones and earth, and breath saw-toothed in the throat. Candle lanterns stood round the rim of the pit they had dug themselves into, but the rim was far above them now and they could no longer see what they were doing, lit only by the miserly light of the new moon. Cleaver, stooping to shift a stone that had jarred his blade said, 'Here is water.'

Viner had not known how he would feel when they found it, but he knew now. He remembered the terrible dawn of the storm when his mother had cried out to the village headman, 'He's nothing now, but in time he'll repay you a hundredfold. He has the power!' He listened to the astounded voices in the dark all round him, thickened by fear, awe, and at bottom, relief.

He had the power, all right.

He was not left to bring up the ignominious rear on the way

home. This time he rode ahead, alone, and no one presumed to join him until he beckoned to Cleaver and Hern to ride alongside.

'When do we tell the King?' he asked. He let his tone indicate that he was asking for advice, rather than directions; that he could, moreover, reject the advice if it failed to please him.

'Soon as maybe,' Hern said. 'You didn't see him yesterday, after the dance.'

'What happened after the dance?'

'He danced again,' said Hern. 'In his sleep.'

'Who saw him?' Cleaver asked, dismayed by the sound of it.

'I did, not for the first time. I found him on the terrace, going ve-ry slowly and turning as he went.' Hern demonstrated with a curious gyration of the shoulders, dark against the stars.

'Did you tell Herself?'

'She was watching him from the window.'

Viner, listening, pictured the King dancing in the dark, under the unforgiving eyes of his wife; Morning Light at midnight. 'What did you do?' he asked.

'Led him back to bed. He never woke. He won't know what happened, unless Madam told him.'

'I'm sure she told him,' Cleaver said. 'It's not something he'd want to know. I wonder what they did today, with none of us there to cushion the impact.'

'What they always do after a dance, I suppose,' Hern said. 'He stood on the terrace and watched the sky, while she sat at the window and watched him. Can't you just see it?' he asked, savagely. 'People running in and out from the villages, bring us rain, bring us rain, and he stands there, because there's nothing else to do, and she sits, because there's nothing else to do,' said Hern. 'That's how they spent today, and that's how they'll spend tomorrow, and tomorrow, and the day after that, until he dances again. And then it will start all over.'

Viner could see it exactly.

'The sooner he knows, the better, then,' Cleaver said. 'Don't you think, Viner?'

Viner thought it was obvious, but he was gratified by Cleaver's deference, until he remembered that deference was now his right. He was entitled to it.

'Tell them both, or just him?' Hern asked.

'Tell him, and let him see for himself, and then let him tell her. It would give him pleasure,' Cleaver said.

'That's not all it would give him,' said Hern. 'She treats him worse than a louse, for all she's carrying his child.'

'When do we tell him?' Viner said. 'Tonight? Or in the morning?'

'It's already morning,' said Cleaver.

Viner rose sore and stiff and slowly that day, but with a new sense of purpose. He went to the well for his bucket of water thinking, as he turned the whining handle, that from now on he could very probably have as much as he liked. He would be entitled to it. Come to that, they could all have as much as they liked. He thought of the thin moon, shining on the water as it welled up in the excavation last night; of the sun that would be shining on it now, morning light on the water, water for Morning Light and a new mere for Madam. He was not given to playing with words but these danced effortlessly in his head. After he was dressed he went in search of Cleaver instead of waiting, as before, for Cleaver to come looking for him; boldly demanding assistance from total strangers until he ran Cleaver to earth with Hern and Catskin in Catskin's own room, a sparsely furnished apartment, with a bed only slightly larger than it needed to be. Catskin favoured upright chairs and played host with a stern unbending back.

'Where's the King?' Viner said.

Catskin waved him to a chair. 'Watching clouds.'

'*Clouds?*' Viner had not seen a cloud since he went Over the Top and had looked back to find one below him.

'We do have clouds here,' Cleaver said, with leaden pleasantry.

Viner ventured a pleasantry of his own. 'Why does the King watch them? Does he think they'll stop when they see him?'

'Perhaps he thinks that if he stares hard enough they'll be shamed, and fall,' said Hern.

'They won't fall for him,' said Catskin.

They won't fall for anyone, Viner thought, remembering that they genuinely believed that a man could call water out of the sky.

Their faith was marginally more credible now that he knew they as honestly believed that he himself could call water up from the ground. Nothing he could say would make them believe that it was there already, and that all he had done was to tell them where to dig. They admired him for all the wrong reasons, but they admired him, nonetheless. For now, the reasons were irrelevant.

'Where's Madam?' Hern said. Viner noticed Catskin's face register violent disapproval.

'The Queen is in her arbour,' he said, stiffly. He did not favour the use of sobriquets, in spite of having one himself.

'And long may she stay there,' Cleaver said. 'I suggest we go and tell him now.' He nodded to Viner. 'Who comes with us?'

Viner stood up, and Hern. Catskin stayed where he was, interested only in the water, not in the effect that the news of it might have on the King. The others hurried out of the room and Viner was content to follow behind, this time, as he did not know where they were headed. He hoped that one day circumstances would take him to an upper floor, where he too might stand at windows and look down, but Cleaver led the way to the room where Viner had first seen the King, and the King was there again, one of three men who stood near the far end, in urgent conversation.

'Someone's found him first,' Cleaver said, motioning to Viner and Hern that they should wait, and squinnied through that convenient rent in the curtain that Viner had developed, last time. Viner peered over his shoulder. The King, obviously harassed, was backed up against the wall, outweighed in numbers and in passion by the gesticulating petitioners who had come to beg, or demand his intercession. In loud and monotonous voices they listed their failing wells and counted them on their fingers. Between the two of them they had not enough fingers.

'Come into the town,' said one. 'Come to the town and dance.'

'I can't do that,' said the King. 'I can only dance here, in the dancing place.' He sounded, to Viner, concerned and distressed, but even so, detached. For all he had failed to make rain, he was still the King. 'There is nothing to stop your people trying to make rain,' he went on. 'Here in the villages they call upon the clouds themselves.'

'We passed through one of those villages today,' said one man.

Viner caught his breath sharply, but if the men had spoken of the ruined village then they had evidently seen nothing. The water lay far from the road.

'Why keep a dog and bark yourself?' said the other, offensively, and Viner saw the King flush, so that for once he looked like sunrise.

'Go to the dining hall,' he said, 'and food will be brought to you.'

'And water?' his antagonist asked, unkindly.

'As much as you can drink,' said the King. 'This afternoon I shall dance for you.'

'There's no shortage of water here, then?'

'We shall watch you,' said the second man, seeming fearful, perhaps reasonably, that if he were not watched the King might skimp the ceremonial and so lessen his chances of success. How little they know him, Viner thought, derisively, superior in the certainty that he knew more; and then realized that probably they did not know the King at all, and neither did he.

The men were led muttering away. Viner stayed at his spy-hole, expecting some reaction from the King, but he simply remained where he was, unmoving, being a king. But never, Viner thought, a Rain King. You will never make it rain.

'Now we go in,' Hern said.

'Give him a moment to collect himself,' Cleaver said. 'He has the whole land on his back, now.'

'Then the sooner we lift it off, the better,' Hern said, and brushing aside Cleaver's restraining hand, he pushed past the curtain and entered the room, with Viner close behind him, determined to assert himself from the moment his power was revealed. He did not intend to allow the accolade to fall on Cleaver. Cleaver might take credit for finding Viner, but Viner would take credit for finding the water.

He saw at once that Cleaver had been right in advising them to wait. The King remained uncollected, against the wall, where he had stood all along, looking more taken aback by their sudden appearance than he had been by the townsmen's attack.

'The wells in the town are drying up,' he said, in a shaken voice. Viner reminded himself that he knew nothing about

89

Morning Light, whether he was a wise man or a fool, honest or dishonest. Whatever else he might be it was clear, however, that he was not a quick thinker. 'And it won't rain,' said the King.

'There are more ways of getting water than out of the sky,' Cleaver said. He was smiling already, in spite of himself, longing to break the news, or anxious to be first with it.

'Out of wells, and the wells are drying up,' said Morning Light. Viner began to doubt that he would understand anything that they told him while the news of the latest catastrophe was still in his ears.

'Then we must dig new ones,' said Hern.

'Dig? Where shall we dig? Didn't you hear what they were saying?' If he knew they had been eavesdropping, he was past caring. 'They *are* digging, and there's nothing there.'

Viner was about to add, 'Because they don't know where to dig', but Cleaver got in ahead of him.

'Do you remember I told you of the sorcerer who could call water up? Who could find it by his art, in dry places?'

Morning Light looked hopeful, then his customary aura of defeat settled about him like fog. Viner guessed that he had been consoled too often with false hopes to dare to hope again.

He said, 'I remember you told me you'd *heard* of him.'

'That's right, and now we've found him,' Cleaver said.

'He's here in the palace?' A light that was not hopeful started in his eyes. 'Another liar with knives and flints?' His earlier eagerness had deflated. 'Sorcerers want blood. They promised rain, but all we got was blood – my blood,' he said, spitting out the last word.

'Not this one,' Cleaver said, touching Viner lightly on the shoulder.

'*Him?*' Morning Light retreated a step but, finding the wall behind him, fought to regain his poise, such as it was. Viner spread his hands foolishly to show, he supposed, that he was not equipped with knives and flints. 'How did he come here?'

'We met him on the road,' Cleaver said, vague and casual. 'He wishes to serve you.'

'How does he wish to serve me?' The King lost control of his voice completely and choked over the words. 'With more lies? I will not bleed any more for a liar.'

Cleaver stood his ground. 'What he says he can do, he can do; I've seen him do it. Water calls to him out of the ground. With his rod he conjures it to him, and where he tells us to dig, there it is, waiting.'

Viner saw that his judgement of the King had been correct. The eyes, dark with suspicion, came round to meet his.

'You've seen him do it?'

'Two days ago,' Cleaver declaimed, 'we went to the ruined village on the road and he marked the place where he said water would be. I didn't believe him; I could see no water, but yesterday six of us went back there and dug from before sunrise till after moonrise, and the water was where he said it would be, and at the depth he said, too. Even if the sky will not answer you, Morning Light, the earth will obey him.' Cleaver seemed to appreciate that this last remark might not sound entirely tactful for he gave up all efforts at rhetoric, ending shortly, 'One way or another, we'll have water.'

Morning Light was watching Viner.

'Is this true?' he said. 'You can do this thing? You can call water to me here, in this room?'

Viner resigned himself to the usual rigmarole of half-comprehended explanations. 'No,' he said, 'I can't do that. But I can tell you where water is, under the ground. If you come with us to the village, I'll show you a pool where two days ago there was only dry earth. If there's water near the palace I will find it for you; in the town, I will find it for you. Then all that must be done is to dig.'

Morning Light looked at him closely. He did not smile, he did not relax. 'Who *are* you?' he said. 'Where do you come from?'

'I'm Viner,' said Viner, 'and I come from a place where there's more water than any man wants.'

'Are you a sorcerer?'

'I'm a dowser.'

'Whatever you are . . .' the King's voice sank to a conversational whisper, 'if you are deceiving me, I'll tear out your heart

with my own hands. If there's to be blood it'll be your blood.'
Viner was grateful for Cleaver's insistence that he find water
before they told the King that he could do it. 'As for you two,' he
went on, rounding on Hern and Cleaver.

'No one's going to bleed. Is it my fault if you play with lunatics
when I'm not here? Knives and flints, my arse,' Cleaver said,
amiably. 'I promise you, he's found water.'

'They have webbed feet where he comes from,' said Hern.

The four of them rode out to the village on horseback, at speed;
at such speed that Viner was at first afraid that he would not
complete the journey, but somehow he stayed in the saddle. He
was becoming proficient on horseback. He was a success. Pro-
ficiency was his right, and so he did not fall off. There was no
conversation. They rode all four abreast until they reached the
village, when by common consent they strung out in a line, with
Viner at the head, to lead the way through the ruins to the place
where he had called water out of the ground, so he was the first to
see his pool, his miracle. It was no moment for words. Uplifted by
the momentousness of the occasion he simply drew rein and
stretched out an arm over the water. Morning Light brought up
his horse alongside, and looked where he pointed.

His face remained absolutely expressionless. Viner knew that
he had not believed a word that they were saying to him, until he
saw for himself what Viner had done, but when he finally turned
his habitual look of stunned dismay had vanished. As Cleaver had
predicted, days ago, he smiled. It was failure that had stunned
him; hope was bringing him round.

'How did you do it?' he said.

Viner brought out the new hazel rod, one fit to show a king,
which he had providently stowed under his shirt.

'This is your charm?' Morning Light took the rod and turned it
in his hands, gingerly, as though it might be hot and perilous to
hold, searching for some sign of the power that summoned water.
'Will you show me how it works?'

Viner thought he had a nerve, and showed it. Cleaver and Hern
too looked disapproving. It was not done to ask a sorcerer for his
secrets, but Morning Light looked so happy that Viner could

forgive him his solecism and his curiosity. Not that it mattered, in any case; he had no intention of satisfying it.

'It moves in my hands, when water is near,' he said, repossessing the rod, 'but it won't move if the water has already shown itself.' He guessed that Morning Light would demand to see it put through its paces now, over the pool. 'But if we go back to the palace, I'll try to call up water there.' He decided that there was no hope of making them understand what the rod did and did not do, unless he explained how he interpreted it, and that was unthinkable; but he began to hope very devoutly that when he dowsed around the palace there would be something there for him to find. He did not want to falter now, standing as he did in the full glory of the King's gratitude.

Morning Light had dismounted and was crouched in the pit at the edge of the pool, lifting the water and letting it run over his arms and through his fingers. Viner felt very tenderly toward him, a king brought to his knees by the handiwork of an orphaned and derided outcast. Morning Light stood up abruptly and climbed out of the pit. 'I'm going back,' he said, 'to tell the Queen. Come with me!'

Without waiting for an answer he leaped back into the saddle and wheeled his horse round; Viner kicked his own mount into action and followed him, without waiting to see if Hern and Cleaver were coming too. It seemed to him that suddenly they were of no importance at all.

Again they rode in silence, but from time to time Morning Light looked across at him, and when their eyes met Viner knew that he had found the person who needed him and might become his friend, and it was not Cleaver.

They abandoned their horses to the care of a groom in the stable yard, and ran indoors, two men in a hurry, not master and servant. This, said Viner to himself, is the King, and I am walking beside him. Let me find him all the water he needs, and stay at his side.

6

Shoulder to shoulder they mounted the staircase by Cleaver's room. Viner, who had gazed curiously and enviously up those stairs, every time he visited Cleaver, looked about him in gleeful wonder as they passed along a passage which, unlike the echoing derelict labyrinth below, admitted no sound save that of their own footfalls.

It was bright, it was clean, the walls were intact and the ceiling unbroken. In the quietness Viner became aware of a distant and subdued pattering which made him think first of rats, then of spilled pulses on a stone floor, then of rain. He glanced sidelong at Morning Light, but Morning Light made no sign that he heard anything unusual. It could not, then, be rain. The King halted at an archway, hung with a thick curtain; the small random percussion rattled on, beyond it.

'In here,' said Morning Light. He moved the curtain.

In a little courtyard, roofed with a trellis and furnished with evergreen shrubs in red clay pots, sat the Queen, on a cushioned bench, her toes resting on a footstool. In what remained of her lap she supported a small skin drum, and beat lightly upon it with the tips of her fingers to make the rainfall that Viner had heard in the corridor. Almost under her breath she was singing a thin wordless song, very high, that set his teeth on edge. He could not at first understand why, for her voice, though toneless, was tuneful enough, until he noticed that the rhythm of the song was at odds with the drumbeats, and he was so perplexed as to how she did it that he hardly noticed when she looked up at her husband, for she did not stop singing; very deliberately she did not stop singing. Morning Light's eagerness withered as a plant pulled up by the roots. The tiny song spiralled round the enclosure like an invisible gnat, and Viner had recognized the same phrase three times over

94

before she stopped, but even then she continued to pattle on the drum head.

'Is it raining?' she said. She hummed inconsequently. 'I said there was no need to come back until it rained.' Viner was more than ever glad that it was he who had enabled the King to ignore this remark, or at least to withstand it. He did not imagine that the King easily withstood the wounds that his wife inflicted on him.

'There is someone I want you to see,' he said. The Queen regarded Viner through the crook of her husband's arm. Accustomed to more robust insults, he had never known that a look could so disable.

'I have seen him already.'

'Do you know what he can do?'

She lifted her shoulders. 'Why guess? I thought I knew what you could do, once.'

'He can call water from the earth,' said Morning Light. 'I have seen it.'

'You have seen him call it?'

'I've seen the water.'

'How do you know he called it?' the Queen said, her voice a languid yawn. 'Can he call it from the sky?' The drumming stopped.

'No, but – until it does rain, we can dig new wells.'

'We have wells. What use are new wells with no rain to fill them?'

'That depends,' Viner began, boldly, but she ignored him and looked again at Morning Light.

'And you will stop dancing?'

'No!' he said, and went down on his knees before her. 'But now, no one need suffer while I dance. There will be water, enough for everybody.'

'*I* suffer while you dance,' the Queen said. Morning Light held out his arms to her. She put down the drum and folded her own arms over the baby, fencing it and herself from its father. Viner saw it kick and shifted his gaze, uncomfortably, but Morning Light had no such inhibitions. He turned still, incredibly, smiling, and looked at Viner.

'We're going to have a child,' he said. 'That is, I – *she* is going to have a child.'

'What he wants you to know,' the Queen interrupted, 'is that he fathered it. There appears to be some doubt in certain circles.' Viner stared pitifully at him as she stood up and without further comment walked from the arbour. Morning Light, kneeling, watched her go, smiling radiantly and with such misery in his eyes that Viner could not bear to look any more.

'It's because of the baby,' he said, assuming that he need say nothing more and that Viner would understand. Viner understood, well enough, but for quite a different reason; having watched his mother bring four live children into the world, and two dead ones, he was unimpressed by the mystery of childbearing and the rules that governed it. Morning Light was bound for life to a woman who detested him and would always detest him. He could not believe that he did not know it.

Meanwhile Morning Light, still on the floor, was peering at Viner's shoes so intently that Viner began to shuffle. Morning Light said shyly, '*Have* you got webbed feet?'

The next morning he took his new hazel rod and for the first time circumnavigated the sprawling block of the palace. At his measured working walking pace it took him half an hour to get right round, followed at a respectful distance by Cleaver and Hern, and at the end of it he had left three markers behind him, placed at his direction by Cleaver who showed an evident desire to please, or an evident desire to keep an eye on him. The King, who had been watching covertly, he imagined, from indoors, came out then. Possibly the Queen was at one of her many windows, also watching.

'Do you know where we should dig, yet?' the King asked.

'No. There are three places that might do, but I can't tell so soon. I shall be at this all day,' Viner said, trying to indicate politely that he was tired of being watched. He could see that he would have to invent some formula condition that would keep them all away from him while he worked; something along the lines that the rod would turn against him if it were too closely observed, or that its powers would wane. To say simply that he found it hard to concentrate would not impress them any more, it would only reduce their awe of him, whereas the rod was inexplicable, incalculable. If he said it must marry a tree and sire nuts they would believe him. It crossed his mind, although he suppressed the thought instantly, that he need not even be polite.

Morning Light's face fell. Yesterday, as he had promised, he had danced the rain dance for the townsmen, and although the gossamer clouds had thickened to cobwebs, no rain had fallen. Viner was glad for his sake that the clouds had gathered; at least he had been seen to achieve some result. Viner had watched him dance, feeling the ground shake under the impact of hands and feet, himself exhausted by the violence of the King's efforts as he twisted and leaped in what should have been a frenzy of exaltation. He had seen Morning Light come in afterwards, chest heaving and the sweat running down his neck over his shoulders, when he pulled off the wig, and he thought that he knew now the King's great and insurmountable failing; he was neither exalted nor frenzied. He danced with dedication, persistence, agility, but it was all done so conscientiously, without inspiration. However simple Morning Light might be, he was not simple enough for the rain dance; aware of every movement he was at one with the earth, never with the sky. Did he go to his wife with the same humourless determination, and there fail again for the same reason? Viner's pity increased, and he did not want to pity a king, even when that king turned out to be an undistinguished young man of middle height, with worried eyes and a wife who despised him. Now he looked at Morning Light under the burden of his defeat, and longed to comfort him.

'It may be,' he said, 'that the first place I try will be the best, and we can begin at once.'

'How will you know it's the best if you don't try the others?' Morning Light asked, so quickly that Viner's estimate of his intelligence underwent another sharp reversal.

'The rod will tell me,' he countered, equally sharp, and Morning Light withdrew, rebuked. Viner was ashamed of himself for gaining such an easy victory with such an easy lie. So long as he maintained his hold on the slender hazel he could do very nearly what he liked with these people. At all costs, he must make sure

97

that no one ever observed him closely enough to imitate him. While he wielded the rod, the cleverest man was a fool in his hands, and if one of these fools found out his mystery, he was instantly diminished. He did not mind making fools of Cleaver and, particularly, Hern and Catskin; he would enjoy making a fool of the Queen, but he did not want a fool for a king.

In the end he fixed on a place on the north side of the building, where the water was close to the surface. He thought they might build a cistern, if they knew how, and suggested that if they wanted a well for the kitchen quarters, they should dig by the south wall, beyond the stables. He was sure that now they would understand that the rod had directed him to the water, but no; they were still convinced that it had called the water up, selecting the optimum position. He became jealous for its safety and, as he walked back to his corridor, alone now that he was not performing, decided that he would have to find a really secure place to hide it, and its fellows. Perhaps he could make it known that he had put a curse on it, but he doubted if he could carry this off with conviction, for he knew no curses except the day-to-day anathemas of the Webfeet, which had been notoriously ineffectual. As far as he could remember, no one's eyes had ever been blasted, no one's teeth grown inward, no one's loose bits dropped off. His father had once told him that a loop of human hair tied round a rod would render it useless, but he had tried, and it had made no difference.

When he reached his room he found Cleaver there before him, reclining on the bed and looking more than usually sardonic.

'Don't bother to come in,' Cleaver said. 'You're moving. Up.'

'Up?'

'I said you'd rise, didn't I? Well, you're on your way. The King expresses amazement and displeasure that you should be quartered here and has chosen a better room for you, himself.'

'How did he know I was here?' Viner said, detecting a democratic unfriendliness in Cleaver's voice that was quite different from his previous good-natured condescension. In the twelve days that he had known Cleaver their relationship had shifted so many times that every morning he met a stranger. Parting from him would be no hardship.

'He asked where he could find you, when you stopped work,

and I told him. "Oh," says he, "that won't do. We must take good care of him."' Viner found it hard to imagine Morning Light expressing himself in such terms. 'He always has taken good care of his property,' Cleaver said, making sure that Viner, wherever he might lie, knew where he stood. 'Follow me, and when we get there you can let me have those clothes back. New ones are provided – *and as much water as you want*, so you can wash them, first.'

'Shall I be nearer you, now?' Viner asked, as they traversed the passages that he was coming to know so well.

'And above,' Cleaver said, tersely, and to Viner's astonishment led the way past his own room and up the forbidden staircase to a half-landing with a doorway in one wall.

'Won't this offend anyone?' He remembered the order of precedence.

'Sure to,' said Cleaver.

The new room faced east, like the old one, but instead of the narrow slit in the wall, he now had a wide window that could be opened and closed, with panes of horn and one or two of glass, so that he could see out, albeit obscurely, even when it was shut. The bed was not so massive as Cleaver's, although larger than Catskin's, but it would have accommodated Viner's entire family, inserted at various angles. His first thought was to fling himself down and wallow on it, but under Cleaver's appraising eye he merely gave it an appraising glance which took in quilts and cushions, no grey blankets here, and the promised new clothes, spread over it, more than his family had ever owned between them. He firmly closed his mind to memory, lest the family take up permanent residence. However little they might have had, they had grudged him anything at all. Rot the lot of them.

On the walls were paintings, like the one in the hall where he had met the King, but on a smaller scale although equally faded. Viner was unwillingly reminded of the Queen, for opposite the bed was a pastoral scene of grazing sheep in a green meadow, and in the foreground a dark pool of water, secluded among flowering rushes, reeds, osiers; on the still surface a patina of lily leaves. When he woke each day he would find a mere before his eyes, a mere and morning light. He considered moving the bed.

'Suit you?' Cleaver asked. 'I wouldn't prepare for a long stay; if you go on rising at this rate you'll be sleeping on the roof before the end of next week.' He turned to go. 'Oh – I should have told you, no more solitary meals or humble repasts with boring old Cleaver. In future you eat with the rest of us. Boring old Cleaver will be there, of course, but you won't have to notice him.' His leery wink disappeared round the door. Viner thought that boring old Cleaver was altogether too acute, but before he could say anything, Cleaver was gone, and he was left alone with his picture and his bed. Retreating as far as he could he took three great strides, at a run, and sprang clear into the middle of it.

At his new altitude the atmosphere was noticeably rarefied, and so were his neighbours. The area where he now lodged seemed to be quite structurally sound; the people near by clearly a cut above his associates from his days at the end of the corridor. When he met them about their business, and he could not guess what that might be, they were not laden with buckets, baskets, brooms and mops, but went about the building empty-handed. They appeared to be decorative rather than useful, a means of disguising the vastness of the place, like embroidered cushions. He told himself, grimly, that he was most likely the only necessary member of the whole entourage and in this he included, quite arbitrarily, Cleaver, Catskin and Hern. He was doubly convinced of this when he saw them all at table: pigs round a trough, he sneered, only pigs earn their keep, eventually, and this lot do nothing. He supposed that they stayed because there was nowhere else to go. He tried counting heads and reckoned there must be upwards of a hundred sat down, feeding their faces, but the following night he looked more carefully and saw newcomers who had not appeared before. They seemed, like the building, to be infinitely multiplying.

The pictures in the room where they ate were wistful reconstructions of abundance. Where Viner sat a gigantic ox looked over his shoulder, knee-deep in buttercups and mallow. Beyond it a herd of milch goats wound its way through pastures of long grass and on the hill behind them white woolly sheep complemented the fat clouds that flocked promisingly overhead. Viner was seated next to a young lady, one of the Queen's attendants, who nibbled delicately at her dish of boiled beans and propped her elbows all over the table. He discovered that his fame was spreading.

'They tell me,' said the young lady, whose name was Red Hen, 'that where you come from the land is like that all the year round.' She waved her hand at the painted pasture.

'It would be, if it ever stopped raining,' Viner said, ungraciously.

'You mean, it rains all the time?'

'Near enough.'

'It must be like that Good Place we may go to when we die.' She rolled her eyes at him.

'Not exactly. Our Good Place is very hot and dry. Men stand about all day fuelling the flames, and there is never a drop of rain in the whole place, it being underground. That's how much they value water.'

'But they say you all have webbed feet.'

'That's a joke,' he said, sourly. '*I* don't have webbed feet. D'you want to look?'

She gave a squeal of laughter which made everyone stare. Viner saw himself gaining a reputation as a wit. 'I tell you what, though,' he said, sorry to have been so abrupt with someone who had tried only to be friendly, 'it's so wet in spring that the sheep have grass growing on their backs.'

She squealed again. 'I don't believe that!'

'It's true, though. And daisies, some of them. They have to be weeded before they're sheared.'

Red Hen laughed so much at this that her yellow hair flopped into the beans and she unwittingly shovelled in a mouthful and chewed it, like noodles.

At the High Table Mere and Morning Light sat side by side and said nothing to each other. He ate very little and drank often. She gobbled hungrily at everything that was put before her and talked demonstratively to Catskin who sat on her right, his eponymous jerkin put off in favour of a suit of green leather. Cleaver sat between Hern and Morning Light, watching the latter sidelong and exchanging looks with the former every time the King raised his cup. Viner wondered objectively how long it would be before he was up there with them: when the wells were dug, he supposed, which would be soon. He hoped that if ever he found himself sitting next to the King he could bring back the smile that he had seen when Morning Light had ridden with him from the ruined village. As his eyes left the King's face he caught the Queen staring at him and quickly looked down at his plate. *She* had begun to smile, and he did not care whether she smiled or not; but before the end of the meal a message was sent down to him from the High Table, that the Queen wished to speak with him in her room, afterwards, and when they all rose to leave it was Catskin who came to conduct him there, while Cleaver and Hern observed his movements from below raised eyebrows.

In Mere's room a thunderstorm was raging, whipping to oily cream a sea energetically painted by someone who had never seen the sea. Viner had never seen the sea, either, but travellers passing through the village had left corroborating descriptions behind them, so he knew that it was not a rock-rimmed cauldron girt with willow trees and peopled by monstrous fish with beaks and teeth that tore whole boats in half and scattered the crew piecemeal among overgrown waterlilies. This sea was a pond got out of hand. The storm was very well done, though, with great blades of lightning that scythed the mountain tops and clove the clouds that hung like dirty dumplings in the livid sky. Unoppressed by all this turmoil, Mere sat on a couch in her usual position, feet on footstool, drum in lap, singing her perverse little song. She stopped at once for Viner, as she had not stopped for Morning Light, but she said nothing. Viner understood that he must speak first.

'What are you singing?' he asked. 'How can you play one beat and sing another?'

'I learned young,' Mere said. 'My mother taught me and I must teach my daughter,' she patted her baby, 'if it is a daughter.'

'Must?'

'It's a song for rain,' said the Queen. 'Sit down. If you go into the villages you'll hear the women beat on the ground with sticks and wail and cry to bring rain. Sometimes they beat their children, and the children wail and cry. We do things better, here.'

'Does it bring rain?'

'The singing or the beating?'

'The singing.'

'No, but it becomes a habit, and while I'm doing it I don't have to listen to anyone else.'

'Morning Light?' Viner said, without meaning to. The Queen threw down the drum and stood, awkward but imperious. She began to walk up and down the room, striking her palm with her fist and gnawing at her lip.

'How can he think he brings rain, how can he *think* it?'

'They say he brought it once,' Viner said. He had not come expecting intimacy, and he had no idea how to handle it, nor did he want it.

'Once.' The Queen turned on the spot, her skirts swinging, and paced back again. 'I'll tell you what,' she said, 'I don't think it was his rain at all. He was the twenty-and-seventh man to dance the rain dance, and he did it immediately after the twenty-sixth. Rain never came that suddenly even for my father, but Morning Light danced and the sky opened. As he threw up his first javelin the clouds burst. It was like – as if – as if he'd run a knife through a water skin; and it rained till midnight. I sat here and watched it, through the window, and smelled it. I held out my hands and caught it, I drank it out of my hands. I listened to the people yelling, they were all rushing about with buckets, and then they brought him in here, soaked. He'd been standing out there, just standing; he could hardly believe it, either. Dripping. He stood where you're sitting and all the rain ran off him, off his hair, it was long then, he stood in a great puddle. And they said to me, "Here is the Rain King, Madam," and I realized, I remembered, that I had to marry the man who made the rain, and I looked at him, standing there with the water running off him . . .'

She stopped, breathless, and looked down at Viner.

'And you didn't want him?' He was horrified. He did not wish to know what passed between the Queen and Morning Light.

She stared at him in amazement and began to snuffle with laughter. 'Didn't want him? Didn't want him? Oh, I wanted him, all right. He didn't want *me*. I could see it. He said, "Lady, I was a stranger here and they called me to dance. They said it was the custom and I danced to make rain for the people. I never knew I must marry afterwards." Can you imagine that? Saying it to me?'

'No.' He could not imagine it. He could not imagine Morning Light saying it.

'I said, "What is your name?" and he told me. I said, "That's a worthy name for a king." I actually said that. Think of it, a worthy name for a – for that – that *stick*. I thought it was a splendid name, then. I loved it. I said it to myself, over and over again.'

'It is a splendid name,' Viner said. Splendid was not a word he would have chosen, but he supposed it had associations of splendour.

'Yes it is, but not for him. Someone was looking the wrong way when he was born. I said, "Stay in my palace for tonight and we will talk in the morning." In the morning he was in a fever from the dancing and the rain. He couldn't have left his bed, even if he'd wanted to. So I sent for my old nurse and I said, "Make him well. What will you give him to make him well?" and she said, "Elder and hemlock and elecampane to clear his lungs." "That's not all it will do," I said. "Give him vervain as well, as often as maybe." She knew what I meant. Perhaps she gave him other things, too, while he lay there and didn't know day from night, but in three days he asked for me, and so I had him. I married him that same night,' she said, bleakly, '*and it hasn't rained since.*'

'I'm sorry,' Viner said. He was sorry; sorry for Mere who had snared the man of her choice with a philtre, only to find that she did not want him, and sorrier for Morning Light who had been held against his will and was no longer wanted, but he did not know why she was telling him all this, and kept his sympathy under control.

The Queen picked up the drum and sat down again.

'I don't care what you think,' she said. 'I didn't bring you here to talk about *him*.' He watched her composure reassert itself. She said, bluntly, 'I want you to tell me how you do it.'

He was shocked and let her see it. 'The rod? I can't do that, it's my mystery.'

'Explain "mystery". I don't understand this word.'

'All craftsmen have a mystery, ask any smith, or mason. It's the way a thing is done. It takes many years to learn. How can I *tell* you?'

'A craftsman? But surely this is sorcery?' She did not pronounce the word with any sense of awe or caution. Thinking of the philtre, he guessed that she could take sorcery in her stride.

'I am a dowser.'

'But the rod is sorcery.'

She was telling him, not asking him. All right, then, the rod was sorcery. 'Yes.' It was safe now, to admit it. It had worked.

'But only a craftsman knows how to use it?' She was coming uncomfortably close to the truth, however wide her angle of approach. He had to scotch her progress.

'Only those who have the power can become craftsmen, in this mystery.'

'I see.' She pondered. 'So if Cleaver held the rod, it would do nothing for him?'

'Nothing at all.'

'And Morning Light?'

What was she after? For all he knew, Cleaver and Morning Light and menial Anvil, come to that, might easily learn to dowse if he taught them, but he would not yield a fraction of his power, even to Morning Light. Morning Light was in his power now.

'No.'

'Can you tell if he has this power?'

'He has no power.'

'So,' she said, 'you can call water and he cannot. The Rain King has no power over water.'

He said, rashly, 'Would you love him, if he had?'

She said, 'No. But I could live with him.'

The wells were dug and the water was good. Viner was promoted to the High Table where he took care to sit on Hern's left side, as far as possible from the Queen and under the lugubrious eyes of a painted heifer that breathed down his neck.

'He remembers us; isn't that nice?' Cleaver said, when he first took his place. Beyond Cleaver, beside the Queen, sat Morning Light, animated with relief and pleasure now that it was within his means to give water to the people, even though it was a second-hand gift. He had sought Viner out and begged him to make an expedition with Cleaver to all the villages where the wells had failed, and especially to the town. Viner understood an order, however well disguised as pleading. In the nicest possible way, Morning Light never said please, or thank you. He seemed to take it for granted that people would know he was pleased, and he was at least beginning to look it. His pleasure was all the thanks that Viner needed. He watched the King continuously, wishing he could be happy as well as pleased. Morning Light had wanted water. The Queen wanted rain, and until he gave it to her he would have no peace, and she would make sure that he was never happy.

The Queen watched Viner continuously. He had reviewed their conversation many times, but could make nothing more of it. He thought she wanted him to teach the King the mystery of the rod, so that he could call down rain with it. Could it be that she thought he too could call down rain? How could he admit the rod's limitations without damaging its reputation, and his own? When Cleaver came to him and said that, with his consent, they would begin their travels next day, he was so relieved that he found tears in his eyes. They would be gone for weeks. By the time they came back it might have rained and anyway, with luck, the Queen would by then have something else to occupy her thoughts. Surely the baby must be born soon. When she had her child she might relax her determined persecution of its father.

Hern and Cleaver set joyously about preparing for yet another hunting trip.

'I thought we were only hunting for water,' Viner said, stiffly, suspecting that they did not take the object of the operation seriously enough.

'Of course we are, but only you'll be doing the hunting,' said Hern, his knives honed slit-sharp at his belt, and a handsome quiver of newly flighted arrows at his back. 'We'll find other game.'

'At this time of year?'

'I can always find something to kill,' Hern said.

'I bet you can.' Viner watched him in disgust as he sat cross-legged on Cleaver's sumptuous bed and peeled a rabbit, for he had lately been reduced to setting snares round the palace for the little animals lured there by the unlooked-for supply of green shoots that had begun to show. 'Are you going to blindfold me, as we travel?' he asked Cleaver, only half jokingly.

'Why should I?' Cleaver said.

Why indeed? He was admired by the people; he stood high in the King's favour; why should he ever want to find his way back to the cave on the hillside, and from there retrace his steps through the wilderness until he came unwelcomed among his own people again. *These* were his people now; they needed him. He turned to his packing with a light heart, only slightly carked by some intrusive thought that rankled without ever defining itself; something to do with the baby. It was not until next morning, when the three of them had said good-bye to Morning Light and wished the Queen a safe delivery should the birth precede their return, and had ridden far beyond the ruined village, that he recalled the conversation between Hern and Catskin, overheard as he lay hidden among the fallen leaves of the Low Forest.

When we have a princess will be time to think of a new king.

7

They were gone for five weeks and by the end of the journey Viner had forgotten that such things as storms and floods existed to trouble the world. His head was filled with yellow images of death and famine; of wizened children and haggard cattle, ploughed strips near villages where corn had grown to the length of his little finger before dying; a walled castle where the people queued for their daily dole of bread, of the lord's charity, while the lord and his lady fasted alongside them; the town where rats were spitted and roasted; the ritual entreaties beneath dry skies that would not yield to entreaty; the dust; the little graves: always in his nostrils the sweet infected stench of drought.

He found water for them, sometimes so deep that he feared to contemplate the task to which he was committing them, but wherever he went he left diggers; men with spades that they had scarcely the strength to wield, women and children with baskets to drag away the earth that they were too weak to carry, and he prayed, continually, that tomorrow he would not come to a place where he would find nothing. Word of his coming went before him, and when he approached, with Cleaver and Hern on his either side, he was greeted as the-man-who-can-make-it-rain-upwards. At first, Cleaver rode ahead to announce him as the King's envoy, come to give water in the King's stead, but after a while the King's name ceased to be mentioned. No one cared where the-man-who-can-make-it-rain-upwards came from, nor who had sent him; it was enough that he was there. Viner however did not forget the King, or the Queen, or the child who might by now lie in the Queen's arms. When he walked alone with the rod in his hands, he was haunted by the memory of the King's unmemorable face; optimism caused tenderness to soften the Queen's features. He saw a pretty woman with a pretty child at her breast. A first child at least was always welcome.

One evening, toward the end of their travels, he sat with Cleaver, scratching insect bites, outside an inn, while Hern went away to stable their horses. Cleaver, weary as a result of their efforts but, lacking Viner's sense of achievement by way of stimulus, lethargic with it, slouched against the wall in the evening sunshine and was disinclined to talk. This did not suit Viner at all. In a few days they would be on their way home, and he was determined to know what he was going back to.

'Do you think the baby's been born yet?' he said. Cleaver yawned until his eyes closed, and did not trouble to open them again.

'Maybe.'

'What if it's a boy?'

'Nothing. They'll have to try again. That could take another two years, heigh-ho.'

'Don't you care?'

'I'll start caring when we've got back. Why meet trouble halfway?' said Cleaver, slapping flies away from his face.

'And if it's a girl?'

'Then that's what we've all been waiting for.'

He was getting nowhere. 'Cleaver,' he said, bluntly and firmly, 'why might it be time to find another king if the baby is a princess?'

Cleaver's eyes opened instantly. 'Who told you that?'

Viner remembered, in some confusion, that he had not been told. 'I don't know. I must have heard someone say it.'

'Then you must have heard it wrong,' Cleaver said. 'The next king will be the husband of the princess, if it is a princess, but that mayn't be for a long while.'

'Mayn't? Supposing something happened to Morning Light?'

'He's healthy. Like I said, why meet trouble halfway?' Cleaver leaned back again, but his eyelids flickered.

'But you said, once, you didn't know what happened to a failed king.'

'Now that you're here, that hardly matters, does it?'

'Then you don't get rid of a king as soon as his daughter is born?'

'Of course we don't.' Cleaver still looked edgy. 'I can't think where you got all this from.'

'Perhaps I misunderstood,' Viner said, more than ever convinced that he had not. 'This one won't be married at birth, then?'

'Why should she be?'

'Madam's mother was married at three months.'

'Madam's mother's parents died within a week of each other, of a pestilence. There's no pestilence now.'

'Nor there is.'

'No,' said Cleaver, 'but there may be if the drought doesn't break. Who can dance away the plague? Here comes Hern,' and he began to talk with hectic enthusiasm about beer and women. Viner recalled his first impression of Cleaver and his friends, as he had watched them from among the trees: that they did not trust each other.

They returned two days later, under an evening sky that was as hot and cloudless as it had been at dawn. Viner was pleasantly surprised to feel excitement as he recognized landmarks from the outward journey, and when they came in sight of the ruined village, as the sun was stooping to the horizon, he felt as though he were coming home. His own home had vanished from his mind as if it had never been. They made a brief detour to look at his pool, and exclaim over the green things that had begun to sprout on its banks; from the once trackless wilderness all round, a hoof-beaten path was just discernible. Travelling people had found the well.

'You are famous, now,' Hern said, to Viner.

'Not me, only the rod,' Viner said.

'Such modesty!' Cleaver murmured, mockingly. 'And I thought he wanted to better himself.' They turned their horses and rode toward the palace.

While they were still some distance from it they could see that at the foot of the walls, like braid on the hem of a tatty cloak, small vegetable plots were flourishing, young vines climbed shyly on newly-built trellises, and the green scent of things growing hung in the air.

'Your doing,' Hern said, to Viner.

'It may have rained.'

'It may not.'

When they reached the stables Anvil came out to greet them, and lead away the animals as he had always done. Hern's girl was waiting for him but she had a friendly smile for Viner before she was claimed. Even Catskin came out.

'What's the news?' Cleaver asked him, as they walked indoors together. Viner thought of the first time he had entered there, to an alien household; now he knew what awaited him, looked forward to his room and his bed, to familiar faces at supper, familiar voices calling remembered names. Their sticky gulping accents caressed his ears.

'No news.'

'No baby?'

'No baby,' Catskin said. He had added some more pelts to his jerkin. Nine tabby tails hung round him and knocked softly against his knees. 'Mere is still carrying, but that can't last much longer. Morning Light is still dancing and still it hasn't rained.'

'Well . . .' Cleaver looked discomfited. 'At least you have enough water.'

'Oh, yes, we have enough water,' Catskin said. '*Here* we have, but it's not a pleasant sight to see the land perish all round us. The green in the gardens just makes everything else look that much more dead. After all,' he said, looking at Viner, 'sooner or later these new wells will dry up too. Then what? We can't go on for ever, digging holes.'

'You can if you must,' Viner said, tartly.

'That could be a lot of holes,' said Catskin. Catskin, Viner remembered, was the Queen's friend, not the King's. Catskin was Hern's friend.

'The King will want to see you as soon as you've rested,' Catskin said, contriving to imply that this was an unreasonable request, although it seemed understandable enough to Viner that Morning Light should wish to see his friends. He accounted himself a friend. He wished he could account for Hern.

They went to their separate rooms, agreeing to forgather later in the painted hall to wait for the King. Viner was there before the others, and sat at his ease on a bench, admiring the murals. The whole room had been redecorated since he saw it last, and he noticed that his story of the grass-ridden sheep had born fruit. It had improved too, since he told it to Red Hen, and he supposed that it had been embellished as it was passed round, until it reached the man who had painted the pictures. One wall was devoted entirely to sheep. Even the most distant and inferior of the flock were freckled with tiny flowers and leaves, butterflies sunned themselves on the petals, but the finest specimens were foliate beyond his wildest dreams. Hollyhocks and foxgloves sprung from their backs, lilies, loosestrife, spires of mullein; fleece was wreathed in briony and woodbine; one ram had a sapling birch between his horns and another autumnal beast sprouted puffballs and spotted toadstools and a magnificent bracket fungus, like a starched dewlap, beneath his chin.

As he sat and stared, Red Hen herself came through the hall, carrying linen and on her way to the Queen. She seemed delighted to see Viner, as it were among the flowers of his flock.

'Do you remember telling me about them?' she said, apparently taking credit for the whole design.

'I told you grass,' Viner said, laughing, 'never all this.'

'People have come from the villages to see it. One woman was so near her time that she had her babe right here, in the hall. She called it Flowering Sheep.'

'Poor thing,' Viner said, referring to the baby. He hoped it would not grow up to curse him, but for all he knew, Flowering Sheep might be considered a gracious name among these people, who had accepted him as one of themselves and honoured his most chance remark by painting it on a wall. Perhaps he would appear on a wall himself, in time, with webbed feet. He would not mind. They were his people now, even if they did saddle their children with names like Flowering Sheep, Dead Brother, Lintel, Morning Light.

The talk of babies jolted him. 'How is the Queen?' he asked. 'We hoped to find her a mother when we returned.' He was pleasantly struck by the neatness of his remark; it was courtly.

Red Hen looked secretive, yet anxious to share the secret. 'You're in time,' she said. 'There's another week by the calendar, but,' she leaned close to him, 'the Queen thinks, and the nurses think, and I think, that it will be sooner. It's a heavy child, very low, and kicks Herself like a man would, but we pray that it won't be a man child.'

'No.' How soothing to think of someone, even an unborn baby, kicking the Queen. As yet he was still confused about the rights of succession, but he knew that a son would be nothing to celebrate. How strange, he thought. Kick away, while you can.

Hern and Cleaver came in then, and with them the King whom they had met in the corridor. Morning Light came toward Viner with a look that was all friendliness, and unexpectedly put an arm across his shoulder for a second. Viner shivered with such happiness that he felt his homecoming lacked nothing more to make it perfect, but when the King stood away he saw him more clearly, and shivered again, not from pleasure. Morning Light had purple bruises under his eyes and the rims were reddened. His hands trembled, but his smile was as gentle as ever.

He said nothing.

'Pleased to have us back, then?' Cleaver said, loudly. 'Miss us, did you?'

Morning Light looked bewildered and put out. 'Of course I'm pleased to see you come back safely. Did you think I wouldn't be?'

'Hard to tell with you,' Cleaver grumbled. His voice was amiable but Viner heard in it the irritation that he too felt from time to time. Morning Light was a good deal too ready to take for granted what other people wanted to hear uttered. Was it his tactless reticence that drove the Queen to insult? Morning Light turned to Viner, anxious to repair any omission, now that the omission had been pointed out to him.

'We need you here,' he said.

'Are the wells failing – *my* wells?' Viner asked. Morning Light shook his head.

'No. But people feel that if you are here the rain may come. They think you may have power over it, to call it here – not to call it *down*,' he added, in a hurry.

'I couldn't call it down,' Viner said, politically. 'Only you can do that.' He did not deny his power, however.

'When I dance tomorrow I should like to feel that you were near by. Cleaver tells me that everywhere you went, you found water. It may follow you here.'

'It may.' He did not think it would. 'I'll be near by,' he promised. He did not want to be. He could not bear to think of the misery of watching the King dance.

'Good. I wanted to talk to you all, but the Queen needs me,' Morning Light said. 'She's getting near her time . . . it makes her fretful.' He mumbled further excuses and went out, blindly colliding with Red Hen who was hovering near the doorway. Cleaver called her to them.

'Is that true; the Queen needs him?'

Red Hen, embarrassed at being questioned and uncertain how to answer, would not meet his look.

'She hasn't sent for him. If he goes to her she sends him away.' She ducked under his arm, and ran. Cleaver, Hern and Viner were left to exchange looks of wordless dismay. At last Hern said, 'Is he drinking?'

'That's what I'd have said,' Cleaver answered, 'but they say no – no more than usual. He's not drinking, friends, he's dancing. Every day.'

'He can't dance every day,' Hern said, flatly. 'No one could. It's impossible.'

'It's not impossible, but look what it's doing to him.'

'Does the Queen drive him to it?' Viner said.

'I don't know, but I wouldn't be surprised. Still,' Cleaver said, 'he might listen to you, you powerful person. Tell him that now you're back he needn't dance so often.'

'Why should he listen to me? He needn't dance at all, if the wells are full.'

'Tell him anyway.' Viner looked at Cleaver and thought of Cleaver in the firelight in the wood; Cleaver laboriously nonchalant, outside the tavern; and of Catskin: *When we have a princess will be time to think of a new king*. Viner did not relish the prospect of telling Morning Light what he must and must not do, but thinking of the King's ravaged face he nodded, and said he would try.

They went into supper with reduced appetites and sat uneasily at their end of the High Table, while people wandered up to them, throughout the meal, to congratulate them upon their safe return. Everyone made a point of telling Viner how well the gardens were growing. He was not sure that he wanted to know, and watched the Queen, who had not moved herself to greet them, thinking that if he had reached that state of convexity nothing would persuade him to move from his bed in case he split down the front, like a peasecod. He stared in horrid fascination as she walked slowly to her place, supported by two of her women, and settled down to pack as much food into herself as time permitted. She'll burst, she'll burst! he thought to himself. It must be twins. How can she stay upright when she walks? How can she lie down? It must be triplets, a whole litter. It's not natural. He tried to rationalize his ridiculous reaction by telling himself that she looked so gross because he knew her to be a very little woman, but he could not keep his eyes from straying to her end of the table. As soon as he could he made his excuses and went to join Red Hen who was signalling to him from across the room, but before the end of the meal a message was sent down to him from the High Table, that the Queen wished to speak with him in her room, afterwards. He did not want to go at all, but he went.

'If I die having my baby,' said the Queen, 'and I may, I may, then my daughter will need a husband.'

Viner wanted no more talk of infant weddings. 'And if it's a son?'

'Then they will find someone else from my family to take my place. There are enough to choose from.'

'Your family?'

'All my family is in this place. Catskin is my cousin, and Red Hen. The old nurse is my great-aunt, and the young nurse is her daughter; many others. I can't remember them all.' She implied that she was surfeited with relatives, that supply outweighed demand. 'But either way, my cousin or my daughter, they must find a king for her. He will be a man who can bring down rain. I think that would be a man who can call water to him, don't you?'

Viner felt his eyes widen in disbelief. He *could* not believe that he was understanding her drift. 'But has Morning Light no relations?'

'I've no doubt he has, but they have nothing to do with it. The King is the Queen's husband, it doesn't matter who his family is. I think it likely that if a man can call water out of the ground he can call it down from the sky. If I die, young-man-who-can-make-it-rain-upwards, I want you to be the first to dance the rain dance. Promise me.'

Viner, who had been squatting before her, rose to his feet. 'Madam, I do not want to think that you may die.' He meant it.

'Many women die in childbirth, and I am very small. I do not want to die, either, but I know it is more than possible. Promise me.'

'But if it is a son – '

'Then dance for my cousin, or whoever they choose.'

'I cannot call down rain.' He would have to tell her the truth. 'Or call it up.' The Queen was not listening.

'Of course, it might not rain for you, but I think that will not matter. Water from below is as good as water from above. I think you will marry anyway, soon.'

'If you die.'

'If I die. But if it is a son, and I live, we must try again, and again, and again, until we do have a daughter. I'm told it becomes easier each time, but each time it will be Morning Light . . . that won't be easy.'

'Madam, Mere, you must understand, the rod doesn't call water from the ground. It can only find what's there already.'

The Queen stopped pacing and looked at nothing. Her face had stiffened into a frightful smile. 'It's true, I may not die. But the King may . . .'

She no longer saw him. Stumbling in his haste to reach the door, he dismissed himself, and fled to his room.

He sat in the wasteland of his wonderful bed, bowed over his arms and clutching his terrible knowledge to him like a pain in the gut.

She wants him dead. He will dance himself to death and she will let him.

All his joy at coming home to his people had evaporated. They were not his people, they were monstrous foreigners with filthy unnatural practices in which they wished to embroil him. He thought of her talk of herbs, the last time they had met; was she ready to poison the King if she lived through her labour? Oh, let her die, he whispered let *her* die, and only then realized what she wanted from him; a husband for her baby, or her cousin, if she died, but what if she lived, and Morning Light died? His first thought was to seek out Cleaver and tell him what had been said, but while he knew that Cleaver was loyal to the King, he knew nothing of his adherence beyond that. Was he loyal to the office, or to the man? He called himself the King's friend, but was he also Morning Light's friend? He might consider Viner an ideal substitute for Morning Light, and he was Hern's friend. Hern was Catskin's friend, Catskin was the Queen's friend. He knew now that his euphoria over the last two months had been a delusion, a deceiving sickness. He was not among friends; he was alone, and trapped: and terrified.

The palace became still. He heard hunting owls outside, outside, outside were the stables, the horses, the road that led away from this place. If he slipped out now, unseen, he would be in the town by tomorrow's nightfall, and there he would find people who knew him, without knowing his circumstances, who were grateful to him, who would help him. With a little effort and ingenuity he might eventually find his way to the cave on the hillside, above the river where the alders grew, and from where he could see, in the uttermost distance, the hills beyond the hill that overlooked the big stones; and then he could find his way home, or go somewhere, anywhere, else.

Unwilling to be thought a thief, even after he had gone, he laid aside most of the clothes that had been given to him, and selected only the warmest and thickest against his return to a colder climate. He rolled them tight and stuffed them into his brother's bait bag, with the bacon bone and the pot bottle which he filled with wine from the jar by his bed. With luck he might find something to eat as he passed by the kitchen, but food was the least of his worries. His only concern was to get away. He was used to hunger, and if he needed water, he knew how to get it. His last action was to take his divining-rod from its hiding place under the mattress and put it under his shirt. Then he blew out the light and crept onto the landing.

The passages of the palace were in deep shadow, relieved here and there by the pale glow of a lamp on shelf or bracket. Keeping close to the wall, in case he encountered other prowlers, he made his way from shadow to shadow, toward the room of painted sheep, from where he could find his route to the kitchen and the yard. He had almost reached his goal when a movement at the further end of an adjacent passage told him that someone else was abroad and coming his way. Holding the bag to his chest he shrank into an alcove and waited, not daring to draw breath as the figure approached, walking with a curious weightless step.

Viner felt his armpits prickle and break out in a sweat of fear. It was a ghost that came toward him, a night spirit; it was a fearful thing conjured up by Mere in her evil thoughts, sent to pursue him as he fled. It was a demon on tiptoe. It was Morning Light, walking in his sleep. Viner, almost sick with relief, was thankful that he did not dance as Hern had seen him dance.

A moment only, and Cleaver came flying after, soundlessly along the corridor, in pursuit, overtook the King, taking him by hand and shoulder, turned him carefully without waking him, and guided him back the way he had come. Viner, his own hands twitching enviously, remained in his alcove for several minutes afterward, unable to make any move. It was a small consolation to know that Morning Light was in gentle hands for the time being, but it was not enough. He pushed himself away from the wall and made his way back to his room, where he lay on the very edge of the bed and curled up, staring into the darkness.

If he ran away he would save himself, and he might save Morning Light, but for how long: how long would he be spared to walk the corridors of his dreadful palace before the dance killed him, or the Queen killed him? Viner's conscience was new, but it was tender. He was well and truly trapped, now.

He did not know what to do. He did not know how long he had before he was forced to do *something*. He avoided talking to Hern and Cleaver and devoted his attention to listening to them, but their talk was all of hunting, more than usual. He could not tell if they knew what he knew. He supposed that Morning Light was safe at least until the child was born and that could not be long, now, but what would happen after that? He felt as if he were under water, not floating, not sinking, but suspended and unable to move either up or down. All the time, he looked out for the King. The next day, and the one after, he watched the dance, and saw that the woman who handed the javelins to the King was no longer the indisposed Queen but Red Hen, the cousin, the sinister claimant, who had been nothing more than a silly young girl two days before. Who would hand the javelins to Viner when he danced? He could not, would not dance.

On the third day after his return he found himself short of water and went out to his new well, on the north side, to draw himself some more, intending to souse his hair which stood on end and crackled angrily when he touched it. He grew daily more oppressed, but when he stepped out of doors he saw that this time the oppression was not all the Queen's doing. There was a dampness in the heat that had not been there before, and he felt sweat on his face. A turbid light lay over the landscape as if something unseen in the sky obscured the sun. Although he could find no clouds there was a distinct thickening of the air above the eastern horizon. Something bad is going to happen, he thought, but in his mind's eye he could see only Morning Light lying dead in the dust at the end of his dance. Would the sky fall for that? His head ached, he felt quick pains in his palms and fingers.

He walked fretfully round the side of the building to the well, fetched his bucket of water and as fretfully, walked back again. When he returned to the kitchen yard he found Morning Light there, alone, and not dancing. He stood, feet apart, hands on hips and head tilted, staring up the wall to the roof.

'What are you doing?' Viner said, for the King looked as if he might, at any moment, leap upward and scale the wall like a fly. Morning Light turned, startled, with his elbow raised as if to ward off a blow, but he smiled when he saw who stood there.

'I think it will rain,' he said.

'But you haven't danced,' Viner said, without tact, taken aback by his groundless assurance.

'No, but if I danced now, I think it would rain.'

'I wish you wouldn't,' Viner said. It was no time for mincing words. 'It doesn't do you any good.' And it doesn't work, he thought. 'Anyway, how can you tell?'

'How can I tell? How can I not tell?' said Morning Light. 'For two years, Viner, I've come out here to look at the sky before I dance. That's why,' he added, 'I don't dance every day, unless the people demand it.'

'You're dancing every day now.'

'The people demand it, but there are days when dancing is useless. I know it won't rain.'

'How do you know?' Viner said. He thought, *Do* the people demand? Do you really know why you're dancing every day?

Morning Light laughed, shortly. 'Experience, I suppose.' This was not a word that Viner had expected him to use. Experience was a craftsman's stock-in-trade, not the property of a ritual dancer.

'You mean, you can tell what the weather's going to be like just by looking at the sky?'

'Not just the sky,' Morning Light said. 'The wind, the light, the sunshine. You can tell by watching insects, even. I think it will rain. The first time I danced the rain dance was on a day like this, and it rained.'

'They tell me it hasn't rained since.' This was tactless too, but Viner was suddenly aware that he was talking to the King at last, as one man to another, easily, without spectators. He could not let the opportunity pass by. If he could only keep the conversation going until it became the casual and unguarded talk of friends, he might achieve some success with whatever he had to say. He had to say something, soon.

'It has rained,' Morning Light was protesting. 'But,' he admitted, 'not very much. Only little showers, and you know how quickly they go into the ground.'

'That day, the first time, did you know it would rain, before you danced?'

'Oh, no. Up till then I'd never needed to know. Dancing was just dancing. But I learned, quickly enough.'

So, he's defeated in advance, before he even begins, Viner thought. At the same time he was enormously impressed. Without trying to, Morning Light had turned himself into a prophet who could foretell the weather, something that the Webfeet, with all their weather, had never learned to do. Suppose he did go home again . . .

'Could you teach me?' he said. With this further accomplishment he would be invincible. Morning Light looked at him out of the tail of his eye.

'If you show me your mystery.'

Viner's dismay must have been obvious in his face for Morning Light looked immediately disheartened. 'I'm sorry. I shouldn't have asked.'

'It wouldn't be any use,' Viner said. 'It doesn't bring rain.' He was telling the truth and tried to let it show in his voice, but Morning Light was not listening. He had behaved improperly in asking a sorcerer to reveal his art. He would not use his desperation as an excuse.

'I shall dance,' he said, suddenly decisive, and turning abruptly walked towards the doorway with more purpose in his step than Viner had seen for some time. Viner stayed with him.

'Everyone says you must rest – one day at least . . .'

'I must dance.'

'But you said it would rain anyway.'

'I didn't say that. I think that if I dance it will rain.'

Viner knew that he dared not miss the opportunity. If he danced and it did not rain he would be no worse off than he was now, but if it rained and he had not danced, the rain might be attributed to someone else's influence. Viner could not tell if he knew whose, or if he knew that he knew.

'You'll kill yourself.'

'It's as good a way to die as any.'

'Oh, life's cheap here, isn't it?'

'Isn't it cheap everywhere?'

'Not where I come from. Too many of us were drowned every year for us to think that.'

'Imagine it,' said Morning Light. 'Dying of too much water.'

Viner did not know where they were going, but he was reluctant to let the conversation founder now that he had launched it so successfully and it was making headway. 'Don't you know where I come from?'

'Some wet place,' Morning Light said, enviously. 'How did Cleaver find you?'

'By accident,' Viner said.

'But he told me he'd heard about you, while he was away searching for water. He promised to try and seek you out, but I was surprised when you turned up so suddenly.'

'He was lying. He found me while he was away searching for water, all right, but he didn't want you to know until he was sure I could find it here.' He pressed the point. 'What he told you wasn't true.'

Morning Light was abysmally unconcerned by this evidence of perfidy. 'He often lies to me,' he said. 'That is, he only tells me what he thinks I should know. I trust him, he's my good friend.'

'Do you know what he did when he found *me*? First he tied my arms and dragged me back to a place where I might find gold for him. Then he made me ride blindfold for three days till we came here. Is that friendly?'

'I didn't think he'd be so rough. I don't suppose he'd do it now,' Morning Light said, reasonably. Viner did not suppose it, either, but he thought the King was taking it rather too lightly.

'It was Hern, mostly,' he said, looking for some reaction.

'Hern's a wild man. He might do anything. I wish he wouldn't carve up the furniture so, though. There's not a lot left. Someone else will want that bed when he's finished with it.'

Viner was not interested in the fate of Hern's bed. 'Doesn't it *worry* you, having people like that around you? Look at Catskin.'

'He wouldn't do anything to me. Why should he?' Morning Light turned sharply at the corner by Cleaver's room and bounded up the stairs, past Viner's own landing.

Can't you even guess what danger you're in? Viner mouthed at the back of his head. For pity's sake, who can you really trust? Have you ever given it a moment's thought? Even I'm a threat to you.

He would have put his exasperation into words, but before he could decide what to say, they reached the short passage that led to the Queen's arbour. He listened at once for the rainy staccato of drumbeats, but no sound came from behind the curtained doorway save for a sudden and sharply indrawn gasp. Morning Light tugged the curtain aside. Mere was sitting on her bench, with two of her women (cousins, great-aunts, sisters, even?) and they had moved up close to her, supporting her on either side. Her face was pinched and looked reduced, as if the life were being sucked out of it, and on the floor lay the little drum, the skin torn at one end and crumpled from the spasmodic grip of a clenched fist.

One of the women looked up and said, 'The child. The pains have begun.'

Morning Light moved forward, arms open to take hold of his wife, but she muttered to the women at her side, 'Take me to my bed. Keep him away from me.'

Viner did not know if Morning Light had heard what she said. At any rate, he took no notice.

'Let me carry you.'

'I'll walk – I will *walk*.'

'But the child . . .'

She gave him a look of almost good-humoured contempt.

'Do you think it will drop out like an egg from a hen? This is only the beginning.'

'Then how long?'

'Hours. Or days. If I am lucky, hours.' The last words were spoken through tightly clamped teeth, but she rose to her feet and began to leave the arbour without waiting for help. The women converged in the doorway to hold her up, and they all passed out of sight together. Viner's dislike of her, even while it grew, was temporarily displaced by admiration. Morning Light, looking utterly abject, pushed past him and followed the women; clearly he had no further thought of dancing. Viner let him go, and went to find Cleaver and Hern, and so spread the news round the palace.

8

On the whole it was received quietly. People lowered their voices and went on tiptoe, even in rooms and corridors so far from the Queen's apartment that no sound could possibly have penetrated. Viner had expected screams, not only from Herself. In the valley, during a childbirth, the women of the village, as a sign of solidarity, gathered round the house of confinement and keened in sympathy, coming away almost disgruntled if the birth were an easy one and the labour short. After dinner, a scant meal taken in haste, Viner found himself mounting the stairs again. He had never before been there alone, or uninvited, but he doubted that anyone would challenge his presence; he was above challenge, now. He wanted chiefly to know what Morning Light was doing, and rather expected to find him making one of his aimless tours of the building, in an agony of anxiety, but when they ran across each other at the head of the staircase, he was moving in the same direction, taut and twitching, as expected, but brisk.

'Is it going well?' Viner asked.

'So far.'

'Are you going to be with her?'

'No,' Morning Light said. 'They wouldn't allow me and she would forbid it and,' he said ashamedly, 'I should be afraid to see it.'

'It's not a frightening thing,' Viner said.

'It's not your wife.'

'Will you wait in the anteroom, then?' It was in his mind to offer to wait as well, if Morning Light seemed to like the idea, and already distracted and nervous as he was it seemed as if he might. Morning Light however shook his head.

'I've better things to do than that.'

Viner was surprised, shocked even, by his callousness.

'Things to do?'

'They tell me nothing will happen before midnight.' He turned and said, with unwonted firmness, 'There's no need to stay. I can do this alone.'

Do what? Viner thought, as the King moved away. He went back to report to Hern and Cleaver.

'How should I know what he's going to do?' Cleaver said. 'There's no need for you to follow him round like a hen that's hatched out ducklings. He managed quite well on his own before you came,' he said, sourly, 'and if he needed company he called on us. We're his friends. You're his dowser, not his darling. Stick to what you're good at. Your business is with the earth. Stop climbing.'

'Who was it said I'd rise?' Viner returned, quickly, but he did not argue further; Cleaver had unintentionally supplied him with the answer to a question that he had not cared to risk asking. Evidently Cleaver had no idea how high he might rise if the Queen had her way. He knew that Cleaver was resentful of the King's growing dependence on his dowser, but did his resentment extend to Viner's own person? His future had looked so secure when he had galloped back to the palace with Morning Light, all those weeks ago; now he could look forward to nothing until they heard if the baby was a boy or a princess, and if the mother still lived.

He left Hern and Cleaver playing draughts and drinking, and making occasional vulgar remarks about babies and the begetting of them which he considered ill-timed. Cleaver hooted after him as he went, and the sound followed him all the way down the corridor, where he found a group of the Queen's women, or relatives, companionable round a jug of weak beer and exchanging cosy tales of miscarriages and monsters, the bloody tittle-tattle of midwives, unfit for a man's feeble sensibilities, and they fell silent and sly when he passed them. He escaped to his room, where he sat on the bed, wishing that he had left when he intended to, on the night of his return. He had been mistaken, the King did not need him. He chewed over his wrongs and saw them in a different form. The King needed him and did not know it. What could he do?

He became conscious of a strange sound outside in the darkness, an insistent thud and shuffle that he almost recognized and yet could not identify. Extinguishing his light, so that he would not be seen at his window, he opened the casement noiselessly, and looked out. The moon was up and shining over the plain, over the stable yard, carving sharp bright buttresses and bulwarks from the black ramshackle mass. In the angle of the stables and the wall where his own window lay, he saw a figure moving in the night, not furtively or thievish, but overtly, upright. It was the King, alone and dancing the rain dance in the humid darkness. He was without the wig and silver trappings that he wore to dance by day, dressed in his ordinary clothes, and barefoot, but beyond him, ranged in a kind of stockade, points in the earth, were the javelins. As Viner watched he put out his hand, seized the nearest javelin and flung it up against the moon. Common sense told Viner that although he could see where they were going Morning Light could not; nor could he tell where they would fall, and Viner, fearing to find him spitted at daybreak on one of his own weapons, watched until the last had landed, and was about to draw in his head when he saw that the dance was not over, as it should have been. Morning Light was still dancing.

Viner watched him, and fell asleep, woke, watched again, slept again, and when he woke, the King was still at his moonlit dance. Viner had no notion of the hour, but the moon was out of sight and the shadows long. Morning Light was absorbed in the night, invisible, his presence betrayed only by his footfalls, his laboured breathing, and by the sudden shining swipe of a javelin, like a meteor among the stars. Viner could only guess, but he was sure that Morning Light was dancing for his wife and his child, and lying on his bed, walled in, he could have wept at the devotion, the wasted devotion.

He woke to the sound of heavy footsteps approaching at speed, and before he could lift his head from the bed, the door crashed open and Morning Light stood before him, flushed and breathless. He sat up, panicking.

'What's happened?' He dared not think what had happened. The Queen was dead. The child was a girl and the Queen was dead. Oh, if the Queen is dead let the child be dead too. But Morning Light was laughing. He leaned over and dragged Viner out of bed.

'Come and see,' he said. 'Come and see my little baby.'

Viner swayed and blinked and would not be moved.

'It's a girl?'

'Yes.'

'And the Queen?'

'She's well. Perfect. They're both perfect. Come and see – you're the first to know.'

'*I?*'

'You were the nearest.'

Thanks for the compliment, Viner said, under his breath. Finding that he was still dressed after last night's vigil he allowed Morning Light to pull him headlong up the stairs and down passages to the Queen's rooms, one of which had been turned over to the nurses. An angry old woman guarded the door.

'You can't come in here,' she said, unimpressed by rank and revelling in her right to be so.

'I want to see my baby,' Morning Light said, making as if to push her out of the way, but she was immovable.

'You've just seen her.'

'Viner wants to see her.'

'Then want must be his master,' said the nurse.

'Bring her out,' said Morning Light. He was regaining his stature. The two of them strove to outface each other, in the doorway, the old woman and the young man, and the young man won. She went grumbling and snarling back into the room and returned with what Viner would elsewhere have identified as an immature bolster, swathed in sheets. Without ceremony Morning Light took possession of the bolster and held it under Viner's nose. At one end of the wrappings was an elderly little face, squashed and scarlet with rage, its eyes compressed into finely pleated slits. A spare crop of gingery hair, the colour of a tom-cat, curled over its head.

'My daughter,' said Morning Light.

'Well done,' said Viner. It seemed the kindest thing he could say about this approximate sketch of a human being. The nurse recovered the baby and bore her back inside the shuttered room. 'What's her name?' He only then understood why Morning Light had spent the night as he had. 'Rain Dance?'

Morning Light looked at him gratefully; and hung his head, as if ashamed of his pretensions. 'You saw? When Mere began her labour I said to her, "When it's all over, look first out of the window and see what is there," and she did. But she looked up, not down. The baby is called Dark Cloud.'

Viner thought it was a terrible name for a baby. 'She ought to have known what to look at,' he said, sharply. He guessed that Mere had known only too well what not to look at.

'Oh no, it's not what one looks for, it's what one sees,' Morning Light said with a curious intensity that made Viner wonder if he thought he had done wrong in trying to engineer a different name for his daughter.

'She should have seen *you*.'

'It doesn't matter,' Morning Light said. 'Dark Cloud is a wonderful name. Look out of the window.'

He looked. There were dark clouds as far as the eye could see, that heaved and groaned with thunder as though, he thought, the sky itself were in labour.

What will become of me, if it rains?

Viner stood at a window and watched the sagging clouds, out of which fell leaden pellets of water, severally, heavily, warm like tears that had been withheld too long. They did not land with the light precision of Mere's fingertips on the drum head, but struck the ground with thuds, kicked up dust, made craters, while the air grew treacly and clung to hands and face, but after an hour of twilight, before the dark coins of moisture on the ground had melded, a narrow gleam appeared along the horizon, below the clouds, like a line of light under a door, and before another hour had passed the sky was clear, the earth steaming faintly in the sunshine. On the terrace in front of the palace there assembled a little group of people who had left their rejoicing to watch with disbelief the rearguard of the clouds as they sank over the western hills, and last of all came Morning Light, who had danced all night, to dance again and hurl his javelins at the impregnable underbelly of the sky.

So, I'm safe, Viner thought, watching him, but what about you? When we have a princess is time to be thinking of finding a new king, and the Queen still lives.

If he expected the King to be cast down by this last and most devastating failure, he was mistaken. Morning Light continued to dance every afternoon, but in his free hours, instead of stalking, shrouded in hopelessness along the corridors, or attempting to engage the Queen in conversation, he spent all his time with the baby, and neglected everyone else. Hern and Cleaver sulked. Viner would have sulked with them, but Morning Light dragged along with him anyone who would consent to join him. Since the baby was much like any other to look at, and her status established, few people wanted a second visit after their initial curiosity was satisfied, but Viner went when he could for the King's sake, sure of a welcome, even if uninvited. The baby was sometimes sick, frequently damp and generally objectionable, but Morning Light was crazy with love for her. It gave Viner pleasure to see the two of them together, not least because he had noticed that it made the nurses angry. They thought it unwholesome for a young man to want to play with a baby; grandfathers, yes, and childless uncles too sinfully occupied to beget lawful issue, aunts and sisters, anyone with fond memories, anyone, it seemed, except Morning Light. They were jealous of their supremacy and it infuriated Viner to see these gleeful women conspire to deprive him of his joy.

They were not, however, noticeably successful. If he went into the nursery at any hour of the day, he was sure to find the King there before him, with the baby in his arms, pacing gravely about the room to lull her, or singing for her pleasure. Viner's experience of two-week-old babies led him to doubt if she cared for music above suckling and sleeping.

'She's pretty, isn't she?' the King said, pulling back the shawls to exhibit his treasure.

'For a baby, yes,' said Viner. Morning Light was having none of this.

'No.' He laughed. 'Any way she's pretty. She'll be lovely when she grows up. Won't she?' Viner did not, at that moment, give much for the baby's chances of growing up. Her father would surely drop her first. 'And she's so warm! Come on, my little lily, my rain child. Do you want to hold her?'

Viner declined, politely. Morning Light seemed more relieved than offended. He held the baby so that her head rested against his neck, and crooned to her. The nurse swarmed upon him, clicking her tongue in disapproval. 'That's no kind of a song to be singing to a baby.'

'She doesn't understand it,' Morning Light protested. 'She likes the feel of it.'

'The feel of it?'

'Here.' He touched his throat, beside the baby's ear. 'Isn't she smiling, Viner?'

'Yes.' As far as he could tell the child was comatose.

'You see, she likes it.'

Viner rather liked it himself. It had a plaintive lilt.

> '*My lady's face a flower is,*
> *Her hair a sheaf of golden wheat,*
> *Her maiden lips are full and kind,*
> *Her eye is mild, her breath is sweet;*
> *But oh, her robe is long and thick,*
> *And reaches to her feet.*'

The chorus struck a more hopeful note.

> '*But when the piper tunes his reed,*
> *And to the dance we go,*
> *Like doe or hind she skips and leaps,*
> *And I below, below.*'

'To grow up hearing such words in her ears,' the nurse was grumbling, pursuing Morning Light ineffectually round the room.

> '*And when the sun at even sets,*
> *Then up, then up we go,*
> *With she upon the stair above,*
> *And I below, below.*'

'Wait till the Queen hears of it.'

> '*With she upon the balcony,*
> *And I below, below, below,*
> *And I below, below.*'

Viner thought it was a sweet enough tune to sing to a baby until, noting the escalating details, he realized that it was a song about looking up someone's skirt, with predictable consequences. After that he was inclined to agree with the nurse, but Morning Light, whose voice was true and resonant, perhaps his only beauty, sang it with a peculiarly innocent relish, as if he too did not know what it meant. He had a stock of melodious old ballads rife with lust and lechery, sagas of multiple vices and an odd ditty about gathering watercress, with gestures. On reflection, 'Below, Below' was undoubtedly the least scandalous.

One day Viner went out to his well, with two buckets, and found Mere there before him, with the drum in her hands, lightly dressed in veils, in shades of rain and haze. Strangely, without the bulk of her baby, she seemed bigger than she had done before, as though the child had been taking all her substance, and now she could flourish, free of it. They greeted each other formally and she stood aside while he filled the buckets, and then sat down on the well's rim.

'Do you know where the King is?' she said.

'With Dark Cloud, I suppose. Where else?' He grinned.

'Where else indeed?'

'I thought you would be with her,' Viner said, meaningly. He had never yet seen Mere in the nursery.

'Why? She has good enough nurses, and a doting attendant. I carried her, I bore her, I feed her. What else should I do? As soon as I picked her up I should have *him* blowing down my neck.' She pounded the drum with her knuckles, and a muted booming echoed in the well. 'What shall I do?'

'Do? Who needs to do anything?'

'Have you forgotten our talk?' she said. He had hoped that she had forgotten it. 'I asked you to dance for my daughter.'

'But that was if you died.'

She looked up apprehensively. 'Are you sure he's in the nursery?'

'Not sure, but it's more than likely. No one can overhear us.' He was grateful for that. He would be more grateful still if somebody hove into earshot and cut off any more conspiracy.

'If he left me for a year and a day I could marry again. We should have no king, and my daughter would marry too. We need not wait a year and a day for that.'

Viner felt his palms grow wet with anger and embarrassment. How dared she involve him in her intrigue.

'He will never leave you. He'd certainly never leave the baby. Don't you know that the night she was born he danced the rain dance all night for you?'

'*Don't* I know it? I could hear him out there, shuffling and stamping and snorting like a penned bull.'

'Then you might at least have done what he asked and looked out at him.'

'And named my child for that sweating fool? I couldn't look at him. Who wouldn't look up,' she cried, her voice cracking with angry tears, 'if the alternative was to see him dancing?'

'Does he know what you think?'

'No. If I told him to his face he wouldn't know it. He doesn't want to know it.'

'Do you blame him?'

'Blame him? What has blaming to do with it? I'll never be free of him, I'll never be *free*. I'm a flowerpot, that's all; a container for his seed. Imagine, a lifetime of Morning Light and his children.'

'True, he'll never leave you.'

'Then we must think of the other thing,' said the Queen. 'Have you forgotten the other thing?' Viner looked at the woman at his side, curled into a knot of fury and despair. He would have pushed her down the well on the instant, had he not known what her extinction would mean for him. 'If you went secretly and said that you'd learned that I mean to have him killed, would he go then?'

'I told you, he won't leave the baby. And he has friends, too.'

'Cleaver and Hern. Well, they're easily enough got out of the way. They're off hunting now, aren't they? We could have him before they come back, and you can dance the rain dance.'

'And I am his friend.'

'Are you? Is he yours? Well, I have more friends than he has, enough to make sure that what I want done is done. Don't imagine that you can go, either. You would not leave this place alive.'

'If you kill me,' he said levelly, but trembling, 'you'll lose your water.'

'I shan't have *you* killed,' she said. 'I only meant, that you will not leave this place. You will not go. He will, one way or another.'

Viner said, 'Why don't you go?'

'I?' She gaped at him. 'What are you saying? No Rain Queen ever left this palace. What would the people say?'

'Would you care what they said? You don't care what they say about the way you treat your husband. There's nothing to stop you taking your baby and leaving. You told me yourself you had plenty of cousins to stay in your place. Why not Red Hen?'

'Would you dance for her?'

'I might, yes.' Better Red Hen for a wife than Dark Cloud. 'But it might not rain for me.' It won't rain for me.

'That doesn't matter. You've proved yourself already.'

Once he had cursed because he would never find a bride among the Webfeet. He was not sure that he wanted to marry any of this she-wolf's relatives, but he was ready to promise anything. With Mere gone and the baby gone, Morning Light would be safe, he would live. His adored daughter was his death warrant.

'And what,' said Mere, 'will you do to Morning Light when I'm gone?'

'Do to him?'

'You'll be king and he will not. Put it another way: what will he do to you when he sees how you've displaced him? Dare you let him live?'

'If he falls it will be you who felled him,' Viner returned, swiftly.

'But are you ready to climb over him? I wonder, are you doing this out of good heart, or ambition?'

He said, 'Lady, I'm not ambitious.'

'No?' She eyed him, curiously. 'Then what's he to you that you want to save him?'

'My friend.'

'You said. And yet you hardly know him. Are you sure you want to marry, dowser?'

Viner lowered his eyes. 'Where would you go? When?'

'Give me a little time to think and I'll speak with you again,' the Queen said. 'Is this all your own work, or will you go and report it to your other friends – his friends?'

'I never thought of it till we spoke,' Viner said, truthfully.

'Then don't think of it again. Wait till you hear from me.'

'When shall I hear from you?'

'Give me time, give me time. I cannot go anywhere yet, so soon after the birth. I must know who would shelter me.' Her eyes turned inward. 'I should not have much trouble finding another husband, do you think?'

He left her there, solitary and scheming, and went back the way he had come, with his buckets, beneath the open window of the nursery where Morning Light was singing one of his unsuitable songs to his baby.

'Sing to her while you can,' said Viner.

He had assumed that the Queen's family might number a dozen or two; he made some cautious inquiries and learned that of the people who lived and worked in the palace, more than half were in some way related to Herself. The whole ghastly family seemed to stretch back into measureless time, arriving, marrying, constantly replenishing itself. So that's what happens to the boy babies, he thought, recalling that he had once thought his own family too big for comfort. Eventually, he imagined, they would occupy the place entirely, absorbing outsiders like himself and Cleaver, until at last the only true outsider would be the Rain King, ever a stranger by tradition, to temper the inbreeding. (No wonder Hern had no chin.) How far they had advanced toward this goal he could not be sure, but he was sure that Morning Light was already so heavily outnumbered as to make his position hopeless. If the Queen wished him to go, he must go. If she wished him dead, he would die. His only salvation lay in Viner's own wild and unpremeditated suggestion that the Queen should go instead, taking the baby with her. With the child gone, there would be nothing to keep Morning Light in the palace; he would leave and save himself in spite of himself. Viner's imagination did not extend to working out what would become of him after that, deserted by his wife and bereft of his child. Perhaps Hern and Cleaver would go with him. He could begin a new life, while Viner also began a new life as the Rain King, with a queen at his side and not in a cradle. With that end in view he began to take a closer interest in the likelier candidates, but without enthusiasm. He was committing himself to a life of dangerous isolation at the heart of the tribe, be he never so reverenced. His rise was taking him higher than he wanted to go. He had wanted to be the King's friend, not the Queen's husband, whoever the Queen might turn out to be.

He wished that he could confide in Cleaver, but Cleaver, who had asked him if he understood what a friend was, had friends of his own. Hern was his friend, but Hern also kept company with Catskin who, so Viner had lately discovered, was Hern's brother-in-law, which meant that somewhere in that close-knit company, one or the other of them had a wife. His head spun.

Dark Cloud at one month was a comely child, with her father's even features, but none of his plainness, and her mother's light eyes, but she had few visitors to remark upon it. Cleaver and Hern, displaced by Viner and the baby, went on leisurely expeditions, Catskin resumed his seat at the end of the High Table, next to the Queen. Morning Light was all for bringing the baby into supper with him, but he was fortunately overruled. At six weeks he swore she recognized him. It seemed a reasonable boast and no one argued, since he had nothing else to boast about. She saw more of him than anyone else, including her mother, who visited her only to feed her, and sing seemly little lullabies at nightfall.

Viner saw the Queen often, but never alone, and she never again sent for him to visit her. He hoped very much that she was giving serious thought to his suggestion, for Morning Light danced the rain dance daily, without result, except that the onlookers muttered more behind his back, and more openly to his face. Viner, knowing that the King wished him to witness the dances, attended with growing reluctance and waited afterwards in an anteroom to help Morning Light disrobe. He did not like what he saw outdoors or in. The once firm and muscular body was growing wasted and lean, its resources exhausted, and the dance suffered.

'You should go hunting again, or play ball,' Viner said, as Morning Light, silenced by exertion, slumped on a bench in the anteroom, motionless except for the caving-in of his chest as he struggled to breathe. The ribs slid under his skin and his heart thumped hurtfully against it. 'You never play now; the others miss you. At least stop dancing for a few days.'

He refused to stop dancing.

The waiting was intolerable. Two things could happen: either the Queen would decide to stay, and Morning Light, however it were contrived, would be removed; or the Queen would go, and Viner would be left to comfort a man who had without warning lost his living, his wife and his beloved child. Three things could happen: the Queen might stay, the Queen might go, or it might rain. He did not think it would rain, and he waited in suspense for Mere to send for him again, and tell him what she intended to do. In the meantime he paid half-hearted court to Red Hen, just in case. She seemed to like him.

Summer drew to its dry close. Now, in the valley, Viner thought, dressing by his window one morning and noticing that the sky had a definite autumnal clarity, now they will be getting ready for the floods. The hill tops will have vanished. The green stuff will be growing on the walls again. The sun shone in through the glass panes of his window, picking out here and there a flower or a bird on the painted wall, a curlicue on his quilt, a square of white among the tiles on the floor. Surely, even here, autumn would bring rain. They might all be saved yet.

Viner turned to find his shoes and stared at the pale patch, thinking that it must be a tile that he had not noticed before, but even then he knew that it was not. It was a sheet of folded paper that had been pushed under the door during the night. He scooped it up, carrying it to the window where he could read it more easily. It was many years since he had read anything – he had been absurdly pleased with himself for being able to pick out A THIEF OF WATER IS A THIEF OF LIFE, over the well head – but he was going to have to read this. There was no one he could show it to.

Scrawled across the sheet in a string of tipsy capitals was the message he had been waiting for:

> I CANNOT WAIT ANY LONGER
> DO WHAT YOU CAN

He read it through twice before he could trust himself to believe what was written there, but once he was sure that there was no mistake, and that she had at last made up her mind, he crunched it in his hand and ran out onto the staircase, to head for the little arbour where he supposed she would be waiting, but before he could reach it Morning Light came bounding down the stairs with a bundle under his arm and followed by Cleaver and all three nurses. He ran up against Viner and clutched his arm. He said, 'She's gone.'

Viner had to feign ignorance, and it was not difficult. He had thought, by the note, that the Queen had made her plans and wished to consult him, but he saw now that he was behindhand with events. She had not waited to consult him, she had run. The note was a farewell.

Morning Light was in a pitiable state. Half dressed, unshaven and with his hair hanging over his eyes, he looked, with his hastily snatched-up bundle of clothes, like a refugee from famine or plague. He said, over and over, 'She's run away. She's gone, she's gone. How could she leave us?'

'Did she leave a message?' Viner asked, hurriedly concealing his own.

'No, only – yes. Yes. Just that she was going away and never coming back. We must find her, we must bring her back. Cleaver, go. Go now, *Go.*'

Viner tried frantically to reconstruct the events of the previous night. Presumably Mere had decided that Viner was as unreliable as the rest of them and, not caring to risk the chance that he might betray her, had fled secretly, putting as great a distance as possible between herself and the palace before anyone went after her and tried to fetch her back, or at least fetch the baby back; the baby. His eyes at last took in the details of the bundle that Morning Light held in his arms. It had never occurred to him that she would leave the baby behind.

9

She had gone indeed, and left him, green and gullible, to contemplate her handiwork; a deserted king and a seven-week-old child in urgent need of a husband. Good-bye, Red Hen, you'll have to look elsewhere. His first panic-stricken thought was to clear out at once, as he should have done weeks ago, and let this appalling crew make the best of what he left behind him, but after one look at Morning Light he knew that he could not do it. Morning Light would not abandon his baby, and Viner could not abandon Morning Light.

Dark Cloud lay impassively against her father's arm; Morning Light, shoeless, dishevelled, his shirt unfastened, sat in the nursery clinging to his child, while the nurses, who had given up trying to prise her from his grip, stood in a threatening circle, ready to swoop the moment he slackened his hold.

'We must search for her; we must bring her back. I thought she was happy now the baby was here,' he kept saying. 'We must bring her back. She didn't mean to go. Women are often unsettled after childbirth, aren't they?' he pleaded, appealing to the nurses' superior experience of such matters.

Not so unsettled that they leap onto a fast horse and bolt in the middle of the night, Viner said to himself. To Morning Light he said, 'They'll find her. Catskin and Cleaver are searching now. She can't have gone far.' He thought that probably she had gone very far indeed, Catskin's own powerful gelding was missing from the stable. She had not risked being delayed by a pack-animal and, assuming that she had left in the early hours of the morning, had won a long start over anyone who might try to follow her, even supposing that they hit on the right track by accident. He wondered where she had gone, recalling her conversations at supper after their meeting at the well head, carefully probing, in the most general manner, the geography of the country, listening open-mouthed and absorbed to Cleaver's answers, as if to travellers' tall tales, and now she had acted upon that information, freeing herself at one stroke from her unwanted husband and her unwanted baby; and the husband was still an unwanted king. How could a woman not want her baby?

Dark Cloud began to whimper and struggle in her swaddling bands. Morning Light tightened his arm protectively about her as a hovering nurse closed in.

'She's hungry, give her here,' she said.

Morning Light shook his head. 'No.'

The nurse, balked, made an unsuccessful grab. 'Give her to me. There's a wet nurse waiting.'

'A stranger?'

The chief nurse looked over his head at Viner, silently begging him to make the distraught King see reason. 'Baby won't care if it's a stranger.'

Baby, meanwhile, pressed against her father's naked chest, had given up hope of anything better and applied herself trustingly to his nipple. The nurses averted their eyes as though an indecent act were being committed.

'Look at that,' Morning Light said, wonderingly.

Viner realized that he was past making any rational decisions. He leaned across and said, 'It's no good, Morning Light. You can't.'

'Can't what?'

'Can't feed her. Give her to the nurse.' Morning Light turned to him with obstinate eyes, concussed with shock. 'She'll *starve*,' Viner said, sternly. Observing Morning Light's divided attention the nurse snatched at the baby who, deprived, immediately set up a wail of protest.

'Take him away,' the nurse said, to Viner, allowing herself to feel a measure of sympathy now that she had finally triumphed after weeks of contention. Viner pulled him to his feet and led him from the room.

Morning Light had recovered at least his sense of direction by the time they reached his room. He went straight to a chest below the window and took out a woollen shirt and a leather tunic. Fumbling and swearing with impatience he dragged them over his

139

head, and over the shirt he was already wearing. Viner would have helped him, but fearing an elbow in the eye stood back and waited for him to emerge, looking round in surprise at the smallness of the apartment. As in his own room, which was larger, the walls were decorated with paintings, and the picture that had been prepared for the Rain King was of the rain dance. A crowd of stiffly sculptural figures stood in a circle and above them, in the centre, was the image of the Rain King at the zenith of his dance, elevated against gathering clouds and bent like a sickle, heels almost touching back-flung head and arms outstretched. As he looked at it one of the figures stepped out of the painting and approached him. It was Cleaver.

Viner, who had assumed that Cleaver would be out searching, as ordered, was too much taken aback to speak.

'Where do you think you're going?' Cleaver said to Morning Light.

'To look for her, what else?' Morning Light said, showing no surprise at Cleaver's sudden materialization. 'Why aren't you doing likewise? I sent you.'

'Catskin's seeing to all that,' Cleaver said, soothingly. 'You can't go out riding on an empty stomach. Drink this.'

'On an empty stomach?' said Viner, but Morning Light took the horn cup that Cleaver held ready, and swallowed the contents in one tasteless gulp.

'It'll do you good,' Cleaver leered, as Morning Light sat down on the bed to pull on his boots. Viner at last saw a chance to assist, but Cleaver nudged him to one side.

'I wondered when you'd turn up,' Cleaver said. 'I'd been waiting.'

'So I see. I thought you'd be out searching.'

'You can come with me,' Morning Light said, overhearing. 'Both of you.' His speech was halting and uncertain, as if his tongue had swollen.

'Right, we'll get kitted out.' Cleaver took Viner by the arm and steered him into the corridor. 'Come on – down to your room.'

'Where'll we start searching?' Viner said, reluctantly.

'We won't, and nor will he. He'll be asleep in about ten seconds.' Viner looked back and saw Morning Light still seated on the edge of the bed, shaking his head like a dog with water in its ears. Cleaver tugged him away and hurried him down the corridor to his room on the landing.

'What did you give him?' Viner thought of Mere's faith in herbs and potions.

'As I said, something to do him good. He wouldn't have enjoyed the next few hours at all.'

'What was in it?'

'A little of this, a little of that; some of the other. It'll only make him sleep. If he left the palace now I wouldn't give much for his chances of coming back alive.'

'But who –?' Viner seemed to see a dagger before him, the handle toward his hand: '– who would kill him?'

'Right now, just about anyone,' Cleaver said. 'You included.'

'*Me?*'

'Well, of course; if someone doesn't do it on your behalf,' Cleaver said, coldly. 'You've got what you wanted, haven't you? I said you'd rise, and it looks as if you've found your level.'

'I don't know what you mean.'

'Yes you do. Sit down and shut up. If they don't find Mere –'

'But everyone's searching –'

'I said shut up. They won't find her. Can't you guess that the men who've gone out to look for her are the ones who know where *not* to look? If they don't find Mere, that squalling scrap upstairs is our Rain Queen, and the Rain Queen must have a king, and I think you know very well who that will be. Yes?'

'Yes.'

'Herself told you?'

'She mentioned it.'

'Work it out then. We can't have two kings at once. Before you take over the previous incumbent will have to go. How long d'you think he'll last, with so many waiting to help him on his way? Don't tell me you hadn't thought of that?'

'No, I hadn't.' He certainly had not thought of it for a very long time. Since his plan for the disappearance of the Queen had included his assumption that she would take the baby with her he had ceased to see himself embroiled in yet another disappearance. He had imagined the King leaving of his own accord, never that he would remain to be forcibly deposed by his successor. The whole plan had been formulated to obviate that miserable circumstance. He had no idea how much Cleaver knew of what had been going on, or of Viner's own part in the whole sorry mess. One thing only was clear: Cleaver believed that he was well pleased with the outcome. His reputation for ambition had outstripped his ambition.

'Don't tell me,' Cleaver said aggressively, 'that you actually want to protect him?' He expelled a nauseously sentimental sigh. 'Aaaah, *did* he, then?'

'I don't want to harm him,' Viner said. He shouted, 'I never wanted to be king.'

'Keep your voice low.' Cleaver went to the door and looked outside, onto the landing. 'You never know who's listening. It makes no odds what you wanted or didn't want. You'll be king and he won't be.' He closed the door and leaned on it. 'I'll tell you what will happen. In a few days Catskin will come to Morning Light, with some of his friends, and say, "We've found a husband for your daughter. Sorry, but you'll have to go. We'll give you twenty-four hours, or some such time, to get out." Now, what do you think he'll do?'

'He won't leave the baby.'

'He'll have to leave the baby.'

'What will be done to him if he refuses to go?'

'I don't know. They might not even wait for him to refuse. He could be found on the terrace with a broken neck, having flung himself off the roof, mad with grief, you understand; or drowned in one of your nice new wells; or lying in bed with a knife in his back – having stabbed himself.'

'Would it really come to that?'

'You asked me what would happen if he refused to go. I'm guessing. I've got nothing to go on, this doesn't happen regularly, please note.' Cleaver's voice was flat. 'Now, listen. I'm going out to look for that bitch myself. If it's possible to find her, which I doubt, I'll find her, but I'll mainly know what everyone else is doing. I reckon we've got about three days before Catskin comes back, and if I work things my way, I shall be back first.'

'I thought you weren't going.'

'Oh, I'm going all right. I just wanted to be sure what I was leaving.' Cleaver sighed again, a weary groan of genuine sadness. 'No, I didn't think *you* would kill him, Viner, but now you know how things are, and how long you've got, start thinking.'

'Thinking of what?'

'Of what you're going to do. In the meantime, don't let him out of your sight, him or the baby.'

'Why the baby?' Following Cleaver's thought processes was like climbing a tree in the dark.

'Because,' said Cleaver slowly, 'as if to an idiot, 'he *might* go if he thought he could take her with him, and if he did, we'd have no queen at all. You don't want to see your little bride vanish into the night, do you?'

This being exactly what Viner did want, he was slow to answer. 'Wouldn't they choose another?'

'Yes, but it's a long and arduous ritual with which I, for one, do not wish to be involved. I don't think he will go – it wouldn't occur to him yet – he'll wait here for the Queen to be brought back, poor fool. He thinks no harm of anyone.' Cleaver opened the door, but as he strode through it turned, in a vortex of swirling cloak, and raised his hand. 'But Viner, if you love him, stand at his back, sit at his side, eat from his plate and sleep at his door.'

Viner, emerging from the oasis of his room, expected to find himself in a howling wilderness of lament and consternation. In that room, and in the nursery, he had been aware of shrieks and wails, urgent footsteps on stair and corridor, commands bellowed, questions bawled, but flatly, distantly, like an audible painting. Now it had all subsided; only whispers were exchanged, sidelong glances, sudden speculative looks cast in his direction. He thought at first that they must know what he had done, but he began to see that they only wondered what he would do. He waited.

They waited, and with all the tact they might have shown to a man who was dying and did not know it, they gathered to condole with their King when he woke giddy and sick from Cleaver's ministrations. Morning Light, his eyes straying towards the nursery door, listened dully to all that was said, and answered only, 'She'll come back soon. They'll bring her back,' staring out of the window as if he expected to see her approaching from the blank landscape into which she had disappeared. Viner feared that his lassitude would give way to vacant madness, but after three days, and still no word of his wife, he roused himself, bathed and shaved, and danced the rain dance.

It was the first time since the morning of the Queen's flight that he had been out of Viner's reach by daylight. At night Viner forsook his room on the staircase and slept on a palliasse at the threshold of the room where Morning Light lay sleepless below the frozen figure of the dancing painted king. He could not tell if anyone had noticed that the living King had acquired a body-guard, but he doubted that any blow would be struck before Catskin returned and declared the Queen irrecoverably lost to them. Until that day he was still the Rain King, and Viner was only Viner.

Viner watched him from an upper window, as he had dreamed of doing, and waited for Cleaver, ruminating on Cleaver's warning. On his lap lay his future wife, tacitly committed to the care of her future husband by the nurses. Morning Light, still entirely ignorant of the impending relationship, trusted him to guard her as if she were his own; in a little while, Viner knew, he would drag himself upstairs, half dead with fatigue, to reclaim her and lay his feverish trembling mouth against the tender fur that now capped her head. Viner, sickened by the prospect, and more sickened still by subsequent prospects, lifted her from his lap and replaced her in the wicker cradle at his side. Catskin, according to Cleaver, might return at any time now, and when he did, Morning Light's kingship would be at an end, and he must go, dislodged at last by his devoted friend and dowser.

And you will go hating me, Viner thought, looking down at him where he danced.

'I don't know how you can watch him, knowing what you do,' said a furious voice at his back. Viner whipped round, horribly startled to hear his thoughts so accurately voiced, and saw Cleaver leaning against the wall at the head of the staircase behind him.

'She isn't found?'

Cleaver, dirty, sweat-streaked, and tottering as if he might collapse where he stood, was beyond sarcasm. 'No, she isn't, and never will be, now. Catskin and his party will be back inside half an hour. I've barely been out of the saddle for three days; what have you been doing?'

'What you told me to do – thinking,' said Viner. He rose from his seat and pushed Cleaver onto it. 'Listen, Cleaver; if he went, would you go with him?'

'Someone would have to, or he'd be back again. The problem,' said Cleaver, 'isn't only getting him away, it's keeping him away.'

'You and Hern then? What would you do with him?'

'Just what we did to you, I suppose,' Cleaver said, glumly. 'We couldn't turn him loose until we were sure he'd never find his way back.'

Viner, remembering what Cleaver had done to him, recoiled from the thought of Morning Light, blinded and pinioned and dragged, a prisoner, ever further into the wilderness, but little as he liked the picture, still less did he like the image of Cleaver and Hern on his either side, while Viner, as much a prisoner, remained in the palace. He was still trapped. They were all trapped.

'Time's passing,' said Cleaver, nudging him out of his reverie. 'How do we make him go?'

'Why do you ask me?' Viner said, flattered in spite of himself. 'I'd have thought you'd be good at this sort of thing.'

'Intrigue? I may be twisted,' said Cleaver, sombrely, 'but compared to you I'm as straight as a rush.'

How d'you make that out? Viner wondered. He said, 'You told me yourself, he'd go if he could take the baby with him.'

'Of course he can't take the baby with him.'

'No, but if he *thought* he could – he'd go, wouldn't he?'

'How d'you make that out?'

'Suppose we told him that we'd planned an escape –'

'He'd like that, wouldn't he? Finding out that we've known all along what was going to happen to him.'

'Then let him think *he's* planned it. We've got to make him believe that if he goes, the baby goes too. We could tell him that you and Hern would go on ahead, with Dark Cloud. He'd meet up with you at the ruined village, or somewhere like that, do you see? By the time he found out the truth it would be too late to do anything about it.'

'You *have* been thinking, haven't you?' Cleaver said, grudgingly. 'But how could we be sure he'd left?'

'I'd see to that.' Viner saw himself seeing to it and quailed. 'Can Hern be trusted?'

'He's my friend.'

'Oh, don't start all that again. He's Catskin's friend, too. Is he the King's friend?'

'If I say so. He's safe,' said Cleaver. 'Hern won't care where he goes, or who he's with, so long as he gets some killing in.'

'Exactly; and he doesn't much care who he kills, either, does he?'

'I meant game,' Cleaver snapped. 'He's safe – so long as he doesn't know what's going on.'

'Would he betray us?'

'No, but he might get confused. Don't worry about Hern.'

'And what about you?'

'What about me?'

'Well – would you stay with Morning Light; *always*?'

'Only as long as need be. I'd come back in the end, I dare say. Oh, don't fret.' Cleaver's tired voice struck its usual bantering note. 'You'll be seeing *me* again. Good old boring old Cleaver always turns up eventually.'

But not Morning Light, Viner thought, who will live out the rest of his life knowing that I took his place and tricked him into leaving his child. He'll never come back.

Cleaver was standing up again at the window, not watching the dying of the dance but frowning, red-eyed, into the distance. 'I can't see anything,' he complained. 'My eyes are raw. Is that dust kicked up out there?'

Viner looked to the horizon. 'Horsemen – about a dozen.'

'Catskin's coming,' Cleaver said, 'and you'll be the one he comes to first. Now get Her Little Self back to the nursery and wait in your room. You won't have long to wait.'

'Wait!' As Cleaver headed for the staircase Viner gathered up the cradle and headed after him. 'I know what he'll say, but am I supposed to know?'

'How am I supposed to know what you know?' Cleaver said, and having mangled his question beyond answering, took off.

By the time Viner had returned the baby to the nursery Catskin was home. Viner, at his own window now, watched him ride into the stable yard with his little band of followers all, unlike Cleaver, looking remarkably alert and unwearied after the rigours of their sad quest. Stiff with anxiety he watched them dismount and stride indoors, knowing that at the same moment, on the other side of the building, the Rain King was also entering, also unsuccessful. He wondered if Cleaver might be wrong in his predictions of Catskin's movements; might not Catskin go first to Morning Light, who would certainly be looking for him, however innocently. The minutes of his solitude had lengthened to an hour before Catskin and several others appeared on his landing.

'I think you know why we've come,' said Catskin in the doorway, surrounded by friends, or relatives. Viner sprang to his feet, not altogether surprised but shaken, nevertheless. 'Sit down. I'll come straight to the point,' Catskin said, with soldierly decisiveness. 'If we can't bring back the Queen, and she'll be well away by now, the Princess becomes queen in her turn, and she'll need a husband.'

'The first man to perform the rain dance successfully,' Viner said.

'We've discussed that. We think it's enough that the next king should be able to find water; it doesn't matter where it comes from.'

'You mean, he needn't dance?'

'Oh yes, you can dance, but there's no need to wait. Marry first, then dance.'

'Me?' He sounded astonished. It was an effort. 'Don't fool around,' said Catskin. 'Don't waste time. Who else would we mean? Dance if you like, but marry you must.'

'Marry when?'

'In a day or two, if it turns out that the Queen can't be found.' It seemed to Viner that Catskin knew the Queen would not be found. Catskin had known where not to look, and now that Catskin had spoken openly, before witnesses, Morning Light's eclipse ceased to be a menacing possibility and became an imminent fact.

He said, flatly, 'I can't. Morning Light would kill me.'

'Morning Light will be in no position to object. We've prepared him. You prepare yourself.'

'He *knows*?'

'Oh yes. He doesn't like it, but he knows.'

Viner was afraid to stir out of his room after that in case he ran into Morning Light, on the rampage and seeking vengeance, but Morning Light came looking for him. He stood in the doorway, shivering with rage and humiliation, but kingly with it, for once.

'I hear you are to be wed before the week's out,' he said.

'They say I must.'

'They can't force you. You could leave – people have left before,' he said, without hope.

There was no point in pussyfooting. 'You're the one who will leave,' Viner said.

'And leave you to marry Dark Cloud?'

'It would be no marriage,' Viner said, wretchedly. 'She's too young to be my wife. She always would be. I'd never claim her.'

'Age notwithstanding,' Morning Light said, 'you are not the husband for my daughter.' He looked almost haughty and Viner would have cringed, had he had the time to feel the edge of his contempt.

'Listen,' he said, 'if you don't go away, they'll kill you.'

'They only told me to go,' Morning Light said, and flattened himself against the wall.

'But not what would happen if you didn't?'

'No.'

'Well, now you know how badly they want you gone. What will you do?'

He leaned against the door frame and hid his face in his hands. 'My wife has gone. How can I leave my baby?'

How can I stay? Viner thought, and if I don't, how can I leave *you*? 'Take her with you,' he said, 'and I'll come too.' He had not meant to say that, but hearing his own voice outrageously phrase his feelings, he stumbled on, 'I don't want to be king. I don't want to take your place.'

'I don't care if you take my place.'

'I don't want to take your baby.'

The clenched fingers parted and a dark incredulous eye blinked warily behind them. 'You'd help me? You'd come with me?'

'I'm your friend.'

'But you'd be giving up everything.'

For you, Viner said, with his own eyes. For you. He wished and wished it were true. 'I can't take what I haven't earned. I'd have left before, if I'd known you'd be safe.'

'Then let's leave now – at once. Right away.'

'In broad daylight? How far do you think you'd get?' Viner was aghast at his lack of practicality. 'Without any preparation? If we're taking Dark Cloud we must plan carefully. How would you feed her? We're not taking the wet nurse along, I suppose?'

'That hag? No. But how shall we feed her without?'

'There you are, see? We must plan.' Since they were not taking Dark Cloud Viner had given no thought either to the problem of feeding her. 'Sit down and be quiet for once.' Morning Light sat obediently on the bed. Viner was appalled to think how he had addressed him, but they both understood that he was no longer King in anything but title, and that soon he would not have even that. He could not be quiet, however, overcome as he was by the baby's dietary needs. Viner began to wish he had never mentioned them.

'We use a bottle,' Viner said, 'with milk in it. And we put rags in the neck of the bottle, to plug it, and she can suck the rags; I've seen it done, and I've a bottle that will do.'

'Rags?' said Morning Light. 'She won't like that.'

'No, she won't,' Viner agreed, 'but if it's a choice between the bottle and nothing, she'll take the bottle. Babies don't have any pride. They can't afford it.'

'Can any of us?' said Morning Light.

'As soon as you can you must get her to take pap. It's best she's weaned quickly.'

'You know a lot about babies, don't you? More than I do,' he said, jealously.

'There were four at home,' said Viner. 'Talking of home,' he remarked, with apparent carelessness, 'where shall we go, when we go? To your home?'

Morning Light was looking out of the window. It was some time before he answered. 'I have no home.'

'Well, where did you come from?' He had hoped, for a moment, that wherever he came from, Cleaver might take him back there. It seemed not.

'Somewhere out there,' Morning Light said at last, 'there's a little wagon, drawn by two horses. Last night perhaps it put up in a village, tonight maybe in an open field, tomorrow in a town. Wherever that wagon stops is my home. No one knows that, here. When I came I told a different story.' He paused. 'But I think they may have guessed, from the way I talk.'

Viner, to whom they had all sounded exactly the same, thought he knew how he felt. 'You were a traveller?'

'All my family was in that wagon. They were singers, tumblers, dancers – so was I. I danced the rain dance out of charity, because I *could*, not because I wanted to. I never knew I must stay, but I did stay. I left my family.' He leaned his head on his fist. 'I don't know why. Even now I don't know why.'

'You could find them.'

'They wouldn't have me. Can you blame them? One morning I went out to find a place where we could perform – times were hard: they'll be harder now – and I didn't go back again. I became the Rain King instead. I can never go back.'

'Were you already married, then?'

'Betrothed; as good as married. I broke my betrothal. I paid for it.'

Oh, Mere, you and your philtres; why didn't you let him go when he would? Viner thought. Aloud he said, 'We'll find somewhere to go; someone will want us.' I want you, he thought. 'So long as we stay together,' he said, wishfully. 'But I told you, we must plan carefully. Now, Morning Light, have you any true friends here; people you can trust?'

'You mean, who might help us?' It appeared that it had only just occurred to him that there might *not* be anyone.

'I mean who would go with us. Well, is there? Anyone at all who would help you, or at least not betray you?'

'Cleaver.'

'I hoped you'd say that,' Viner said. 'He was the first one I thought of.'

'And Hern.'

'I don't know about Hern. I wouldn't trust him further than I could spit on him.'

'But he's my friend.'

'I wish you'd stop saying things like that. Cleaver's your friend. I'm your friend. Remember that, will you? Still, I'll find out about Hern,' Viner promised him. 'Now, we must be ready to go, at a moment's notice. Make preparations for yourself and the baby, and I'll sound out Cleaver. If he won't go with us we can go alone.'

'Suppose...' Morning Light faltered. 'Suppose he did betray us?'

'I won't tell him enough to betray,' said Viner. '*I* don't trust anyone.'

Cleaver was in his room at the bottom of the staircase, brooding, in an attitude of meditative gloom, at the centre of his bed, hunched and oblivious.

'Come in, Majesty,' said Cleaver, when he saw Viner at the doorway, and inclined his head in a grisly parody of servile reverence. Viner, propelled by embarrassment, pity and cold fury, climbed onto the bed and smacked him round the head. Cleaver shrugged morosely and did not retaliate. Viner sat down on the edge and clenched his stinging hand between his knees.

'I heard voices as I came down,' Cleaver said, 'so I didn't come in. Who was with you, Catskin?'

'Catskin first,' said Viner, 'then Morning Light.' He found it hard to believe that Cleaver had passed down the stairs without pausing to lay his ear to a crack in the door, but Cleaver looked up with quickening interest.

'You mean you've already spoken to Morning Light?'

'I had to.'

'And what,' said Cleaver, turning on him a cool considering stare, 'did you tell him?'

'Just what we planned – only he thinks he and I planned it on the spot. He'll go with you and Hern if the baby goes too. He's planning her wardrobe right now, only –' Viner hesitated, '– he thinks I'm coming as well.'

'You?' Cleaver lay flat on the bed and laughed hollowly. 'Wouldn't he go without you, then?'

'I had to tell him that,' said Viner. 'I couldn't let him go thinking that I'd plotted to take his place.'

'Oh well, he'll know soon enough,' Cleaver said, sitting up again. 'Can he be ready to leave tonight?'

'He was ready to leave immediately – with Dark Cloud.'

'That's what I was afraid of. Right, we'll do it like this. Get his gear out to the stables during this afternoon and Hern'll hide it; let's be nicely conspiratorial, hah? Tell him we'll leave after supper, me and Hern first, which'll be true, taking Dark Cloud with us, which won't. He'll not know we haven't got her until he catches us up, and by then it'll be too late. Let him believe that you'll wait to make sure he's got away safely before following. Can you do that?'

Viner could think only of Morning Light at the moment when he discovered the precise nature of his escape. 'There must be an easier way,' he said.

'Wasn't this your idea?'

'Yes, but . . . can't you just give him some more of your sleep drink and carry him off before he wakes up? Who'd stop you?'

'I haven't got any more,' said Cleaver. 'I gave him twice as much as he should have had, as it was. That cleaned me out. How long did he sleep?'

'A day and a half. Can't you knock him on the head?'

'You knock him on the head, if that's what makes you happy. It'll take time to prepare for this journey. I just want to keep *him* happy until we go,' Cleaver said.

'That's kind of you.'

'If he isn't happy,' said Cleaver, 'he may take matters into his own hands.'

Oh, how I wish he would, thought Viner.

'We leave tonight,' Viner said, to Morning Light. 'After supper. Cleaver and Hern will go first, with Dark Cloud –'

'How will they get her out?'

'I'm not sure.' Viner improvised rapidly. 'Cleaver knows what he's doing. Something to do with herbs. I think he means to put the nurses to sleep.'

'Suppose it doesn't work?'

'It worked with you, didn't it?'

Morning Light scowled at the memory. 'But it could take time.'

'Two minutes flat.'

'Why can't I take her?'

'You'll be watched, you know you will.'

'Why can't we all leave together?'

'We'll be less noticeable if we all go separately.'

Morning Light's enthusiasm was flagging. 'Are you sure we can trust them?'

'Trusting them was your idea, not mine.'

'Yes, but with Dark Cloud . . .'

'Morning Light, they're your *friends*.'

Morning Light nodded unhappily. Viner wondered if he knew his friends better than anyone suspected.

Towards sunset Viner went out to the old well in the kitchen yard, with a bucket, pausing on his way for a chat with Hern who had been out riding and was rubbing down his horse in the stables. During the course of the conversation he transferred the contents of the bucket to a sack that Hern had thoughtfully left hanging by the stall. Then he went on to the well. Cleaver was there, turning the handle and whistling aimlessly.

'All set?' Cleaver said.

'All set.'

'And Morning Light?'

'He's with the baby.'

'Oh, yes. Teaching it some more naughty songs, no doubt. Now listen, tell him this: when we go we'll leave two horses saddled up and tethered to those trees beyond the byres, one for him, one for you. He's to leave next, after about half an hour, and meet us at the village. Then you. Keep him occupied until he goes or we'll have him sneaking off to the nursery.'

'Why should he?' Viner made heavy weather of winding up the bucket to prolong the exchange. 'He'll think you've got Dark Cloud with you.'

'He's supposed to think it, but he may be in two minds whether to believe it. Perhaps we ought to make him go first.'

'I'll keep him away from the nursery. If he goes first someone might notice he's missing.'

'He's meant to go missing. Do you think people don't know what we're up to?'

'You told them?'

'Here a hint, there a hint, but no word about his thinking that the babe comes too. They might get worried and keep him from her. Let him be happy while he can.'

'I'm sorry,' Viner said, recalling an earlier sneer. 'You *are* kind.'

'Hard to believe,' Cleaver said lazily, 'ain't it?'

They had agreed to go into supper as usual, and Morning Light occupied the centre seat at the High Table, as he had always done. They greeted him easily as they sat down, and then froze, collectively. He had the baby on his lap.

'Why have you brought her in?' Cleaver asked, elaborately off-hand.

'I always wanted to,' Morning Light replied, equally relaxed, 'but her mama wouldn't allow it.' They all became conscious of Catskin, listening intently from his end of the table, ears pricked at any mention of the Queen. 'I shall be leaving her soon,' Morning Light went on, tremulously, 'so I want to spend as much time with her as I can.' Viner was conscience-stricken. Morning Light, under the impression that he was lying, gave a magnificent impersonation of grief, unaware that he was telling the truth. 'Here is your husband, my darling,' he said, turning the baby to face Viner, and Viner noticed that he could not quite control his mouth when he said that. I'm surprised he hasn't pushed *me* off the roof, Viner thought. It's no more than I deserve.

Toward the end of the meal the head nurse came in wearing an expression that threatened dire consequences.

'Let us hope,' said the nurse, loudly, 'that when she is safely wed she will be kept in her proper place and sent to bed at a respectable hour.' Morning Light turned so red with anger that all over the room people stared at him, but it was a natural enough reaction under the circumstances. Taking advantage of his disadvantage the nurse plucked Dark Cloud from his arms and stalked out again, confident that she had done as much damage as she had intended.

'That wasn't very clever of him,' Hern said.

'On the contrary, it was a sight cleverer than I would have expected,' Cleaver muttered. 'Now everyone thinks he's resigned to giving her up. I'd never have thought he'd have the wit to work it out.'

'Not that it will do him any good in the long run,' said Hern.

'He doesn't know that.'

The meal proceeded, ended, dragged out its dying fall in a litter of crumbs and spilled wine. People yawned and belched and wandered away. Finally even Catskin went out, with Red Hen tucked under his elbow.

That might have been my wife he's going to sleep with, Viner thought. If Morning Light *did* take the baby, she still might. *Might.* Fish might sing.

'Right lads.' Cleaver stood up and stretched. 'I'm off. Don't sit up too late, will you?' He strolled out, without a backward glance, and after a few minutes Hern followed him. Morning Light watched them go and poured himself more wine than Viner cared to see, considering the delicacy of the operation ahead. He did not want Cleaver and Hern confronted by a raging drunk, nor himself landed with a man who was too sleepy to move.

'It's all under way, now,' he said, quietly, and shifted along the table until he reached the seat beside the King, where he leaned back and folded his arms to hide what he thought must be the evident thudding of his heart; now followed the difficult part; keeping Morning Light occupied for half an hour.

'Will they have left the nursery yet? Will they have reached it?' Morning Light did not turn his head and continued to stare pensively into the lees of his wine. Then a thought struck him, and he jumped. 'Perhaps we ought to go along and make sure –'

'No! That would be fatal.' It would, too. Viner poured a little more wine into their cups 'We mustn't go anywhere near the nursery. Cleaver knows what he's doing.'

'What if someone finds out that she's gone?'

'No one ever goes there except the nurses, and you.'

'Well, then . . .'

'No. Cleaver worked all this out. If it fails we shan't get a second chance.'

When Viner judged that half an hour had elapsed he rose, with Morning Light, and they sauntered together from the room, through the broken veins of the palace, toward the kitchen and the stables.

'The horses are tied to a tree beyond the byres. Take yours and get on to the ruins as fast as you can. I'll see you soon.'

Morning Light walked a few paces, turned and looked back at him, imploringly. 'Are you certain . . .?'

'When I see you again, you'll have her in your arms, I promise. Morning Light, don't you trust us?'

He spread his hands, helplessly. 'What else can I do?' he said, turning, and walked on down the corridor. Viner almost ran after him, to wish him farewell, good fortune, to say anything that would delay the final severance. He watched the slouching figure dwindle in the shadows, and silently called him back.

See you soon, he whispered. See you soon? After you turn that corner, I'll never see you again, never again. He blinked, and in the instant that his eyes were closed Morning Light reached the corner and turned it, and was gone for ever. Somewhere in the distance a door closed, and that was the utter last of him.

'No!' Viner said, and swivelling on his heel fled back the way he had come until he reached his room and flung open the window. Looking out into the moonless night he heard the faint jingle of harness and solemn beats as a horse moved at walking pace over the bald turf. He strained his ears to listen for the pace to quicken to a gallop, but the night swallowed the sounds and he drew in his head, uncertain that he had heard anything at all.

Viner sank to his knees by the window and thought of Hern and Cleaver, waiting in the ruins for the deceived man who now rode so hopefully toward them. How could they ever repay Morning Light for the thing that they were doing to him? How could they persuade him that he was better off alive, without his child, than he was dead at the hands of her supporters? How could they keep him alive, how could they comfort him?

'But I could, I could,' Viner said, aloud.

How?

'Oh, I could. This is all your doing, Cleaver,' he said. 'I've lost him and taken his child, and he'll hate me forever. You should never have brought me here to be king in his place. I never wanted to be king. I don't want to marry a baby. You should have let Hern kill me when he would. How can I live now?'

And then he knew how. At the foot of his bed hung the bait bag, packed, under Morning Light's supervision, with food, clothes, and the pot bottle filled with milk and plugged with rags. Not pausing to unpack it he swung it onto his shoulder and circled the room, grabbing at articles of his own clothing, stuffing them in on top. In went the bacon bone, too, for old time's sake. From out of a snatched-up shirt fell a crackling scrap of paper, Mere's letter, ragged and crushed. Leaning on the window sill he smoothed it out, added a few words of his own on the back, and tossed it on the bed among the discarded possessions that time would not permit him to pack. Then he strode from the room, leaving the door to swing behind him and send the lamp flame flaring, and went out onto the staircase. He could not run yet. There were still one or two people abroad in the palace. They took little notice of Viner as they passed him, beyond a nod or a complicit smile. In a day or two he would marry, he would be king, and Morning Light and the drought would be gone for ever. He was almost sorry for their misplaced confidence, guilty at the thought of what they would have to suffer when they discovered that he too had gone for ever. It was this thought that had caused him to leave behind on his bed the rods, with a note for anyone who might be able to read it.

NOT SAUCERY

HOLE TITE AN THINK OF WARTER

His horse was waiting alone among the broken trees beyond the byres where Hern had tethered it, the last false clue to mislead Morning Light. Viner had intended to fetch it in at dawn. Now he untied it and led it towards the road, as he had heard Morning Light do, not daring to mount and gallop until the building was far behind him and its few lights no more than a cluster of earth-bound stars. The night was cool but dry. Ahead of him, beyond the ruined village, a faint flush bloomed over the skyline where the moon would presently rise, and by the time he reached the dry pond it was clear of the land, casting the first shadows of the night. Viner dismounted and led his animal between the fallen walls, toward the well that he had found so many months before. On his right the moon's light was mirrored by a sudden flame that showed in a roofless dwelling. Cleaver's voice said hoarsely, 'Morning Light? What happened? Were you stopped?'

He said, 'This is Viner. Where's Morning Light?'

Cleaver, holding aloft a candle lantern, stepped out of the cottage, followed closely by Hern. 'Viner! Did something go wrong? Where is he?'

'Isn't he here?'

'No he's not. What are you doing, anyway?'

Viner, who had been preparing himself for a very different confrontation, looked Cleaver in the eye and said, 'I had to come. I couldn't just let him leave and think I'd betrayed him.'

'Why not? You have betrayed him.' Hern took such things for granted.

'But he *didn't* leave,' Cleaver said. 'That is, he hasn't arrived. We thought something must have delayed him. When did he leave?'

'When you said – half an hour after you did. I saw him go.'

'How far did you see him go?'

'He went out into the yard. I'll swear he got as far as his horse – I heard him walking it away, from my window.' Viner tried to remember exactly what he had heard; surely, a horse, walking. 'He must have reached it. When I got out there was only the one horse. No one would have stopped him.'

'He must have gone back,' Cleaver said. 'He must have got frightened.'

'Or suspicious. Now what do we do?'

'Listen.' Hern, in the candlelight, held up one hand. 'D'you hear it? Hoofbeats, coming this way.'

'It must be him.'

'It might not be. Keep quiet and get back in here.' They huddled against the wall of the cottage and listened as the pounding became louder and closer, until the rhythm broke and the gallop slowed to a walk, the solid beat gave way to the clatter of hooves among rubble. In the darkness Morning Light's voice called, incautiously, 'Are you there? Cleaver? Viner? Hern? Are you there?'

'Be ready to hold him,' Hern whispered. 'Make sure he's off the horse before he knows, or we'll lose him.'

'But he may know now that we didn't bring the baby,' Viner said.

'If he knew that he wouldn't be here. He wouldn't have come without her.'

Cleaver stepped forward and raised the lantern again. 'Morning Light? Is that you?'

'Of course it's me, you fool,' said the voice with unexpected asperity, and after a moment Morning Light walked into view. They stood and stared at him. He was draped from shoulder to knee in a dark cloak, and in his hands he carried a long-necked musical instrument, with strings.

'What on earth have you got there?' Cleaver said. 'What happened to you? We thought you'd been caught.'

'It's my rebec,' Morning Light said.

'You went back for *that*?' said Viner.

'It will hang on my saddle,' said Morning Light. 'It's well trained and no trouble to anyone, and it only cries if you hit it,' he added, with a touch of Cleaver's own sarcasm.

'What do you want that thing for?'

'Listen.' Morning Light's eyes glittered in the dull glow of the lantern. 'I take nothing out of that damned place but what is mine. My child and my instrument. I had it with me when I came and I won't leave it. It was my living.'

'So, that's what you were, Rain King,' Cleaver said. 'A mountebank, a wandering singer. Well, you may earn us a crust or two, yet.'

'Don't fight here,' Viner said. 'Let's be moving.' Incredibly they were quarrelling over a fiddle, when they had expected a struggle to the death over a living child.

'Us?' said Hern. 'Where do you think you're going?'

'Wait a moment,' said Morning Light. 'Where's my baby?'

There was a silence. Keyed up as they had been to face this very question, the disruption of Cleaver's plan had diverted them.

'Morning Light,' said Cleaver, stepping toward him, 'you must understand; we had to get you away from the palace –'

'Where is she? Where's my daughter?'

'– to save your life. We knew you'd never leave of your own free will. We're your friends. We had to get you away.'

'Give her to me.' Hern, Viner saw, had moved round behind Morning Light and was standing ready to foil any move he might make. Cleaver was holding something under his cloak, behind his back. Viner tensed himself for the struggle that was coming.

'We did it for your sake.'

'Do you mean,' Morning Light said pleasantly, 'that she isn't here?'

'We're your friends,' Cleaver said, on a pleading note. He was not pleading, he was playing for time. Hern went up on the balls of his feet.

'You left her in the palace?'

'She's in good hands, I promise you . . .'

Morning Light shrugged. 'Oh well, never mind. I know you meant it for the best; it doesn't matter.'

Viner could not believe what he was hearing. Morning Light was actually smiling. Hern faltered. Cleaver stepped back a pace or two.

'You don't *mind*?'

'No. You did what you thought was right,' said Morning Light. 'So did I.' He threw back the cloak and they saw that across his chest he wore a sling of leather and canvas, that was fastened over his shoulder. In the sling, sleeping, was Dark Cloud. 'You always were a liar, Cleaver,' said Morning Light. 'Are you going to send us back? Hern, I know what you're doing, I've got a knife here. If you lay one finger on me I'll kill you – I *can* kill you,' he added quietly, 'but I'd sooner not. Don't let's stand here arguing. They'll almost certainly have discovered that she's missing by now; she's always fed at midnight. You didn't know that, did you? Well, are we going?'

They stood round him, speechless, until Cleaver said, 'Do you realize what you've done?'

'Only what you promised to do.'

Hern said, '*How* did you?'

160

'Through the window,' Morning Light said, 'in and out. Even nurses sleep. *Did* you give them anything, Cleaver? I couldn't have done it without the horse to stand on – thanks for the horse.'

'So that's what I heard!' Viner exclaimed.

'So long as no one else did.' His calm demeanour was a disguise, he was stammering with nervousness. 'Now, you can try to take her from me, or you can smash my head in – only I think you said something about wanting to save my life, Cleaver, or we can go on as we meant to, though I don't know what you meant to do with me – but make up your minds quickly, because if they catch us up, Cleaver, no one will believe that you didn't plan the whole thing like this. Are you my friend, Cleaver, or aren't you?'

'I'm your friend,' Cleaver said, at last. 'Get on your horse. We must be leaving.'

'All of us?' said Hern, clearly horrified.

'All of us. You heard what he said. Who'd believe that we had no hand in this? Do you want to go back now and face Catskin?'

Hern said, 'What about him?' He pointed to Viner.

'Viner's coming with us,' Morning Light said. 'You know that.'

'I bloody didn't,' said Hern. His barmy yellow eyes rolled wildly until they threatened to capsize. 'He's supposed to be back at the palace, marrying your daughter and making rain.'

'No one's marrying my daughter,' said Morning Light.

'And no one's making rain,' Hern said.

'*Will* you get moving?' Cleaver shouted, 'or there won't be any question of going back to face Catskin – he'll be here!'

'But what about the water?' Hern said.

'Damn the water. Damn everything. Damn the lot of you,' Cleaver cried. 'Let's get out of here, now!'

They remounted without further words, and swung northwards along the travellers' track that led to Viner's well. When Viner looked back again, the lights of the palace had disappeared into the darkness.

10

Through the easy autumn they moved in a spiral, travelling ever further, but slowly, from the palace and the plain where it stood. Hern, who had suggested the manoeuvre, congratulated himself upon its success.

'If they don't find us during the next few days,' he explained, on the first night, 'they'll keep moving outwards in straight lines. They'll follow roads and think we must be just ahead of them. No one could ever imagine we'd be so close at hand.' Viner wondered if anyone else had received the benefit of this advice, on some other occasion.

As it turned out, Hern was right. After a week they were still only a few miles from the palace, having travelled a full circle, but no one had seen them and they felt that it might now be safe to strike out. They had no very clear idea of where they were going and did not much care. Viner and Morning Light were thankful simply to be quit of kingship; Hern and Cleaver were engaged on nothing more than one of their frequent and extended hunting trips. The weather was good, they could feed themselves. It scarcely mattered where they were going so long as, eventually, they left the palace far behind.

'We'll be free men,' Hern said.

'It won't be the first time,' said Cleaver.

'We are free men,' said Morning Light.

'Wait till you know what it means,' said Cleaver.

To begin with they moved only by night, lying up during daylight hours in caves, ruins, woods. Cleaver and Hern had an apparently infinite itinerary of such bolt-holes, compiled on previous trips. 'No one knows the country like we do,' Cleaver said.

'I've lived off the country before now,' Morning Light remarked.

'I said no one *knows* it like us.' Cleaver, resigned to the fact that they had abducted the Rain Queen, was still short with Morning Light; less for trying to trick him than for getting away with it. They were often edgily bad-tempered with each other not least, Viner thought, because Cleaver knew that if Morning Light had not deceived him he would have deceived Morning Light, and then been forced to keep him a virtual prisoner, albeit for his own good. He and Hern were kind enough to include Viner as a co-victim of his duplicity, forgetting that Viner's involvement was entirely his own fault and imagining, as he allowed them to imagine, that he had wanted to return to the palace. Morning Light, on the other hand, took his presence for granted and never guessed at the full enormity of the deception they had intended to practise on him. Viner's greatest fear was that Hern or Cleaver, in a fit of pique, would tell Morning Light that Viner had meant to return and marry Dark Cloud, at which, in order to defend himself from Morning Light's inevitable wrath, he would be forced to admit that he had intended nothing of the sort. It did not make for a happy relationship.

Cleaver and Hern went off alone, from time to time, on unexplained forays. They never returned empty-handed and gradually the four of them effected telling changes in their appearance. Clothes were taken away and exchanged for others less easily identified; coarse shirts, heavy winter tunics and countrymen's thick leggings. Viner let his beard grow while Hern cultivated a gorsy growth that clung to his lower lip like a prehensile hedgehog and disguised his chinlessness. Cleaver lopped off his plait whereupon, to everyone's surprise, his hair sprung into a myriad of dense curls that clung gleaming about his head like a swarm of brown bees. Morning Light, who had always worn his hair shingled to the nape of his neck, to accommodate the silver wig, let it grow long and shaggy, and shadowing his face it gave a new depth to his features; a gravity that had not been there before. Close acquaintances might have known them but at a distance they hardly recognized each other, and Hern, chancing upon handsome curly Cleaver, swaggering through the forest, nearly ran him through, on impulse.

One by one the horses were replaced by hairy hardy ponies and an ass that no one wanted to ride and had to be taken by turns. The

two hunters continued to hunt. Viner might have earned a little by
dowsing, but they could not risk letting him show himself for what
he was, in case his reputation betrayed them all. Morning Light
did better than any of them, by taking his rebec down into the
villages to sing for their supper. On quiet evenings the other three,
keeping guard over the baby in their near-by camp, heard his
voice drift through the still air; songs of love, songs of war, all the
bawdy ballads he had sung to the baby, and the watercress song to
which he seemed particularly attached. He was invariably successful; villages parted with their meagre stores in exchange for his
singing, and Dark Cloud never wanted for milk.

'He's reverting,' said Cleaver.

'What's that?' Hern did not care for long words.

'I told you he turned up out of nowhere, and no one knew who
he was. Well, this is *all* he was,' Cleaver said. 'A singer. What
made him think he could ever be king?'

'You did,' Viner said. 'All of you that thought he would make
rain.'

'Only one of us married him, though,' Hern said, defensively.

'And he was a dancer,' Viner said. 'He told me. He danced
for you because he was asked – and because he knew how to
dance.'

'Dancing for a living and dancing for rain are different crafts,
friend,' said Cleaver.

'Probably born in a barn,' said Hern. 'Morning Light! What a
name for a mountebank. Horse Turd, more like.'

Viner was glad that Hern had not had this happy thought
sooner. It had surprised him before that a man as unsuitably
named as Morning Light should not have found himself a different
handle: but what would you call him? There was nothing that
suited him, better or worse.

The baby continued to amaze them all, except for her father
who had maintained all along that she would be no trouble so long
as she was with him. When they rode she lay in her sling against
his chest, perfectly contented, and when they camped she slept in a
rush basket that was soft enough to be rolled up for transit. Her
change of diet had done her no harm. She suckled milk from the
pot bottle without complaint and happily ate everything she was

given. When she heard her father's voice singing in the evenings she smiled and waved arms and legs, indiscriminately. Viner had been shocked when Morning Light first unwrapped her.

'She'll grow crooked,' he protested. 'Hunchbacked.'

'No she won't. She'll be a great strong child and walk before she's a year old, like her father did.'

'Not unless she's kept straight, she won't. You said yourself that I knew more about babies than you.'

'Look how she grips!' he cried, as the baby hooked her little fingers round his thumb.

'They can all do that,' Viner said, deflatingly, 'even when they're new born.'

'Not if they're swaddled – aaach! She bit me.'

'She hasn't got any teeth.'

'Yes she has. Look there – at the bottom. Isn't that a tooth coming?'

Viner peered into the baby's smile. 'It's very early,' he said, grudgingly. 'They don't usually have teeth before six months. She ought to have something to bite on now, besides your thumb.' He gave Dark Cloud the bacon bone from his bait bag and she gnawed it happily.

'Teeth already,' said Morning Light. 'She'll be able to sit up, soon.'

'Not for a long time.' Viner was firm. 'You don't want to injure her back. She really ought to be swaddled again.'

'I was never swaddled,' said Morning Light, 'and look at me.' Viner looked at him. Even although he was not tall Morning Light was undeniably straight-limbed. 'Hern was swaddled, weren't you, Hern,' he added, with unwonted malice, looking pointedly at Hern's amphibious bow-legs. 'Let her alone and stop worrying.'

If Viner was worrying about the baby it was not her welfare that concerned him; on the contrary, he was frequently moved to dreams of infanticide. Had it not been for Dark Cloud, he thought, Cleaver and Hern who had almost certainly embarked on the venture out of boredom as much as altruism, would have grown bored again, and gladly returned by now to the palace, leaving Viner himself to assume responsibility for Morning Light. Now that they were unable to return the four of them were tied together

165

in a knot of increasingly overt resentment. Viner wished some-times for a row that would sever that knot once and for all, but the row, when it came and discomfiting though it was, left them still queasily attached to each other.

One evening Morning Light went down to the nearest village and returned after supper with his rebec slung across his back and a bag of broken food under his arm.

'You should have waited,' he said mildly, when he saw that they had started without him and had finished eating.

'I thought you'd eat in the village,' Cleaver said. 'You often do.'

'I did, but if you'd waited you could have had this as well,' Morning Light said, tossing down the bag among them.

Hern tossed it back, angrily. 'I'm not one of your vagrant friends to throw bread to,' he said. 'When I want to eat other people's left-overs I'll beg my own, not send a boy to do it for me.'

Morning Light, though young, could hardly be described as a boy, least of all by Hern, who was obviously several years younger. He bared his teeth, wolfishly.

'Aha! He bites!' said Cleaver, turning the knife. 'Don't fash yourself, Hern, we're lucky to have someone with us who knows how to beg. Why keep a dog and bark yourself?' he asked lazily, of the evening sky. Viner and Morning Light recognized the quota-tion simultaneously.

'You're glad enough to eat what I bring back,' Morning Light growled, and showed his teeth again.

'Don't think we're ungrateful,' Hern said, 'but who was it dragged us out here in the first place, to save his own skin?'

This manifestly unjust accusation was too much to take. Morn-ing Light threw himself down on top of Hern and landed a substantial punch on his jaw that made his teeth grate, but he rolled sideways, jerked back his knee and before Morning Light could dodge, gave him a kick in the eye that knocked him flying. Viner intervened before any worse damage could be inflicted, while Cleaver went foraging in the undergrowth for puffballs to stanch the bleeding. Hern was missing a tooth and Morning Light's left eye was purple and oozing like a split plum. Since both sides had honourably drawn blood the fight subsided as suddenly as it had started, but the uneasy peace that followed it found Viner quivering with a silent scream of frustration. It was not the blow to Morning Light that had shaken him; he had after all struck first, and hard; it was the manner of its delivery that gave the lie to all their veneer of amity. Viner had seen Hern's face when Morning Light attacked him, animated not with rage but with outrage, as if a dog, long tolerated because it was thought to be toothless had unexpectedly bitten him, and, as usual, Morning Light had not seen what Viner had seen.

Blind, he thought, furiously grinding his knuckles together; bat-blind, and not just in one eye. Doesn't he know what they think of him? No, he doesn't, any more than he knew what Mere thought of him, any more than he knows what *I* think. Cleaver puts up with him, Hern despises him, but he thinks they're his friends and doesn't see it. He won't see it. He thinks what he doesn't see isn't there. He's never learned to look round corners. All he cares about is that baby.

Half ashamed he found himself hoping for another quarrel that would finally open Morning Light's eyes to the truth about his friends, but he was beginning to understand that Morning Light expected nothing more from friendship than he was getting, and that whatever it was that Viner offered him was outside his canon. He considered suggesting to Cleaver and Hern that they might return after all to the palace, claiming that they had been gone in pursuit of the errant King, a claim that would ring very true if they took back Dark Cloud with them. No: Cleaver, honest in his fashion and kind, surprisingly, self-defeatingly kind, would never agree to that. Suppose, however, he hinted to Morning Light that this indeed was what they were planning: no, again: Morning Light would stare at him with his hazy uncomprehending eyes and decline to believe it. But sooner or later, he was sure, Cleaver and Hern would leave, and when that time came they must be made to go when he chose, before they decided upon it for themselves. He began once more to imagine himself and Morning Light left alone, with or without the baby, and planned for it.

Sometimes, in the distance, they saw the luminous fringes of autumn clouds that seemed to drop rain, but the clouds always receded at their approach, and the weather remained dry. It was still warm by day, but the nights were growing cool. Morning Light became nervous of the baby's health and wrapped her very carefully before stowing her in her sling. At night he slept with the rush basket by his side. Willy-nilly they crowded closer together in sleep for warmth, regardless of personal differences, Cleaver's snoring and Hern's foetid yawns, but they made Morning Light sleep always on the edge, because he seemed incapable of curling up thriftily, with his elbows drawn in. Instead he sprawled, face down, arms and legs outflung; another habit which must have failed to endear him to his wife. One night, as they slept in a cave, he rolled against Viner in his sleep and Viner, knowing that he would not wake, wakeful and comfortless himself, put his arms round him in the darkness.

'Don't go,' Morning Light said, sad and small. 'Don't go.' Viner knew that Morning Light was not addressing him, but held him closer, and although Morning Light did not waken he seemed to sense some presence that agreed with his dream, for sighing unhappily he turned toward Viner and Viner, encircling him with arm and thigh, eased himself over until he lay on his back, and Morning Light's heavy head rested on his shoulder, supported in the cradle of his arms.

Don't wake, he thought; don't wake; but no longer wanting sleep for himself stared open-eyed into the darkness. A strand of hair trailed across his mouth, and he bit it, gently.

One night they camped in the ruins of a cottage and woke shivering to find that a sharp frost had salted the ground overnight. Viner and Morning Light stoked up the fire and they gathered round it to thaw.

'We'll have to be thinking of a place to stay for the winter, soon,' Cleaver said.

'Does it snow, here?' Viner asked.

'Here? I wouldn't have thought so. I can remember snow at the palace one year – ages ago,' Hern said. 'What are you doing?' he snapped at Morning Light, who gravely intent upon his business was leaning over the fire with a twig, rescuing woodlice and millipedes as, revived by the heat, they scurried across the logs to escape the smoke. 'Haven't you got anything better to do?' He picked up one of the rescued woodlice and flicked it back into the glowing ash. 'Eat them, why don't you, roasted?' Morning Light looked at him with dislike. 'You may be glad to, yet.'

'Snow or not,' Cleaver cut in, 'it's going to get bitterly cold during the next few weeks. Weren't the winters cold where you came from, Viner?'

'Mild and wet, mostly. It always rained more in winter. Sometimes we had snow, but it never settled.'

'Well, they're cold and dry here, as you'll soon find out,' said Hern, and flung a prodigal handful of sticks onto the fire so that it roared up. 'There's a whole family of lice in there, wouldn't you say? Mothers and fathers and little babies, too; little girl babies.'

Viner looked at Morning Light who now sat with the child on his knee, poking food into her lovely mouth and absent-mindedly jolting her up and down to keep them both warm. He did not seem to have heard Hern's jibe, his face was expressionless, his eyes serious. He was finally beginning to understand what awaited him, living off the land in winter, with a small baby to support.

'For now,' Cleaver proposed, 'we find a cave and hole up in it. We're near enough to the border to be taken for free men, and no one will trouble us. We can go on as we are, for a while.'

'Do you think they've stopped looking for us, yet?' Morning Light said, averting his eyes from the writhing insects that Hern was dropping into the flames.

'I should think so,' Cleaver said. 'They must have chosen another queen by now; I dare say men are dancing for her hand already; so really, they aren't going to worry about you any more, Morning Light, or your baby. You're nothing, now.'

'Nothing's all he ever was,' Hern said, under his breath, as Morning Light rose and carried Dark Cloud to her basket among the baggage.

'Why do you stay with him, then?' Viner asked.

'Why not? We can't go back to the palace yet, maybe never, thanks to that little lady. When we left I didn't think we'd have her with us, for a start – or you, come to that. I don't know why Cleaver let him get away with it.'

'What would you have done?' said Cleaver.

'Brained him and taken her back,' Hern said. 'I'm not going to spend the rest of my life on the road, friend.'

Morning Light, crouched over the baby and apparently absorbed in some domestic problem, looked round.

'Where d'you suggest we go, then?'

'We?'

'You just said we're not going to spend the rest of our lives on the road. What did you have in mind?'

'I said *I'm* not going to spend the rest of my life on the road. From what I can gather you've spent most of yours there already. You've got your own plans, no doubt.'

'No.' Morning Light came back to the fire and stood over them, Hern squatting aggressively, Cleaver hunched and sombre. 'Are we not staying together?'

'Of course we're staying together,' Cleaver said quickly, 'but we can't go on like this for ever.'

'He can,' said Hern. 'He's bred to it.'

'I can't see why that troubles you so much, that I earned my own living,' Morning Light said. 'What did you ever do to deserve your place by the fire?'

'I never had to do anything!' Hern yelled, springing to his feet. 'What I have I'm entitled to. I never had to *earn.*'

'And look what that's made of you,' Morning Light retorted. They were both shouting now. 'All you know is killing. What kind of living is that?'

'And what kind of a life was yours – a Rain King who never made rain? All your dancing ever made was money.'

Morning Light looked as if he would fall on Hern once more, and this time finish the job; Viner silently urged him on, but all he said was, 'Well, that's all past. I shall never dance again.'

Hern, wrought up for violence could not let it rest there. 'Never dance again? Better you don't. They should have hamstrung you before you ever danced at all. It was you and your dancing made the world dry up. You never brought rain – you caused drought! There's no sap in *your* stick. How did you get your baby, Rain King – or did you?'

Viner and Cleaver closed in, one on each side. The quarrel was laboriously patched up but, as after all such rendings, Viner saw the fabric of their companionship grow ever more threadbare to the point where the least friction would rip it asunder, were it not for Cleaver, ever patient, ever ready to cobble it together again. They remained at the cottage for the rest of that day, and moved on again in the morning. That was a long day's journey. The country was rising more sheerly now. They were trekking among woods and sudden bald scarps, and although Cleaver claimed to know his way in those parts, it was dark when they finally came to a cave on a hillside. They turned the animals loose to graze and took out the dwindling stock of ash twigs and bark that Hern kept for touchwood. When they had eaten they banked the fire and lay down to sleep. In the darkness beyond the cave's mouth Viner saw the stars, blue in the sky and lower down yellow stars, which he took to be the lights of distant villages. One by one the blue stars moved out of sight and the yellow stars died away. He was reminded of something, but sleep was powerful and would not let him remember. Hunched against Hern's broad back, with Cleaver's bulk on his right, and aching to feel Morning Light in his arms again, he closed his eyes and slept.

When he woke in the morning, before the others, he was still nagged by the certainty that the place had some special significance. He got up quietly, stepped across Cleaver, round Morning Light and the baby, and went outside. Below him, in the valley, a river wound its way between banks that were so far apart that he could see the course must once have held a much broader stream. Along the margins grew drooping willow; alder; hazel; on the hillsides opposite smoke rose from early fires among the settlements; a goatherd ambled across the valley, followed by his flock. It was a brilliantly clear morning, cold and sharp. He could see for miles and seeing, knew where he was. To the south-west, below the horizon, lay the triple-peaked hill that overlooked the plain where the big stones stood in their circle, on the threshold of his country.

This, said Viner, is where we part company.

The others were still sleeping. Only the baby opened her eyes and warmly secure in her basket hummed tunelessly at him and gave him a supercilious smile. (In the face of his predictions to the contrary, she had cut three teeth, and never missed an opportunity to flaunt them.) All he need do was gather up his few belongings in the bait bag, saddle one of the horses, and the whole strange episode would be over. He could ride away, undetected, and leave them there to argue, fight, deceive each other, while he went where he chose, truly a free man again; free to ride in any direction; free to go, if he chose, home.

It seemed to him then, as he leaned against the rock in the icy sunrise, that he had always meant to return at the last, replete with triumph and trophy, to show the Webfeet what a dowser could become and yet, he remembered, the previous time he stood there, while Hern crept up on him, unbeknownst, he had sworn never to go back again, and where were his triumphs and his trophies now? How could he go back with nothing to show for his initiative? little better than a fugitive, owning only the gratitude of the man who lay sleeping behind him, and that man himself an outcast and a failure. How could he, the-man-who-made-it-rain-upwards, return to the rain and the people who suffered it?

He looked round and down at Morning Light who lay on his side with his fist curled against his mouth, so that he looked as if he were sucking his thumb, childishly relaxed in the trusted company of his friends.

I saved your life, he thought. If it weren't for me you'd have lost your life and your child. I gave up a kingdom for you; what will you do for me? And then recalling yesterday's quarrel with Hern, he had his answer. Morning Light, he said, you must dance again.

He walked down the hill toward the river, where there was plenty of firewood. Down here the grass was thick, still green though fouled by fallen leaves, and upstream a little way he found a tussocky glade enclosed by bushes; abundant and secluded grazing for the animals. As he ranged under the trees, collecting branches and filling his bag with late hazel-nuts, and appraising forked twigs, the goatherd came level with him on the further bank. He was having trouble with one of the flock who, followed by her kid, kept cantering off at inconvenient tangents. The goatherd paused to talk with Viner while waiting for the animal to catch up.

'Stranger in these parts?' he asked.

'Travelling through.'

'Many of you?'

'Enough.' He knew better than to give away the size of his party.

The goats milled about aimlessly, except for the truant who skipped foolishly at the river's edge, with her kid at her heels.

'You need a dog,' Viner said.

'Not I.' The goatherd, losing patience, strode back to the frisking animal. When she saw him coming she shied away, but the kid was not so fast on its feet. The goatherd swept it up in his arms and walked back to the flock, where he waited while the kid bleated and struggled. Before he had arrived, the goat was cantering after him in pursuit of the stolen kid.

'Simple,' said the goatherd. 'Who needs a dog?'

'Very simple,' Viner agreed. He exchanged a pleasantry or two with the goatherd and went back to the cave with his load of wood.

The cold morning yielded to sunshine and became a mild and charming day.

'This would be a good place to stay for the winter,' Cleaver said, when the fire was going well and they sat round it. 'No one knows us here, or of us. There's water, wood, animals . . .'

'If we intend to stay,' said Morning Light, 'you'd better not go round borrowing people's goats.'

'Are you calling us thieves?' Hern demanded.

'It's just that I wonder sometimes where the meat comes from,' Morning Light said, 'and what it is. I'm not complaining.'

'Better you don't.' If Viner had hoped for a further retort he was disappointed. Morning Light leaned back against the wall of the cave and engaged his daughter in an antiphon of silly noises. The other three glared at him in exasperation.

'We've food enough to last us two days,' Cleaver said. 'Tomorrow I'll go with Hern and find out how things are round here. There should be deer in the wood, and maybe wild boar. We might even teach you two to hunt.'

'I can set snares,' Morning Light said.

'I said hunt, not play cat's cradle,' said Cleaver.

'Pity you didn't tell us before,' Hern said. 'Pity you didn't set them.'

'I thought you preferred to take care of the food.'

'You didn't mind begging for it,' said Hern.

'I didn't beg, I earned it.'

'How long will you be gone?' Viner said, forgetting his desire for a quarrel as he realized that a quarrel might no longer be necessary.

'All day, I should think. We'll start early. You can stay here and mind the child. We'll be back before dark.'

He left them carping at each other and wandered away to sit alone on a rock near by. Clearly Cleaver had forgotten that Viner too might know where he was; not that it would bother Cleaver if he did. It would be no skin off Cleaver's nose if Viner decided to cross the unmarked boundary into that other country and so find his way home, if home was where he wanted to go. But he had little time left.

As promised they made an early start, riding out at dawn. Viner watched them go, propped on his elbow at the cave's mouth and left alone with Dark Cloud and Morning Light. The baby regarded him with bright speculative eyes, and roused herself to a hungry yell. Morning Light sat up, blinking.

'Have the others left?'

'Just out of sight.'

'We could all have gone,' Morning Light said.

'Better they travel alone, they can move faster,' said Viner. 'Let's eat.'

They built up the fire and Morning Light went down to waylay the goatherd and bargain for milk, before attending to his daughter's demands. Viner stretched out and watched them through the flames until the child was fed and bedded in her basket, and Morning Light turned his attention to his own breakfast.

'This is a good place,' Viner said. 'Would you want to stay here?'

'If Cleaver thinks it's a good idea.'

'What if he doesn't?'

'Then we find another.'

'Why don't you tell him you want to stay?'

Morning Light smiled, ruefully. 'I'm not placed to tell him anything.'

'He treats you like a fool.'

'Everybody does. I must be one, don't you think?'

'Not that much of a fool. Shall I tell you something, Morning Light? I know where I am.'

'Good.' He looked puzzled. 'Should you not?'

'Hern wouldn't think so. After he and Cleaver found me we stopped one night at this cave. I'd already said I'd go with them, but he thought I might change my mind and give them the slip and find my way back, so he blindfelled me, and we travelled three days to your palace, and I never saw where we went. I didn't think I'd ever find my way back and yet, here I am; I recognized it as soon as I woke up yesterday. I could make my way home from here.'

'Are you going to?'

Morning Light sounded not only unsurprised but unconcerned. Viner thought that he deserved better than that. 'Would you mind if I did?'

'I mind? No, not if you wanted to.' He set the rush basket across his knees and rocked it.

'Would you be sorry to see me go?'

He looked up, sensing perhaps that he was not reacting as expected. 'Well, yes, but I wouldn't try to stop you. Only, I thought you once said that you were driven out of your village, and I didn't imagine you'd want to go back.'

'It would be better than wandering round the world for the rest of my life, and arguing with Hern. Do you enjoy it?'

'I'm better off as I am than I was when I was the Rain King,' Morning Light said. It was the first time that Viner had heard him refer to the past.

'Don't you ever worry about what's going to happen to you – and Dark Cloud?'

He never referred to the future, either. 'I'll manage.'

Viner understood why conversation with Morning Light had such a deleterious effect on Hern; in the presence of such numbing vagueness much gentler men might turn violent, but he persevered and said, urgently, 'Morning Light, why don't you come with me?'

Taken unawares, Morning Light stopped rocking the cradle and at last gave Viner his full attention. 'Come with you where?'

'Anywhere. To my home . . . anywhere.'

'But you said it was a terrible place. If they threw you out for calling water, they're not going to welcome you back with a rainmaker in tow. I couldn't take Dark Cloud to a place like that.'

'It's not the only village in my country. We could try somewhere else.'

'I don't want to, even so.' He seemed to be searching for reasons, and stammered, 'I don't want to leave my own land.'

'Even if it means hiding for the rest of your life?'

'I don't think it will come to that. It's good of you to ask me, Viner, but I don't think Hern and Cleaver would agree.'

'I didn't mean Hern and Cleaver.'

'We can't go off without them.' Morning Light looked shocked. 'How could I do that, after what they've done for me?'

'What have they done for you?'

'They're my friends. They helped me to escape.'

'So did I. They won't stay with you for ever. You know that. Hern would leave you now, if he could. Suppose they didn't come back today?'

Morning Light looked into the cave. 'They've left all their gear. They'll be back.'

Viner sat shaking with fury, remembering how kingship had been within his grasp and that on an impulse he had turned his back on it to follow Morning Light. I gave up everything for you, he thought, and you won't do anything for me. I could have been king in your place. I could have wed your puling brat and you'd never have seen her again. Hern was right, we should have brained you and taken her back. He'd brain you now, given half the chance, but you'd rather stay with him than be with me. Cleaver asked me if I knew what a friend was. Do you? *Do you?*

Aloud, he said, 'But if they don't come back; would you come with me then?'

'But they will come back.'

'We wouldn't have to go to the Webfeet.'

'But Viner, they'd never go off and leave us. How can we leave them?'

'We could stay here, even.'

'I thought you said you wanted to go home.'

You don't want me at all, do you? Viner thought. Here, there, or anywhere. I've served my purpose, haven't I?

He said, 'You *can't* stay with them. You know what Hern thinks of you.'

Whether he knew or not he was not to be drawn. 'No, Viner, I'm sorry . . .'

'I want you with me. They don't.'

'. . . I'm sorry. I can't come with you – but I won't stop you. I'd never forget you.'

Viner stared through the quivering flecked air above the hearth. Morning Light, that was your last chance. I won't ask you again.

'When will you go?' Morning Light said.

'I don't know that I shall,' Viner said lightly. 'It was only a thought.'

Morning Light bent once more over the baby. Viner sat up and looked pensively across the open countryside to where the line of hills hulked against the skyline, scarcely more than a swelling on the horizon, like a bruise on a cheek-bone. It was pleasantly peaceful in the sunshine, above the river, with Hern and Cleaver absent. The baby dozed. Morning Light began to sing, softly, and Viner began to think.

After their late breakfast, noon was upon them before they knew it, and they stirred themselves guiltily to mend the dying fire, knowing that they should have spent the idle hours in amassing a substantial stack of wood to last them through the cold evening and colder night.

'Shall we go up into the wood?' Morning Light said. 'We could take the ass; the logs are larger, there.'

'It's too far,' Viner said, quickly. 'Half an hour's walk. It would be a pity to collect a lot and lug it back here and then have Cleaver tell us we're not stopping.'

'He'll tell us a thing or two if we let the fire go out,' said Morning Light. 'Do you think we can find enough by the river?'

'There's plenty there; I looked yesterday. No – don't bring the baby,' he said, as Morning Light bent over the basket. 'She'll be quite safe here. We shan't be out of sight for long.'

'Suppose she wakes?'

'We shan't be out of earshot, either. Why don't you feed her first and then she'll probably sleep while we're gone.'

He concentrated on making a trivet of flints, over the embers, so that they could warm the milk and gruel for Dark Cloud, and Morning Light gathered up the remaining logs to bank the fire when they were done. While the baby was dining Viner delved among the baggage in the cave and fetched a length of rope that Hern had used as a spare pack strap and which had proved itself practically indestructible.

'If we cord up some of the wood we can drag it behind us. We'll shift more of it, that way.'

'I never think of things like that,' Morning Light said, busy again with the basket.

'You don't think much at all, really, do you?' Viner said, waspishly.

'All the time.' Morning Light was not insulted. 'Only the things I think about don't seem to be of much use to anyone else. Are you sure she'll be all right?' He still deferred, from time to time, to Viner's wider knowledge of child-rearing.

'She's asleep already. Come on.'

They descended to the river, Morning Light looking back continually over his shoulder to the sunlit bowl in the cave's mouth, that was the rush basket.

'I should have put her in the sling,' he said. 'I think I'll go back –'

'That would be no use,' Viner said. 'You wouldn't be able to carry much for fear of crushing her.'

At the foot of the hill the river ran shallow, brown and clear over the stones of an old ford. Some were as big as flags, others smooth and small, like bannocks. Viner picked up a stone to heft it experimentally, and it curved into his palm like an egg into a nest.

'All that water,' Morning Light said, wistfully, 'and *running*. If it weren't so cold I'd roll in it.'

'You could drown in a river like this,' Viner said.

'Don't spoil it for me. When we've taken the wood back perhaps we should bring the skins down and fill them. Then if Cleaver wants to move on when he gets back, they'll be ready to load,' Morning Light said, altogether more industrious, and his arms already full of wood. Viner stepped out of the shallow water into the shade of the trees, where Morning Light was stooping to free a long and gnarled branch that had become entangled with the roots of an alder.

'I'll give you a hand with that.'

'I can manage.'

Viner came up quietly behind him, and as he was in the act of standing upright, swung the stone against the side of his head. Morning Light let fall his armful of wood and collapsed on top of it, without uttering a sound. It was very cleanly done.

It was some moments before he could bring himself to look at what he had done. Morning Light lay across the heap of branches like a corpse, head hanging down and motionless except for a small blister of blood that swelled among the roots of his hair and burst, and trickled. Viner crouched beside him on the river margin and regarded his handiwork, mumbling, 'I didn't do it. I didn't do it,' barely able to believe that he had done it. He was not yet committed. There was nothing to prevent him waiting until Morning Light recovered and then explaining that he had met with an accident, had struck his head against an overhanging branch, as he stood up. He could probably carry him, at least drag him to the cave, to await the return of Cleaver and Hern who would come back never knowing what had happened in their absence. There was nothing in the world to stop him except for the horrible and growing certainty that as the stone had come down Morning Light had begun to turn round, and had seen what was coming.

He took the rope from his belt and, handling Morning Light as carefully as Morning Light handled the baby, wound it round his waist and arms, firmly but not, he hoped, painfully, and knotted it at the back, whispering all the while, 'It's your own fault. What am I doing? What am I doing? *It's your own fault.*' It was exactly what Catskin had done to him at their first encounter, and he knew from experience that the prisoner would be able to walk, slowly;

eat, just; scratch if he needed to and relieve himself, but he would not be able to run, he could not pick anything up. He could not pick up a baby and run.

Viner twisted his hands into the rope and into the slack of Morning Light's tunic and, moving backwards, dragged him through the miry grass and fallen leaves until he came to a place where the alder boughs and willow fronds sheltered him from all but the most inquisitive eyes. He rolled his burden into a thicket of dry reeds and straightened up, his arms aching. A few nights back they had ached to close once more round Morning Light. Now they could hardly drop him quickly enough.

'Wait there,' said Viner to Morning Light, deaf and immobile in the reeds, and stepped out through the curtain of willow branches. Hern and Cleaver might return at any time, and from now on he had to work quickly. He ran back up the hill to where Dark Cloud lay in her basket, beaming at the sky. Stepping round her and taking care to stay out of her line of vision lest she see him and become chatty, he went into the cave and gathered up everything that belonged to himself and Morning Light, whistled up the ass and the pony, loaded them and left them standing in the mouth of the cave. Taking a charred stick from the remains of the fire he scrawled on the wall

CLEEVER

WE AR GOIN ON ALOAN

YOU WON T TO EE RID OF US I NO

GOOD HUNTING

He threw the charcoal down in the hearth and turned his attention to Dark Cloud. 'Coming to find your father are you?' he said to her. 'Will you come with me?' The baby looked at him confidently. 'You'd go with anyone wouldn't you, you little harlot.' He put her into the sling and hooked it over his shoulder; rolled up the rush basket and thrust it in among the baggage on the ass's back, with the remains of the food inside it, and then with Dark Cloud bouncing gently against his hip, picked up the rebec and led the animals downhill to the water, under the trees.

In his cavern of alders, screened by the willows, Morning Light slept on, unaware of all that was happening to him. He looked as if he might sleep for ever and, sick with remorse, Viner would not look at him except to ascertain that the pulse still beat in his neck, wishing that he were better versed in the science of knocking people on the head. His problem now was to shift Morning Light's dead weight across one of the animals and fasten him there without his falling off, until he recovered consciousness and could keep his own seat. Preparatory to this he laid the baby in the grass and was about to attempt some kind of a purchase on Morning Light, when he looked up through the branches, quite by chance, and saw on the hillside across the river, two mounted figures moving downward, slowly, and coming in the direction of the ford. He could not be certain at that distance, but he was fairly sure who they were; against all likelihood and luck Cleaver and Hern had come back early. At the speed they were approaching it would be some time before they would be close enough to be a threat, but there was certainly no time to be practising balancing acts with Morning Light who must weigh at least as much as he did. He gathered up the leading reins and coaxed the two beasts deeper into the trees, along the muddy path that lay by the river, until they came to the little hidden pasture that he had discovered the previous morning, where he tethered them to a low branch and left them contentedly browsing, out of sight, out of hearing, hoping that the ass would not turn skittish and bray.

By the time he had retraced his steps to the alder grove the horsemen were within hailing distance, should he be fool enough to hail them; definitely Hern and Cleaver. Silently he stretched out at full length in the reeds beside Morning Light, took out the pot bottle from where he had stowed it inside his shirt, and plugged it into the baby's ready mouth. At leisure Hern and Cleaver rode down to the water's edge and crossed over. Hern's pony wanted to drink and halted midstream to satisfy itself. Cleaver rode on, up the hill. Viner stared at Hern through the network of twigs and with his free hand rocked the baby in her sling among the reeds.

Cleaver began to shout as his pony approached the cave. When no one answered him he slid from its back and scrambled up the last of the incline on foot. Viner watched him with one eye, the other on Hern astride his pony in the middle of the stream. He wished he had a third eye for Morning Light who, without any warning, had begun to move his head and moan, faintly.

Suddenly Cleaver burst out of the cave's mouth and raced down the hillside, waving and shouting, leaving his startled pony to plod after him. 'He's gone! The bastard's gone! They've all gone, baby and baggage.'

Hern dismounted and the two of them met on the bank. 'How do you know?'

'They've left a message – Viner's left a message. They've decided to go on alone as we want to be rid of them.'

'That's true enough.'

'Would you credit it? After all this? They've taken the pony and the ass; all their gear – *and* the food . . . just gone.'

'Are you sure?'

'Of course I'm sure. There's nothing up there but our stuff. The fire's still warm. They can't have been gone long.'

'Shall we go after them?'

'Are you joking? Anyway, we don't know which way.'

Leading Hern's pony they began to ascend the hill, grumbling at each other. Viner looked down at the baby who, bedewed with milk, had fallen asleep; well and good. Sleep on. He looked round; Morning Light had woken up. Viner turned on his hands and knees and slithered towards him where he lay without stirring, stupid with pain and confusion. Viner hissed in his ear, 'Don't move; don't speak. There are men out there, searching for us.' It had the desired effect on Morning Light. Viner felt a tremor of fear pass through him and he stiffened, only mouthing, 'Where's the baby?'

'Over here. Keep still and they may go away. Don't even try to move. Yes, they're going into the cave.'

'They'll find our gear,' Morning Light whispered; 'did you recognize them? Are they from the palace?'

'Yes. Don't move and don't speak. Sound carries.'

'What are they doing?'

'Searching the cave.' He could see, as Morning Light could not, that Cleaver and Hern were carrying out their own belongings and loading the animals. They did not stop long. Cleaver kicked out the smouldering fire and within minutes they were on their way down again.

'They're coming back. Be quiet.'

Morning Light did as he was told, so great was the fear of discovery upon him, but as the ponies stepped into the water his head jerked in recognition.

'That voice – that's Cleaver.'

'No. *No*. Be quiet.'

'But it *is* Cleaver.' He attempted to sit up. Viner, in a frenzy, slammed his hand across his mouth; Morning Light tried to raise his own hand to push it away and only then discovered what had been done to him. Viner could not let him do anything else. He rolled on top of Morning Light, pinning him down with one knee and pressing his face into the silt so that he could scarcely draw breath, much less cry out.

'It's strange,' Hern was saying, as he and Cleaver gained the far bank. 'Why should they go like this? Why not tell us to our faces?'

'Perhaps they were afraid we might try to stop them.'

'Chance would be a fine thing. I'd have paid the boring little bugger to go.'

'Viner? I thought . . .'

'No, not Viner . . . never imagined he'd have the guts.'

'Got tired of playing at outlaws, I suppose,' said Cleaver. Their voices were growing fainter.

'How long do you think he'll last?'

'A couple of days on past showing.'

'. . . Viner, do you think?'

'Strange creature . . . probably his idea anyway.'

A last aggrieved yell from Cleaver. '*Ungrateful sod!*'

Viner, accustomed to calumny, listened unmoved, but Morning Light's one visible eye widened in distress as he heard his erstwhile friends informing him, unknowingly, exactly what they thought of him. As if it mattered now, Viner thought wearily, half compassionate, but he did not slacken his hold until Cleaver and Hern had disappeared over the brow of the hill, and rode out of his life as abruptly as they had ridden into it.

Then he had to let go, and swiftly. In his overwhelming need to remain undetected he had not noticed that the ground where they lay had become waterlogged under their combined weight. He was kneeling in water and Morning Light's front hair was actually floating as he writhed and struggled to free himself, under the impression, with his mouth and nostrils full of silt, that Viner was trying to drown him. When he knew that they could be neither seen nor heard Viner eased himself back onto dry land, pulling Morning Light with him. Morning Light kicked out in blind fright, gasping for air and rolling his battered head from side to side as if trying to wake himself by sheer violence from the nightmare on which his unwary eyes had opened. His last conscious memory had left him in the company of a trusted friend, and he awoke to find himself a captive, and the trusted friend his captor.

'What have you done?' he said. 'What have you done, what have you done, what have you done?'

'Stop it,' Viner begged him. 'You'll hurt yourself. I don't want to hurt you.'

Morning Light wrenched himself into a sitting position, clawing at the rope. 'Why did you, why did you, what have you –' He broke off and looked round in a fresh access of terror, mouth open, unable to phrase the question that choked him.

'I haven't hurt her. I won't hurt her.' Viner picked up the baby, still sleeping, in her sling cradle. 'Don't shout or you'll wake her.'

'Why have you . . . what . . . *why*?' His bewilderment was painful. 'I never harmed you. You were my friend.'

'I was your property,' Viner quoted Cleaver, unreasonably. 'You kept me because I was useful to you,' he added, with some truth.

'But you had everything you wanted. I didn't force you to leave.

You would have been king if you'd stayed. *You had everything.*'

'Yes, and I gave it all up. Now I want something else.'

'What? I'll give you anything – you've only to ask.'

'You've nothing to give,' Viner said shortly. 'I want to go home.'

'I know. I wouldn't have stopped you. I couldn't have stopped you.'

'But you wouldn't come with me,' said Viner, in a deliberately dispassionate tone. He kept his eyes turned away, knowing that if anyone else had done this to Morning Light he would have fought to the death to save him.

Morning Light straightened his back. 'Certainly I won't come with you.' Something of his old manner was in his voice, and something new, as if the very indignity of his position had given him dignity.

'You will if I say so. Try refusing.'

'I will not.'

'It's easily said,' Viner remarked. 'But why refuse? No one else wants you. Your friends have left you.'

'You tricked them. They thought I'd left *them*.'

'And that didn't surprise them, did it? You heard what they said about you; didn't you?'

He nodded, miserably.

'It's only what they've said all along, only you wouldn't listen. Not listening to the truth doesn't make it untrue, Morning Light. They despised you. They thought you were a fool. I never thought that.'

'But why did you do this? Why did you send them away?'

'I told you,' Viner said with cold patience, 'I want to go home.'

'They wouldn't have stopped you either.'

'No, they'd have cheered me on, I don't doubt, but you'd have stayed with them. Now you don't have that choice.'

Morning Light sat mute, his head bent, absorbing this information. At last he said, 'What are you going to do with me?'

'I'm not going to do anything with you.' Viner stood up. 'You can stay here if you want. The goatherd will find you tonight; someone may find you sooner, if you shout long enough.' He picked up the sling with the sleeping baby in it and slipped the strap over his head. 'But I'm going home, and your child is coming with me.'

He turned and walked away, as if there were no point in further discussion. A terrible howl followed him. 'NO!'

Viner looked round. 'It's entirely your choice,' he said, impassively, although he was sweating with anxiety. It seemed almost possible that Morning Light would simply collapse into black despondency and sit there, while Viner carried his child away (and was stuck with it) until he fell dead where he sat: until Viner noticed that at his sides his hands were clenching and unclenching.

'I'll hunt you down,' Morning Light cried, in a demented screaming whisper. 'I'll follow you in the night, I'll tear your heart out I'll have your head on a pike and the crows will peck out your eyes I'll kill you for this I'll kill you I'll kill –'

'But you don't know where I'll be,' Viner said. 'You don't know this place any better than I do. You're lost. At least I know where I'm going.'

He walked on, through the dead leaves and the miry grass toward the clearing where he had left the animals, and did not look round again until a blundering movement in the boscage behind him told him that Morning Light was coming after. Viner stopped and waited for him on the fringes of the pasture.

'You can ride on the ass,' he said. 'Not so far to the ground if you fall off.'

'Like this?' Morning Light lifted his hands as far as he could and let them fall. 'I can't ride like this. Untie me. I'll go with you, I promise, but give her back to me. I swear I won't try to leave.'

'As you are, you can afford to swear,' Viner said, 'but afterwards you'll be a little less generous with your promises. I won't untie you, get on the ass. Not easy, is it? This is what your friends did to me when they first caught me – yes they *did*. They *caught* me. They threatened to kill me, too, well, I've not come to that, yet. Your neck's safe.' He looked at Morning Light, awkward and unbalanced in the saddle. 'You thought it was funny, when I told you. Do you think it's funny now?'

'I will come with you. I promise I will.'

'I know you will,' Viner said. 'Do you remember what else I

told you they did? When we reached that cave up there, they blindfelled me, so that I'd never find my way back again.' His months of simmering resentment erupted. '*But I did!*'

Morning Light looked at the scarf in his hands. 'Is that what you're going to do to me?' He could barely whisper it. Very slowly, as his panic subsided, the full horror of his situation was dawning on him.

'Yes.' Viner bound the scarf round his eyes and knotting it felt the spongy contusion under his hair. 'You won't be finding your way back, either. Don't ask me to take it off, because I won't. I know exactly how it feels but you'll have to put up with it for a day or two.'

'*Two?*'

'Say a week.'

He mounted the pony, took the ass's bridle in his hand and led the way out of the pasture at a funeral pace.

'Someone will see us,' Morning Light said. 'Someone will stop you.'

'I don't think so. It's nearly sunset and there are few travellers about at this hour. In any case, we shan't travel by road.'

'I would never have done this to you,' Morning Light said.

'It was done on your behalf. Morning Light, I'm very sorry for you, but I have to take you back with me. Don't say anything else, please; it won't do any good.' They rode in silence, after that.

By travelling in the evenings and early morning, Viner contrived to avoid meeting anyone, and by keeping to the high ground he was able to stay away from villages and cultivated land where there might be people about. Any chance spectator would have seen nothing more worthy of his curiosity than two cloaked and cowled riders, one leading the other; but by the third evening the food supplies had run out and only a little milk remained in the pot bottle.

'There's a village up ahead,' Viner said to Morning Light, 'and we're going in. You say nothing at all, d'you understand. Nothing. And keep your head down.'

Morning Light had in fact said nothing at all since they set out, but Viner guessed that if he were going to open his mouth, it would be now, in a place where he might command someone's attention. He turned his head toward Viner as if he were watching him through the scarf. 'What will you do, if I speak?'

'Nothing – this time. No one will take any notice of you; I'll see to that, but next time,' he made his voice low and threatening, 'next time I'll leave you somewhere a long way off, and stop your mouth, and let you wonder if I'm ever coming back.'

Morning Light sank back into his wordless apathy, cowering down in the saddle with his head drawn into his shoulders, as Viner had done in his position.

The twilit village was little more than a street of hovels, where wintry dust drifted between the buildings, and emaciated cattle watched them from the sour grassless fields.

'What place is this, friends?' Viner asked, as the suspicious inhabitants sidled out of their doorways to see who was passing through.

'Never mind that,' said one of them, the relic of a big man whittled down to the bones by privation, but with some blood in his veins yet; 'who are you?' Viner dismounted and walked up to the group that took such care to keep a distance between themselves and the strangers. He was about to make a gracious little speech of introduction when the man added, suddenly, 'And what's that?'

Viner turned to look where he pointed. Morning Light still sat on the ass, but he had somehow managed to shrug back the cloak and its hood. He said nothing, but even in the dim light they could all see him.

'What's he tied up for?' demanded one old woman with the face of a toothless polecat. 'Is he a prisoner? What you doing with him?'

You bastard, Viner thought. All right, then. You asked for this. 'He's nothing to be afraid of now,' he said, contemptuously, 'but you should have seen him a week ago, with a knife in his hand. He's one of those free men. I was travelling with my wife and child and he came to rob us while we slept. My wife was dead before I woke, but I brought him down as he tried to run. Now I'm taking him back with me.' The crowd made restrained threatening noises, like throttled mastiffs.

'Back where?' snapped the man. 'Where d'you come from? Eh? Eh?'

'Over the border.'

'The border's that way.'

Viner thought furiously. 'The other border, beyond the big stones.'

They stopped cross-questioning him and began to chunter together.

'You've been past the big stones?'

'Yes, and I'm going back again. But this fellow,' he nodded toward the ass, 'this fellow's only going as far, and no further, get my meaning? Blood calls for blood.'

'We wouldn't hold you back from a task like that,' said the man. 'In fact we wouldn't want to delay you. Best you move on.'

'I would, but I need help.' Viner judged the moment right to appeal to their sympathy, having waked their fear. He opened his cloak and let them see Dark Cloud lying asleep against his chest. The women crooned and came closer to look.

'My daughter,' Viner said, 'motherless. I'm taking her back to my village, and maybe find her another mammy. I need food for her, and milk. Can you spare me anything?'

'Do we look as if we'd owt to spare?' said the withered old woman. 'We would an we could.'

'I can repay you.'

'How? Money's no use to us.'

'Maybe your well's failing?' Viner said. 'Would you like me to tell you where to dig another?' Suddenly a rod was in his hand.

'Be you a sorcerer?' one of them asked him, as they all stepped back a pace.

'Yes,' Viner said, without hesitation. 'I can find water for you if water's what you need.' He watched them exchanging looks among themselves, looks of greed, longing, and unease. They looked at the rod, at the baby, and at Morning Light who as if aghast at the crime imputed to him tried to hide his face against his shoulder.

'No, Master,' said the man, finally, all surliness gone, unctuous, almost grovelling. 'We wouldn't keep you from your task at the stones. We wouldn't presume upon your Honour.'

'It would be no trouble.'

'No sir, you keep going, and accept this loaf and milk for the little one.'

Viner took the food and remounted. He was just moving off when Morning Light cried out, 'It's not true what he says. I never killed anyone, never. Help me!'

'Help you?' The old woman ran out into the road behind them. 'We'll help you to the Dry Place, you filth.' A stone was flung after them. It missed Morning Light but he felt it pass his face, for he jerked his head back and almost fell from the ass. The screams and curses died away.

'That was foolish of you,' said Viner.

Morning Light said nothing, for a very long time, but when they next halted he said, 'Those big stones . . . what are they?'

'I don't know,' Viner said, 'but there are bones there.'

'Is that why you brought me with you?'

Viner gaped at him. 'As a sacrifice? That's Hern's mystery, not mine. But I had to tell them something or they'd have felt sorry for you. Next time, do as I tell you.'

'Aren't you going to leave me behind, next time, like you said?'

Viner looked at the pale defeated face beside him, in the fire-light.

'No. No one will take any notice of what you tell them. I can always say you're a sawney. If it's a choice between the gaoler or the prisoner, they'll listen to the gaoler.'

'I'd rather you left me behind, next time.' His voice shook.

Viner had travelled for three days with Cleaver and his band, between the big stones and the cave on the hillside, but he was beginning to realize that the return journey was going to take four times as long, unless they quickened their pace, and with Morning Light swaying insecurely on the ass's back he could see no way to do it, unless he were prepared to move by day and come down from the hills, onto the roads. Growing more confident of his ability to explain away the circumstances of his prisoner, he decided to run the risk of meeting with curious questions and braved the daylight. He kept the pony's head turned always towards the triple hill that sometimes appeared as if floating, among the small choppy clouds of autumn, blue, pink and golden in the cooling sky; and sometimes reared solid from the solid earth. Morning Light, who could not see it, suffered himself to be led toward his unknown destination, unquestioning. Viner did not ask him what he was thinking about, as he sat, hour after hour, his face half hidden by the scarf and his weakening hands clinging to the reins; one with the ass, mute, patient and heavy-headed; but he guessed that he was mindful of the big stones and wondered how he pictured them in his daylong night, his daylong nightmare. As the author of that nightmare he was afraid to ask what he had wrought.

Towards dusk, one afternoon, he saw indistinct figures on the road ahead, and knowing that it was time for more bartering he urged the animals forward.

'People – coming this way,' he said to Morning Light.

'Aren't you going to get off the road?' Morning Light said, breaking his silence for the first time that day.

'There's only two of them and I need to make an exchange, if I can.'

'Get off the road, get *me* off the road,' Morning Light said, hysterically. 'I don't want to be seen like this. I don't want to hear what you say about me.'

'I shan't need to frighten them, this time. It's only a man and a woman.'

'But I don't want them to see me.'

'You won't see them seeing you.'

'Ah, but that's it; that's it; I can *feel* them looking.' He began to tug defiantly on the reins, and the ass stopped in spite of Viner's contradictory pull on the bridle.

'Very well, we'll wait,' Viner said. 'They'll be up with us in a minute.'

'What did you mean, an exchange? What are you going to exchange? Where's Dark Cloud, what have you done with her, where is she?'

'I'm not going to exchange *her*,' Viner said. 'What do you take me for?'

'I don't know,' said Morning Light, swinging his blind head slowly to and fro in a way that Viner found peculiarly horrible to

192

watch. 'I thought I knew what you were. I don't know what you've become.'

The figures drew close and resolved themselves as a packman and his wife, or woman; he riding, she walking, leading an overloaded mule. Viner dismounted and leaving Morning Light stranded in the roadway, went over to address them.

'Good evening, friends,' he said. 'Do you have any pelts to trade?'

'What've you got in exchange?' said the woman. The man looked over his head.

'Who's that?' he said. 'What's the matter with him?'

'My friend,' Viner said. 'His wife ran off and left him and his child died. I'm taking him back to his family, poor fellow.'

'What's wrong with his head?'

'He's blind. Kicked in the eye by a horse. That's why she left him. She said he was no use to her any more.' He liked to temper falsehood with truth, where he could.

'It's a hard life,' said the packman, airily. 'I've got pelts. What do you have in exchange?'

'This,' Viner hitched up his cloak and produced the rebec. 'It's in good order.' He swept his hand across the strings. 'It needs a bow, but that's easily found. It's a fine instrument.'

'What are you giving them?' Morning Light called out, unexpectedly.

'Nothing important,' Viner called back. 'We need a fur wrap for the baby now the nights grow cold,' he said to the packman. 'Will you handle?'

The packman took the instrument and plucked at it. His wife leaned forward to look at Dark Cloud, revealed wide-eyed beneath Viner's cloak like a little owl in a hollow tree.

'Is she yours?'

'Yes.'

Morning Light screamed, 'It's a lie. That's my child he's holding. My rebec, *my* child.'

'Wait a minute,' said the packman, sententiously, 'what's going on here? Whose child is it?'

'His wits have gone,' Viner said, in a lower, but still carrying voice. 'That's why we have to keep him restrained. He might

harm himself – or me,' he added, as though this latter considera-
tion were of minor importance. 'He's convinced that the baby's
his; the one that died. They were of an age.' He rather regretted
this particular part of the charade, but it did not fail to goad
Morning Light into a striking impression of insanity.

'It's not true, it's not true. She's mine. Give her back to me, give
her back. Look what he's done to me . . .. taken everything, taken
my baby. She's mine.' He slithered from the ass's back and
stumbled toward their voices until he turned his foot against a
stone and fell full length in the road, spitting out dirt and curses,
impartially. The packman, with shocked pity, helped Viner to lift
him back onto the ass.

'Poor soul,' he said, 'crazed as a grasshopper. How long has he
been like this?'

'Since he lost his child,' Viner said, with perfect honesty.

'Ah well, keep the rebec. I'll give you the skin for charity's sake.'

'It would be a kindness,' the woman suggested, diffidently, 'to
let him hold the babe, sometimes.'

'I do,' said Viner, 'but it's so hard to get her back again.' There
was no truth at all in this. Morning Light had not set hands on his
daughter since he had so lightly laid her down in the rush basket at
the cave's mouth. The packman's wife looked into the sling.

'She's bonny, isn't she? And so like you! Anyone can see she's
yours.'

Viner dared not look at Morning Light then, but when the
packman and his wife had passed on he saw tears on the quivering
face beneath the bandage, and the lips bitten white.

In the early morning of the eighth day, Viner rode down into his
last village and exchanged the pony for a skinful of water, a bag of
oatmeal and a crock of milk. He was sorry to see the pony go, but
he knew it would never make the journey across the barren scree
beyond the big stones, and would certainly founder on the sheer
slope of the hill above the Webfeet's village; he surmised that the
animal would be eaten before the winter was out, and left the
villagers, muttering that they drove a hard bargain. In fact, he had
without doubt got the best of the deal. Greedy though they were for
fresh meat, they were jealous of their water. He turned back and

looked at the little group who stood in the street, watching him go.

'Has your well failed?' he asked.

'It's a day's walk to water,' said the headman.

'Will you let me try and find more, closer to hand?' He could not forget their miserable eyes as they handed over the water skin, as though it were a favourite child.

'Can you do that?'

Viner went back and took the rod from his belt. 'I can try.'

'You're a sorcerer, then?'

'A dowser. If there's water here I'll find it for you. Will you hold my babe while I do it?'

The women gathered round to relieve him of his burden, cooing at Dark Cloud's ready smile, and sucking their teeth when they saw that she was not swaddled. He declined their offers of fresh linen bands and set out with the rod. He would not hurry, but he hoped that he would find water quickly. Above the village the triple hill reared against the morning sky and in the sunshine, on its lower slopes, he could see the dark mass of the Low Forest, that fateful place where he had first met Hern and Cleaver and Catskin. He was determined not to go back there, but somewhere between the hill's foot and the parched meadow where he walked, there was a bleak and secluded hollow where he had left the ass and Morning Light, both tethered to the same tree. He had not intended to come alone, but when he left at dawn Morning Light had been still sleeping and he could not bring himself to pass up the chance of a few hours away from his sightless accusing face and his crippling silence. At the last two villages Viner had risked describing him as dumb as well as mad, without fear of contradiction, for Morning Light was now so eaten up with shame that he had fallen into the pretence of not being there at all, like a child who thinks that because he cannot see his mother from behind his closed fingers, she cannot see him. But he would certainly be awake by now, and finding himself alone, terribly frightened. However, dowsing must not be hurried, and Viner owed these wretched people something.

The water, when he found it, was plentiful and close to the surface. It did not take him long to map out the place to dig, surrounded by the wondering and incredulous villagers.

'I haven't time to stay while you find it,' he said. 'Will you believe me when I say it's there? Half a day's work should reach it.' They believed him, and as an earnest of their good faith pressed upon him some strips of dried fish, leathery and blackened, like bats, an egg, and a bag of withered vegetables.

'Is it the power you have?' the headman asked.

'No,' Viner said, gently, 'not power. This is a craft like any other. Maybe one of you can do it too, if you need. Cut a green twig like mine, from any tree. Willow and hazel are best, but any will do. Always think of water, while you're looking for it, and hold the rod tightly. Look – I'll leave you one of mine. I shan't come this way again.'

'We once heard tell of a place where they had a man dance to bring water. They called him the Rain King. Is that true, do you know?'

'No,' Viner said, 'it isn't true. They had a king, but he couldn't make it rain.'

It took him two hours walking rapidly, laden as he was, to get back to the place where he had camped. The hollow was cut out of the hillside as if by a giant spoon, and he wondered what men had cloven stone out of the living rock, and why they had done it. He did not enter the quarry straight away, but approached it from above, and looked down, over the lip, to the distant ground where the ass browsed and Morning Light lay becalmed at his moorings against the tree where he had spent most of the day, and all the previous night. From that height it was impossible to see the blindfold, or the ropes that held him to the trunk. With his bowed head and limp posture he might have been any weary traveller, resting awhile from his journey. Viner walked down round the side of the quarry and pushed his way through the broom and gorse. Morning Light heard him coming and, by the time he arrived at the tree, was sitting upright and alert. His head came round as Viner walked toward him. Viner stopped and looked at him, at a loss for something to say. They remained there, a few feet apart, the one staring, the other straining to stare. At last Morning Light said, 'Who's there? Who are you?' whispering, and only then Viner realized that he had had no idea who or what had stolen up on him.

'It's me,' Viner said. Morning Light slumped again. 'Who did you think it was?'

'I hoped it was a stranger.' His voice was cracked and almost inaudible.

'Have you been shouting?'

'Shouting? With you here?'

'I haven't been here. I've been gone for hours – didn't you know?'

'Gone; in the night?'

'Night?'

'Isn't it night?'

'Morning Light, it's nearly noon. I didn't leave you till after dawn.'

His voice broke again. 'I thought you were here asleep. How could I know? It seemed such a long night . . .'

'I don't see that it matters, night or day,' Viner said, briskly, to quiet his conscience. He remembered how afraid he had been of the darkness behind the blindfold. 'Still, only one day more and you won't need the bandage.'

'I don't need the bandage,' Morning Light said, coldly.

'You know what I mean. It'll be the hardest part of the journey, what's to come, so we'd better get going. I've got rid of the pony but you can keep the ass. On your feet.'

He was too stiff to stand unaided.

By nightfall, in cold and powdery moonlight, they passed the first of the landmarks etched so indelibly on Viner's memory, on the day when he had walked there with Hern's sword at the back of his neck. It was the now mummified carcase of the goat, and a little further on was the ruined hut which since he last saw it had collapsed upon itself entirely.

'We'll stop here,' he said, pulling on the ass's rein. 'Tomorrow we'll cross the plain.' He did not want to pass the night in sight of the plain, where the big stones stood with black shadows at their feet.

The next morning he spent a long while gathering sticks which he tied into faggots and loaded onto the ass.

'You'll have to walk from now on,' he said to Morning Light. 'We'll need as much wood as she can carry.'

'Why?'

'Because there's none on the other side.'

'No wood at all?'

'No wood at all. And no water. No villages, nothing.'

'What about milk?'

'I can't call milk out of the ground,' said Viner.

'But Dark Cloud –'

'There's plenty here, but when it runs out she'll have to take gruel and like it.'

'If I've to walk, will you let me see where I'm going.'

'Tomorrow. Hold on to the ass, for now.'

They reached the stones a little before noon. Viner made unerringly for the place where he had found first the gold ring and then, next day, the water that had saved his life. Although the skin was still almost full, he could not pass up the opportunity to collect some more.

He said nothing of this project to Morning Light who stumbled behind him, unwilling to part with any information that might give him some idea of where he was, but Viner paused so long by the stone, looking into the hollow at the foot of it, that at last Morning Light raised his head and asked, 'Is something wrong?'

'Nothing's wrong,' Viner said, 'but this is the place where I found water for Cleaver, and there's no water now. It's dried up.'

'Cleaver said that place was among big stones.'

'We are among big stones – in a circle; a hundred or more.' Without meaning to he had given away their position, but Morning Light did not notice. He stood by Viner, looking all round with great deliberation, before saying savagely, '*I* can't see them.'

'You know the ones I mean. At that first village –'

'*Those* big stones?'

'Yes.'

'The sacrifice place?'

'Well, burial place, anyway.' He had forgotten what else he had said to the villagers concerning his plans for Morning Light, who had not forgotten.

'Let me see them.'

Viner was staring into the other hole. There was no sign of the gold ring that Hern had thrown in as an act of propitiation;

someone else had passed this way since, or else the owner of the ring had come back to collect it. He took from his belt one of the hazel rods and began to traverse the ground between one stone and the next. Morning Light, hearing him move away, cried out, 'Where are you? What are you doing? Don't leave me here!'

There was no water there any longer. It was as if it had dried up at their approach. And maybe it has, Viner thought.

'Where are you? Come back. Don't leave me to die *here*.' Viner, bawled out of his reverie, looked round the stone and saw Morning Light, alone in his darkness, turning round and round, his rigid fingers hooking at the empty air. 'Viner! Come back. I want to leave this place. *Don't leave me*.'

Viner had not meant to frighten him, and hurried to his side. Morning Light grasped at his sleeve, not from choice, Viner thought.

'What's the matter? I told you before, I didn't bring you here as a sacrifice.'

'I'm afraid of this place.'

'So was Hern – so was Cleaver,' said Viner. 'So am I. Let's get out of it.'

'Let me see them,' Morning Light begged. 'I shall dream of them otherwise. Let me see them.' But Viner would not risk that, and Morning Light did dream of them, whimpering and crying out in his sleep that night. Next morning Viner kept his promise and took away the blindfold, but by then it was too late, and look as he might, all round, Morning Light never saw the big stones, and never knew just how big they were.

Viner cut the scarf from his face, since the knot had shrunken too tight to be untied, and left him propped against a boulder, blinking stupidly at the sudden brilliance of the morning, although it was only a comparative brilliance, for there was no sunlight. The sky was grey from one horizon to the other, and a feeble wind whined among the rocks on the slope where they had slept. Then he saw Viner crouched over the fire with the baby on his arm, and closing his newly opened eyes on the sight that he had so longed for, withdrew into his customary wretched silence.

Viner was warming milk for the baby's breakfast. In spite of the rigours of the journey, Dark Cloud was thriving. He had no particular affection for her, but he knew that even if Morning Light ever forgave him for what he had done to him, he would never forgive any harm done to the baby, and if the baby died, Morning Light might die too, of a stubborn disinclination to live, so Dark Cloud was cossetted in her wanderings, and had warm milk, morning and evening. He was very housewifely about his task. He boiled a pan of water, rinsed out the rags, half-filled the pot bottle with milk, stuffed the rags into the neck and stood the bottle in the pan to warm. Then he spread bacon fat on a crust of oatcake and put it into Morning Light's unresponsive hand. Morning Light had to curl himself almost double to eat it, and he would not do it while Viner was watching. Viner obligingly turned his back and fed the baby who, with treacherous complacency lay in his arms as contentedly as she had lain in her father's. Morning Light too turned his back, as far as he could.

Viner shook out the baby's blankets and changed her clothes, before wrapping her warmly in the fox pelt that the packman had given him, furside in. He would gladly have awarded this duty to Morning Light, who would have accepted instantly, but he could have done little for her unless Viner freed his arms, and he would not chance that. Still, by now Morning Light must be completely disoriented. Perhaps in a day or two, when he had seen more of the terrain and understood that escape was pointless, especially with a baby, it might be possible to let him loose. He was quite beyond retaliation.

There was still some hot water left in the pan.

'I'm going to shave,' Viner said, annointing his jaws with a smear of bacon grease. 'Do you want me to shave you?'

He did not imagine that his offer would be refused, for Morning Light had always gone very clean-shaven. and his prickly beard must be a sore trial to him. Furred with ten days' stubble he looked clouded, soluble at the edges, and less than ever like morning; rather the pallid afterglow of a winter's evening, greenish and unpromising.

Morning Light moved himself to shake his head.

'I won't hurt you. D'you think I'd cut your throat?'

'I don't want you to touch me,' Morning Light said, but he watched closely while Viner whetted his razor and scraped off his own beard which had rendered him unrecognizable for so long. There was no more need to disguise himself. While he was mowing the last recalcitrant bristles in the angle of his jaw, Morning Light said abruptly, 'I've changed my mind.'

'So've I.'

'No; I wish you would. I feel filthy like this.'

'Do you?' Viner regarded him carefully for the first time in days and guessed that if Morning Light could know how derelict he looked, he would be unpleasantly surprised. He relented. 'All right; but you'll have to trust me and keep still. If I was going to kill you I'd have done it already, wouldn't I?'

He scooped more grease out of the pan and spread it thinly over the cold skin of a face that twitched and grimaced with disgust at the contact. He drew his hand away quickly, almost equally repelled.

Morning Light said, 'Can't I do it myself?'

Viner almost wished that he could. 'If you think I'm letting you loose with a razor, think again,' he said, with feigned cheerfulness, brandishing the blade. Morning Light pressed his head back against the boulder and the muscles of his neck tightened like two bones on either side his throat. Viner had never shaved anyone before and in spite of the unencouraging circumstances, he thought he had made a good job of it.

Morning Light unclenched his eyelids and said; 'Will you cut my hair, too?'

Viner, disarmed by his conversational tone, sat back on his heels. 'It doesn't need cutting.'

'It hangs in my eyes. I can't brush it away.'

'You wore it too short before. You looked like a mercenary,' Viner said, absent-mindedly.

'Should you care how I look?'

Viner was about to deny it when he realized that in the unwonted relaxation of the tension between them, he had set the razor down on a stone. With one movement he looked and pounced, but it had gone, and Morning Light had gone too, rolling insanely across the sharp rocks and standing erect on the far side of the fire; his arms free, the severed rope trailing from his elbow, the razor in his hand.

'Now then,' he said, and began to move round the fire toward Viner, crouching as he came and muttering, 'Now then, now then, now then.'

Viner, thrown for a second into utter confusion, recovered himself and began to move too, crabwise, never taking his eyes from Morning Light's hands. He saw that in cutting the rope he had also cut through tunic and shirt, into his flesh. He was bleeding heavily, but he seemed not to notice it as he came on round the fire. 'Now then. Now then. Now then.' Viner stooped, as he sprang across the hearth, and lifted Dark Cloud in her cradle. Morning Light, the razor lifted shoulder high for a murderous slash, stopped as though stricken and stood among the scattered ashes.

'Now then,' said Viner. 'Now what?'

They faced each other.

'Put it down,' Viner said. 'Drop it.'

Morning Light looked all round him as though somewhere, somehow, a solution to his dilemma would present itself.

'Put *her* down,' he said. 'Put her down or I'll cut you to shreds.'

'You won't touch me,' Viner said calmly. 'Drop the razor.'

'Oh, give her to me,' Morning Light pleaded. 'Give her back to me.' Their eyes met and locked.

'Throw down the razor,' Viner said, 'and I'll give her to you.'

'No you won't. It's another of your tricks.'

'I'll give her to you. Put it down. I swear I'll give her to you.' He held out the rush basket. She offered her arms, amenably.

Morning Light dropped the razor among the ashes and took one step forward, but in that instant he let his eyes fall. Viner dropped Dark Cloud and launched himself towards the fire, and the two of them rolled over and over the stony ground, knotted together, knees in gut and groin, hands at eyes and throat, thumbs gouging, while Dark Cloud, rudely abandoned, lifted up her voice and screamed passionately. They had never heard her scream before, and that shriek was her father's undoing, as Viner understood very well. For a fatal instant his hands slipped at Viner's neck, and Viner did not miss it. He tore his head free and rearing up dragged Morning Light to his feet and felled him again with one terrific backhanded swipe across the face. Before Morning Light fairly knew what had happened Viner turned him on his face and lashed his wrists together with the remains of the rope, left him lying there and went to comfort the baby.

Morning Light lay among the stones and looked at him with festering eyes through the too-long hair that was sleeked across his forehead with sweat.

'You fool,' Viner said, bitterly. 'I was going to set you free, tomorrow, and look what's happened to you now. You're worse off than ever you were. Why did you do it?'

'You're mad,' Morning Light said, and turned his head away.

'No, I'm not mad,' Viner said, to the baby, grizzling and hiccoughing in his arms, but he did not explain to Morning Light why he had done the dreadful things that he had done, nor the worse thing that he was going to do.

Remembering his outward journey from the valley to the big stones and the Low Forest, he calculated that he had been on the move, sporadically, for seven or eight days, and guessed that with the ass to bear the loads and a scant but dependable supply of water he ought to be able to cover the same ground, going back, in four. But he had reckoned upon the sun and stars to navigate by, across the trackless wilderness, at his back the Dial, the Torque, the Bow: before him the Frog, the Louse, the Three-Legged Sow. What he had not bargained for was fog.

Although the days were overcast and the sun stifled, the nights were cloudy and clear by turns, giving him at least some indication of the route they must follow next day, but on the third morning after the disastrous fight, they found themselves suddenly in a cold dark chasm and hemmed in on all sides by grey vapour. Morning Light huddled against the rocks of their camp site, cast down even further by this latest phenomenon. He would not speak to ask what it was, but Viner, as he coaxed the damp ash twigs into a blaze, saw him searching the sky, warily.

'It's fog,' Viner said. 'Like mist, only more so. We had it all the time at home, but never like this. We'll have to stay here until it lifts.' He piled the fire with dry sticks until it leaped redly in the murk, and laid two slim logs across the rocks of the hearth; and while the gruel heated he prepared their inevitable meal of oatcake and dripping. Morning Light, now unable to do anything for himself, refused to be fed by Viner and bowed his head, his teeth locked, until Viner gave up, leaving him to go hungry, and by now he must be very hungry indeed.

All through the morning, as far as they could tell it was morning, the fog folded them close, unvarying and impenetrable; but later it began to move. A wind rolled over the open hills and in the gloom strange shapes gathered and swelled, hung over them ominously and receded. Morning Light, torpid and irrational, watched from sunken eyes, shivering. Viner offered him a blanket, throwing it across his shoulders when he ignored the advance, but he squirmed furiously until it fell to the ground. He refused food at midday. Viner, as silent, sat on the other side of the fire, guarding the few flames like precious flowers in winter, afraid to pile on wood in case the supply ran out before its time. He had allowed for one faggot for every night's bivouac, but not for a fire that must burn all day, and it would be madness to let it out, and madness to leave it.

He tried moving away to see how far he would get before it was out of sight, and after only a few paces it faded like the dregs of sunset on a cloud. As he returned, treading carefully, he saw movement at the fire, and peered round a boulder. Morning Light, on his knees, was bent over the gruel pan, eating out of it like a dog, licking and worrying at the crust around the rim. Viner fell back behind the boulder and vomited up everything that he had eaten that day. The fog darkened. It was evening, and very cold.

In the night a small sound close by roused him from an uneasy sleep. He could see nothing all round him, but the fog was thinning. Overhead a star or two glimmered for an instant between one drift and the next. The sound came again and close at hand he heard Morning Light struggling to sit up. He heard it again; the baby was coughing. He had built a little bothy for her where she lay in her basket, walled in by the packs and faggots, roofed by a blanket and warmly insulated in all their spare clothes; but not warmly enough, it seemed. She gave another cough, like a little animal, kid or lamb, in the distance.

A voice in the darkness, that he had not heard for days, said, '*Do* something,' and there was quiet again. Viner had heard babies coughing before. At times the carpenter's cottage had sounded like a pen of asthmatic old sheep, and yet no one had been any the worse eventually; a little rickety, a little short of breath, wheezing through the winters, but healthy enough; alive, at any rate; at least, not spitting blood. But Dark Cloud had never coughed and he found it an ugly sound. He could imagine how it must torture Morning Light. He crawled from under his blankets and stirred up the fire. There was still some milk in the pot bottle and he put it to warm; and looking up saw Morning Light's eyes burning at him across the flames.

'If she dies you'll have no rest while I live,' he said. 'What are you going to do?'

'Give her some milk: keep her warm.' Viner tried to sound collected but he was not, and Morning Light knew it.

'Give her to me. Let me hold her.'

'And have you lay me out? No.'

'She's ill.'

'A cough's nothing. All babies cough.'

Dark Cloud coughed again.

'I tell you she's ill. She's never done that before. Do something.'

'I am doing something.' Viner lifted the baby from her basket and holding her close, under his blanket, tried to force a little milk between her lips, but Dark Cloud was not interested. She coughed. Viner could not tell whether or not she were awake; he did not return her to her place among the packs, but kept her with him under the blanket, warming her with his warmth.

Morning Light, cold and alone, said, 'Did she take any?'

'Yes.'

'If she dies, I will kill you.'

'Whatever happens you'll stay exactly where you are. Can you kill me by looking?' He softened. 'She won't die.'

'I'll kill you. Some way, I'll kill you.'

'Be quiet,' Viner said, 'or I'll make you.'

In the morning the fog had gone but the dark day was cold and shrill. The wind had risen during the night and clouds boiled across the sky so low that it seemed as if it were the land that moved while the sky stood still. Morning Light declined to eat. The baby coughed.

'If you don't eat,' Viner said, 'it'll be you that's dead. What good will that do you?'

'I'll take nothing from you.'

Viner went to fetch the ass, leaving the pan of gruel that Dark Cloud would not eat, lying near the hearth. When he came back it was almost empty.

'Do you want a drink?'

Morning Light shook his head, but his dry mouth and sticky teeth were too much for Viner. He grabbed his own water bowl and emptied it down Morning Light's throat before he had time to close his lips or move.

'You're not going to kill yourself,' Viner screamed at him. 'You're not. You're not!'

But he would not mount the ass, although the wood was almost exhausted and his painful walking pace was making their progress dangerously slow. Viner could not persuade him. All he would say was, 'Don't touch me.' The baby coughed.

They moved down into the valley. Ahead of them the loose rock was dusted with soil, and as they proceeded they saw the sallow turf curving down, then up towards an unseen summit, but it was not until the day was well advanced that they had their first sight of the massive granite pile against the milling clouds. Morning Light could not take his eyes from it, and Viner wondered if he were making the same mistake that he himself had once made, thinking that the great boulders were the work of giants, possibly still inhabited; dangerous, but if inhabited perhaps housing some sympathetic soul who would not turn a deaf ear to the crying of a sick baby. Viner prayed only that they might reach it, and shelter, before the fog came down again. Under his cloak the baby slept in her sling, peacefully enough, but now and again she coughed, and he looked up to see Morning Light watching him.

Morning Light, raised in the drought of that far hot country, was learning what it meant to be cold. In the confused and hateful aftermath of the fight they had left his cloak behind, along with a number of other things including the rebec, which he had not yet missed, but he refused any extra clothing from Viner's hands. His own hands were stiff and bloodless at his back. When he stumbled and fell, as he did with increasing frequency, he rose to his feet unaided, although with increasing difficulty, and Viner made no move to help him. He was a walking reproach, and he knew it.

How did this happen? Viner asked himself. It shouldn't have been like this; how did it happen? And under his breath he raged and swore because he could not touch him.

They reached the top of the ridge as it grew dark again, but in time to see that the next hill top was bare of all rocks.

'Beyond that,' said Viner, 'is one other, and beyond *that*, is my valley.'

Morning Light threw himself down on his bleeding knees and would not look.

Viner lit the fire with the last of their kindling and settled down to feed the baby. She woke, whining and fretful, and would not suck. He stroked her cheeks as he had seen his mother do, to rouse her interest, and she obliged with a few mouthfuls, but then resumed her thin complaint. Viner felt something between himself and the fire, and found that Morning Light had dragged himself across to see what was happening.

'She's not drinking, is she?'

'Yes she is. Go back.'

'Don't lie to me. She's had nothing today.'

'At noon.'

'I don't believe you.'

'That's all one to me,' Viner said, levelly, holding pity at arm's length. If he was once moved to release him, the whole terrible journey would have been in vain. 'Only another day,' he said.

'Give her to me.'

'No.'

Morning Light crawled back to his place among the rocks and for a while there was no sound from him, but as the night wore on and the baby slept, Viner heard his voice in the darkness. Had he not known who was speaking he would never have identified the dismal monotone.

'If she dies, it will be my fault.'

'Come again?' Viner could not tell if he were sleeping or waking.

'My fault; I should have left her behind. This is my punishment for stealing the Rain Queen.'

'No, it's not – not a punishment, not your fault.'

'I've lost everything. I've lost my home. My wife has left me, my baby is dying –'

'She's *not* dying!'

'– my friend has bound me and beaten me and made me a prisoner. I am nothing. That's not a punishment? I am nothing.'

'You'll be a king again,' Viner said, thinking that the distressful

208

litany had come to an end. 'Go to sleep. You'll wake the baby.'

'I should have been named Nothing.'

'Go to sleep.'

'My mother bore me at night, without a lamp. She saw nothing. The first thing she saw was nothing.'

'The first thing she saw, I suppose,' Viner said, 'was dawn, and that's what she called you for.'

'She saw *nothing*,' the voice insisted. 'My name is false. I am nothing. My name is Nothing, No Thing, I was never Morning Light.'

'Stop it!' Viner shouted at him. 'You are what you are. My name's not Viner either, do you think I care?'

The feverish voice steadied and strengthened. 'Ah, I know your name. You are what you are. Shall I tell you your name?'

'No! *Will* you shut up?' Viner scraped up a handful of stones and hurled them into the darkness. Two crashed against solid rock, but the third thumped on something soft. He lay down again, with his hands clamped over his ears.

When he opened his eyes it was day, and it was raining. The fire was extinguished and the green sibilant sticks refused to burn. Viner left them hissing and went to look for the ass. All round him, as far as he could see, the rain hung in curtains to the ground. The grass slopped and slobbered under his feet, and there was no trace of the animal. Her broken halter trailed among the rocks.

'Aren't you going to feed my daughter?' Morning Light said, from where he lay, unprotected from the rain that had soaked him as he slept. He was making no effort to shelter from it, and when Viner hauled him against the projecting bulwark of the granite outcrop he folded up, sullen and lumpish, and would not help himself.

'Better not wake her. We ought to be moving soon. The ass has strayed off in the night.'

'If you'd tied it as tight as you tied me,' Morning Light said, 'it'd be here still. Is there any milk left?'

'There's a little, in the bottle.'

'A little?' Morning Light did not realize that Viner was holding the bottle under his cloak. 'Is *she* to starve now?' He kicked viciously at Viner as he passed, and Viner, side-stepping, slipped on the greasy turf. The bottle flew out of his hand and smashed against a stone.

They looked at each other. There was nothing to say. Viner selected the most necessary of their possessions and stuffed them into the bait bag, leaving everything else to lie in the rain; the cooking pans, the blankets, the water skin.

'The rebec?' Morning Light said.

'We left it behind, days ago. I'm sorry.'

'How can you be sorry for that?'

'How not? It was an accident.'

'Sorry for that,' said Morning Light. 'Aren't you sorry for anything else?'

Viner lifted Dark Cloud from her shelter and stowed her in the sling beneath his cloak. Her coughing was more persistent and more resonant, but there was nothing he could do except keep her close to him, restive and hot; a guilty fire smouldering against his chest. He began to descend the hill, without looking back, and after a minute or two he heard Morning Light scrambling and slithering behind him.

The rain came down harder now and the wind rose alarmingly. They walked side by side, not comradely but neither able to maintain a lead, or a lag. Now one would slip and fall against the other, but they exchanged no words, there was nothing to say. They reached the bottom of the hill, climbed again, rested on the summit, and began the second descent. The slope levelled out, they were crossing the place where Viner had found his first stream, but he did not give it a thought. His whole attention was fixed on gaining the top of the hill before darkness fell. The ascent grew steeper, the rain harder, and they were bent almost double in the face of the wind when finally they reached the crest, one dragging the other, to look down upon the clouds that enclosed the invisible valley below.

Your kingdom, Morning Light, Viner thought, did you but know it.

Morning Light turned to him, chest and shoulders heaving with the effort of drawing breath. 'Is she alive?'

'Yes.'

'*Look* at her. Is she still alive?'

He did not know if she were still alive. 'Yes.'

'Give her to me.'

'It will be dark soon. We must go down.'

'Down? Down there?' Morning Light gazed fearfully into the roiling vapour at his feet. 'How can I? I shall fall. I can't go any further, Viner.'

'We can't stay here.' Viner shifted the baby onto his hip and started forward, confidently, but after half a dozen steps he found that without trying to he was beginning to hurry. The descent was more precipitous than he remembered, and slippery now; it was almost impossible not to run, or to fall. Morning Light, already fallen, was on his back, trying wildly to dig his heels into the turf to save himself. Viner managed to seize him by the sleeve as he twisted round, on the verge of plunging into the rainy twilight. He dropped to the ground beside him, and the arm that lay across his chest felt the heart slamming under his shirt.

Morning Light said, 'I can't go any further. I mean it. I can't move.'

Viner, with the last of his resolve, said, 'I still have Dark Cloud. I can move.'

'Then take her down to shelter and leave me here,' he cried. 'Or let me go free. Viner, for pity's sake, let me go, let me go. Viner, let me go.'

If he said anything else his words were lost in a violent intensifying of the rain. It beat them down to the grass where they lay flat, shuddering, face to face. Viner, who had for so long avoided looking into his eyes, could not avoid them. He took out his knife, cut the rope, and waited for Morning Light to fall upon him, snatch it from his grasp and strike, stabbing and rending. Perhaps Morning Light had had some similar idea, but he only sat helplessly in the rain, his arms at his sides, numbed and feeble. It was Viner himself who had to knead and chafe his frozen hands until he snarled with the pain of the returning blood. At last he spoke.

'Give her to me, Viner. Please, give her to me.'

Please. He had had to wait for this to hear it.

He slipped the sling over his head and passed Dark Cloud, hidden in her furs and shawls, back to her father. Morning Light held her to him and bent his head over her, unable to speak. She coughed.

'We can't stay here,' Viner said. 'We *must* get down before the light goes.' He got up, half expecting Morning Light to stay where he was now that his child was in his arms again, but he rose too, clutching her against his sodden tunic, and followed. They could not walk. They skidded, slipped, slid, clawing at grass, stones, each other, to halt the headlong flight. Morning Light, his hands virtually useless still, would have plummeted to the bottom more than once had not Viner pulled him back. They did not speak. There was no sound but the baby's coughing, their own gasping breath, and the relentless hiss of the rain, but as they went lower and the incline slackened, Viner became conscious of another sound, a portentous growling beneath them.

'What is it?' Morning Light said. 'A wild beast? Is it living?'

'It's a river,' Viner said, 'in spate.'

'Must we cross it?'

'There's a bridge.' He corrected himself. 'There ought to be a bridge.'

'How do we cross it if there isn't?'

'We don't. Look out!' Water sucked at his shoes. Before he expected it, the river was there at their feet, already over its banks and still rising.

'Where's the bridge?' Morning Light, finding himself knee-deep in water, when a moment before he had stood on a hillside, lost all sense of direction and was headed for the river itself. Viner grabbed him as he lost his footing in the current's slavering jaws.

'Not there. This way, further down.' The wind, trapped in the valley's funnel, flogged them before it, and Viner's cloak swelled like a sail until he threw it off, afraid that it would drive him into the river. The bridge rose out of the thickening darkness that was alive with booming wind, the rain, the roar of high white water, and one look told Viner all that he needed to know: in another five minutes they would have been too late; in less time than that the bridge would surely be destroyed, and he was not certain, even now, that they would ever get across it. The piles were under water and the handrail swayed loose at one end. Above the tumult he could hear the most frightening noise of all; the grinding squeal of timbers under unendurable pressure. There was no time to decide on a course of action. He clamped his hand round Morning Light's arm and dragged him toward the tottering structure.

'*No.*' Morning Light tried to tear himself away. 'We can't get across that.'

Viner did not argue: pitting his frantic strength against the other's weakness, he swung him round and propelled him toward the centre of the bridge, hurling himself after. Morning Light hit the railing, which gave way where he struck it, and Viner was only just in time to pull him away before he would have somersaulted backward into the torrent, gripping him by the strap of the sling, which parted under his hands so that Morning Light had to let go the rail to save his burden. His mouth opened in an anguished cry, but the wind smacked his voice back into his throat. The water clawed and worried at their ankles and the bridge lurched under them as if it were a river-monster, rearing up on its hind legs. To the sound of wrenched timbers it was torn from its piers and flung the floundering men on its back into the water, against the further side. Viner clung with arms and knees to the railing, and saw Morning Light dashed against the bank, trying with the crook of one elbow to get a purchase on anything that would support him. He was severely hampered by the bundle in his arms.

'Drop it!' Viner yelled. '*Drop it.*' He had forgotten what it was, until he saw Morning Light's agonized face clearly, in the wavering light of a lantern that flared suddenly above them, but the light came as it went, foul water poured into his mouth, his ears, his nose, he was submerged in the river's filthy maw, until arms reached down into the water to hoist him clear, to lie choking and strangled among stampeding feet, and ropes. He sprawled on the bank and saw, without comprehending what he saw, Morning Light and his bundle hauled out to be dropped beside him. To all other sounds was added the bellowing of many voices, and a final death cry as the bridge collapsed for the fourth time in living memory.

Nothing had changed. He knew that as soon as they recognized him. The hands that had pulled him so charitably from the river now seized him by the collar and yanked him to his feet.

'So it *is* you. Why did you come back?'

It was his stepbrother. 'You took my bait bag, you little bastard. Where is it?'

'In the river,' Viner said. Angry faces surrounded him, distorted cavernous mouths engulfed him.

'Viner's back. Look what he brung with him!' He thought they meant Morning Light, but they did not.

His stepfather loomed out of the rain with a swinging lantern that made the shadows on his face lurch grotesquely. 'It's been a good year, since you went,' he bawled. 'A good year, and now look. The worst storm we've ever known. The grange is flooded.'

'The bridge's collapsed,' Viner said, helpfully, as if they had not noticed, and saw a familiar female face at his stepfather's side. 'Mam!'

'I might have known it was you,' his mother said. 'What did you want to come back for?' Other disembodied voices chimed in. 'I knew it was him. As soon as the water began to rise I said, "Viner's about", didn't I? Didn't I say it?'

'Take your floods somewhere else.'

'*Viner!*'

'Where's your forked stick, eh? Eh? Take it and ram it down his throat.'

'Didn't I say he was somewhere around? Viner's weather, I said. Didn't I?'

'Shove it up his arse.'

'Chuck him in the river, him and his friend.'

Jostled and shoved, plucked at from every side, punched and shaken, he found himself in the centre of a ring of jeering people.

'Where is he?' Viner shouted, above the racket. 'Where's Morning Light?'

'Morning light he wants, boys. D'you think he'll live that long?'

The circle split at one side and Morning Light was thrust in to join him. Viner could see that he had no idea of where he was, or of what was happening. He fell at their feet, still clasping his waterlogged bundle to his chest and mouthing, 'Help me.'

The carpenter and his son caught him between them and pulled him upright.

'Who are you? If you're in the same trade as this one –' the carpenter pointed to Viner '– I'll drown you myself.'

'I'm nothing,' Morning Light cried, staring about him with the look of a man who thinks, or hopes, that he is delirious. 'Help my baby, my baby, or I shall have no baby.'

Viner's mother stepped forward and tore the bundle from him.

'A baby?' She hesitated. 'It *is* a baby. Look, neighbours, he tells the truth. What were you doing with her?' she demanded of Morning Light.

'My baby – my daughter,' Morning Light said. 'She's sick, if she isn't drowned. She'll die if you don't help me.'

Surrounded by horrified, pitiful women, the baby was lost from sight. This was not at all what Morning Light had intended. 'Oh no,' he cried, fighting to reach her. 'Don't take her away. Not again; don't take her away from me.' He was forced back, roughly, into the circle, and would have fallen had not the crowd pressed round them so close.

All you need do now, Viner thought, despairingly, is to tell them what you were and we'll be dead men. A near-by shed tilted, as the foundations disintegrated, and slowly subsided, like a cow sitting down. The circle swelled away from it and Morning Light was thrown against him, and reeling, reached out to him. Viner opened his arms and they clung together like lovers, while the mob bore them ever closer to the water's edge, roaring in concert with the rain, 'To the river! To the river! Into the river!' Viner thought, without pity or elation; I have you at last, do you know it? In the sickly swaying pallor of the lanterns Morning Light's hooded eyes and lolling head told him that he knew very little.

'Stop it!' Viner shouted. 'Stop it. You don't know who he is. I brought him here to save you – to save all of us.'

'He don't look like he could save anyone,' said a voice, and the shoving progress continued unabated in the heaving press of bodies, the stink of wet wool, and anger, and fear.

'He'll stop the rain!' Viner cried, in mortal terror. 'He'll stop the flood!'

Now they halted, to hear him out, suspicious still, but willing to listen.

'He causes *drought*. The sun shines out of his eyes. The ground cracks where he walks, the grass turns brown, the ponds dry up, wells fail, rivers shrink, springs are stopped. The clouds fly away when he raises his hand. It will never rain for him. It may never rain again!'

The whole crowd was hushed now, but his words were blasted from his lips by the gale and almost drowned in the tumult of the storm and of the river that awaited them both unless he could make himself believed. He screamed, 'He is the sun dancer. *The Sun King!*'

Against his shoulder Morning Light was muttering, 'I saw their feet . . . not webbed . . . not webbed,' but no one heard him. From the riotous darkness the carpenter spoke.

'That? That's a king?'

'Believe me,' Viner said, 'only believe me. When he dances the rain will stop.'

'Then let him dance now.'

'Not now,' Viner cried. 'He can't dance now; he can hardly stand; look at him. Let him dance tomorrow.'

'Now.'

A chant went up. 'Now. Now. Now. Now. Now. Now.'

The headman stepped forward. 'Do you swear that he can do it?'

'I swear. I've seen it.'

'Then let him dance when he can. Masters, be quiet. This would be an ill night's work to harm a stranger who asked us for help. Viner's right; the boy is as sick as his child. Give me room there.'

The crowd broke up, and Viner was left with his resentful family who could not disown him, as Morning Light was pulled from his arms and carried away.

He slept in his own home that night, before the hearth, since his own place in the loft had been taken by his stepbrother's wife, acquired in his absence. He thought he would sleep at once, but for a long time he lay under his blanket listening to the storm, and vaguely conscious of the unexpected clarity of smaller sounds; water trickling, dripping; the impact of individual raindrops; and watching the quick shadows on the ceiling, cast by his clothes where they hung steaming above the fire. The flames lit up the beams and the provisions that dangled from them; dried fish, onions, sausages, a flitch of bacon. On the nail by the hearth hung a new bait bag. Nothing had changed; he might never have been away. His mother was in the midwife's cottage where together they tended the baby with all the skill and knowledge that Viner and Morning Light between them had so signally failed to furnish. He did not know what had become of Morning Light since the headman had thrown him across his shoulder and borne him into the darkness. Viner hoped that he was comfortably lodged. He hoped very much that the baby would not die. He slept.

He slept late, barely lifting his eyelids when the carpenter's family rose together and left the premises. The cottage was quiet when he woke in dreary daylight, and he assumed that every man, woman and child was out in the storm, salvaging what they might. The wind had not relented, the rain still fell from the clouds that hid the hill tops. He looked out of the shallow window beneath the thatch eaves and saw the village street awash, ducks foraging where hens should peck, the water slopping dourly round the walls. Huddling his clothes about him he went out and crossed the street to the midwife's cottage. Two or three women looked up when he came in, from where they sat about the fire.

'Where is she?' he asked, without preliminary greeting. 'The baby, where is she?'

His mother pointed to a wicker cradle at the fireside. Viner was afraid to look. 'Is she alive?'

'She's alive,' the midwife said. 'She's a healthy child and the cough won't trouble her long. Coltsfoot and horehound will drive it off, and good feeding. Whoever had the rearing of her knew what she was about.'

'He,' Viner said. 'He did, her father.'

'What happened to the mother, then?'

'Ran off,' Viner said, briefly. 'Her father hand-reared her, after that. He didn't trust a wet nurse.' They mumbled, disapprovingly.

'Didn't swaddle her though, did he?' the midwife said, grateful to find some cause for complaint. 'What's her name?'

'Dark Cloud,' said Viner.

'What a name for a little girl,' said Viner's mother. 'We'll have to think of a better one than that; Dark Cloud, indeed; enough to blight her for life. How'll she ever get a husband?'

'Men would have danced for her hand, where she comes from,' Viner said, wishing that he might tell them what the name had signified back at the palace, but he could not divulge even that much. However, he said firmly, 'You should not change her name. She is what she is. She *is* Dark Cloud.'

'Not any more she isn't,' his mother said. 'I suppose it was her father thought that one up.'

'No. These people name their children for the first thing the mother sees after birth. She's Dark Cloud. He's Morning Light.'

'Morning Light? That streak?' The midwife folded up, over her lumpy lap. 'That's a good one.'

'Yes it is,' Viner said. 'Wait awhile, and you'll see how good it is. Now, where is he?'

'In the headman's house.'

'Is he all right?'

'It depends what you mean by all right,' said his mother. 'If he's always like he was last night, yes, he's all right.'

'Well, he may have been wandering –'

'Wandering? He was raving; crying like a woman for his baby.'

'You're a woman,' Viner said, not liking to hear the word used pejoratively.

'But he's not. We couldn't have him in here, creating. We had to call the men back in and they took him over the way. I dare say they managed to keep him quiet. What else could we have done?'

'Given him the baby?'

'It ain't proper, a young man with a baby,' said the midwife. 'What does he want to bother with babies for? Only half a man, it seems.'

'He's a whole man,' Viner said, soberly. 'He fathered it.'

'That's all he need to do. It's not his place to mother it as well.'

Viner took one look at Dark Cloud, flushed but serene and convalescent in her crib, and went out again, into the rain. The headman's house was at the top of the village street, but he did not go there immediately, for on asking where the headman himself might be found, he was directed to the grange. He discovered him in the wreck of the threshing floor, with the elders of the village, his stepfather among them. Walls and roof had gone, flung down on

218

the stone paving in a drenched litter of thatch and clay. A man with a broom was glumly sweeping it away.

Viner addressed himself to the headman.

'When do you want him to dance?'

'What a question!' The headman gestured comprehensively at the village, taking in the clouds, the floods, the river, the broken bridge and the ruined grange. 'As soon as maybe. Is he steady on his feet?'

'I don't know. I dare say he can stand up, if they'll let him. He's being kept quiet, I understand.'

'He had to be. He didn't know what he was doing, last night.'

'Yes he did. He wanted his child. If he dances, you must give him back his child.'

'If he dances and the rain stops, he shall have his child.'

'You swear to that? You won't let the old women keep her from him?'

The headman looked at him seriously. 'Viner, you lived six years in this village. You must know that anyone who could drive away the rain and bring sunshine would be honoured among us. We would pay anything he asked. If all he wants is his baby, he shall have her. If he refuses, or fails, we shall turn him out, and you with him, but we couldn't do that to the child. The women would never stand for it, and rightly.'

'So, if he fails, he loses her.'

'Yes.'

'I see. He will dance.'

He went back to the house, knocked and entered, unbidden. The headman could boast of two downstairs rooms, and in the first Viner found the peace-keepers; the headman's own son and a keel-chested in-law who looked just muscular enough to wrestle with a corn dolly.

'Managed to control him, then?' Viner asked them. They shuffled their feet.

'We was tol' to stay,' said the son, apologetically. 'We was tol' not to leave, so we stayed. He's sleeping. He couldn't hurt anyone.' He recovered himself. 'Who said you could come in here, you dirty swine?'

'Your father. Get out of the way and shut up,' Viner said. 'I'm going in to see him.' They did not offer to prevent him as he walked up to the inner door. Once they had been the first to throw mud and dirt; now they contented themselves with rude names. To-morrow; what would they do tomorrow?

Morning Light was stretched out on the bed, and looking more peaceful in his sleep than he had done since Viner clouted him over the head with a stone, down by that other river, under the alder boughs. He lay, as was his habit, on his face, and one arm, bared by a hitched-up sleeve and scored with rope burns, hung over the bed's side, the fingers trailing on the floor. Viner, who had intended to go straight over and shake him till he woke up, hesitated, looking at the excoriated arm, and then turning his back, looked out of the window. From this elevated position he could see over the whole wasted village; the smoky fires lit to combat the rain, the swilling flood water, the despondent figures that waded, bent, through the wreckage. He could not bring himself to look at Morning Light, and revolted at the thought of touching him, as though he were an animal that he had mutilated horribly but failed to kill, and that now lay at his feet, undead, unable to die, twitching.

The door opened and a head looked round it, hopefully. 'He giving you any trouble?'

'Does it look like it?'

'Just give us a call if he does, and we'll come and quiet him down, for you.'

'Get out!' Viner shouted furiously. 'Lay a hand on him and I'll knock your head off.'

The door banged shut so loudly that Viner clapped his hands to his ears and the man on the bed shifted, drawing up his arm and rolling over onto his back. Viner went up to the bed and said, 'Morning Light. Morning Light?'

The eyes clicked open suddenly, in a face that ill-usage had strangely dignified, elevating it from plainness by sharpening the features, hollowing the jaws, tightening the muscles severely about nose and mouth. He made no attempt to sit up, but lay gazing at his arm, with its abraded wrist, that lay flexed on the pillow by his head, like a broken handle.

'Viner?' He did not look round.

'Yes.'

He said tiredly, 'Why did you do this to me?'

'I never meant to do anything to you,' Viner burst out. 'What I did, I hated doing.'

'But you did it well.'

'You should have come with me when I asked you. I didn't want to force you.' Morning Light turned his head, painfully, and Viner flinched from his look. 'I *needed* you.'

'Is that why you took my baby?'

'I had to make you come with me. I saw a goatherd take a kid from its mother, to make her follow him. I knew you would follow me if I had her.'

There was a very long pause.

'Is she dead?'

'No.' Viner wished he would close his eyes again. He did not blink. 'She's ill, but they say she'll recover.'

'If she does,' Morning Light said, 'they won't give her back to me. I wanted her last night, and they threw me in here. You took her, and I followed you. Now we're here. Make them give her back, they're your people.'

'They are not my people,' Viner said, quickly.

'Oh, they are Viner, they are. You and they are one, thieves and liars.'

'Listen to me,' Viner said, unable to bear any more. 'I brought you here to do something, and you must do it. You must go out there now, and dance.'

'The rain dance?' Morning Light sat up. '*The rain dance?* They don't need rain.'

'They won't get rain.'

'I don't understand you. There's no point in my dancing. This place is flooded – the dance brings rain.'

'Not when you do it,' Viner said, brutally. 'It's never rained for you yet, has it?'

'Yes. Yes it has.' He kicked aside the blankets and knelt, palms up, persuasive. 'The first time I danced –'

'Twenty-six men had danced before you,' Viner interrupted. 'No wonder it rained. After that, nothing but little showers. You became Rain King because the Rain Queen wanted to sleep with you. You've never made rain, Morning Light, you make drought.'

'*No*.'

'Yes you do. You're not a rain dancer, you're a sun dancer. I've seen you drive clouds away. Springs dry up when you go near them. Now you've come to a place where they need a sun dancer. Dance.'

Morning Light shook his tangled head obstinately. If he had imagined that his world had collapsed when his wife went away, he knew now that it was only the superstructure that had gone. This time he saw the foundations crumble.

'I said I'd never dance again. I can't dance, any more. I shall fail. Everything I touch turns to dust. I can't do it.'

'It's easy,' Viner said, implacably. 'Dance the rain dance, as you always did it, and the sun will shine.'

'But I cannot bring the sun. I don't believe I can bring the sun.'

'Who cares what you believe, you poor fool. You thought you could make it rain but it never did rain, did it? It's what *they* believe that matters. If you do this for them, they'll give you back Dark Cloud. You'll be honoured, respected, many things will be given you – you've only to ask; no, not ask; demand. Do your dance and demand your child. Otherwise,' he said, 'you'll never see her again.'

'But if I fail . . .?'

'You won't fail. You can't fail.'

'But I don't know how to invoke the sun.'

'You don't have to invoke the bloody sun!' Viner shouted. 'Wherever you are, it'll come to you. *Dance*.'

'In front of all those people?' Viner saw the last hope of reprieve leave his face. 'Like this?'

'Stark naked would do.'

'Dance and deny myself?'

'No,' said Viner, 'you won't deny yourself. You are Morning Light. *Be* Morning Light.'

'And if I don't I will lose my child for ever?'

'Yes.'

Morning Light lay down again, slowly, and turned his face to the wall.

'Come back in an hour and I will tell you what I shall do.'

In the rainy morning they assembled on the threshing floor in a subdued circle, everyone in the village. The clouds had thinned a little, but the sky was heavy with the promise of more and worse. Near at hand the river thundered threatening by, and the wind ripped shreds from the water.

Viner perched on the wall of a byre where he could see over their heads into the circle, and also, in the other direction, down along the village street, where a solitary man was walking towards the threshing floor. Morning Light was wearing the clothes he had travelled in, ruined by water and exposure. His feet were bare in the mud, his hair hung matted, lank and dull, until the wind caught it and tore it into dark rags about his face. Viner thought of the shining Rain King in his sleek wig and kilt of silver; of the gongs, the javelins, the waiting Queen, the maker of lightning with his blazing torch, the other circle on the terrace, where the people had pounded the pavement with their hands and clapped, and clapped.

But we don't need any of that, he thought. All we need is him.

As Morning Light reached the threshing floor the circle parted to admit him, and he stood in the centre of it, dazed and uncertain, not knowing how to begin. The villagers did not know either how to begin. No one moved.

'Dance!' Viner shouted, from the wall. He struck his palms together. 'Dance. Dance. Dance!' He clapped in time to the cry, and the others joined in, stamping out a rhythm with their wet shoes slapping dolefully on the stones.

'Dance, dance, dance, dance, dance!'

Morning Light began to dance, falteringly at first, with clumsy steps and uneven balance. Viner, afraid that he would fall, shouted louder than anyone, 'Dance, dance, dance,' and he did dance, turning and springing, with his arms raised and his hair swinging. From somewhere in the circle a fiddle struck up, and in time to the stamping a drum sounded, deep and sonorous. Morning Light leaped higher, spun faster, and the circle widened to give him room as he leaped and crouched and spiralled and leaped and leaped, elevated against the clouds and bent like a sickle, heels almost touching back-flung head. The faces in the crowd were breaking into smiles. People looked at each other, nodding and smiling, and the whole sky seemed to lighten with their humour.

'*Dance. Dance. Dance. Dance. Dance.*'

Viner, looking down on them all, felt that he was finally home and welcome. True, they could not keep Morning Light for ever their prisoner, however honoured a prisoner he might be. One day, Viner foresaw, he would run again, as Viner had run, scrambling up the hillside to Over the Top, with a bait bag on his shoulder and his daughter on his arm; but until then the water was tamed, the village was secure, the people content, and Viner their saviour. He smiled benignly upon them, and upon Morning Light, inspired at last, dancing in despair beneath the blue sky, the fleeing clouds, the inexorable sun.